A Pound of Flesh

by

Kenneth Butler

DORRANCE
PUBLISHING CO
EST. 1920
PITTSBURGH, PENNSYLVANIA 15238

This is a work of fiction. Names, characters, places, and incidents are either the product of the author's imagination or are used fictitiously, and any resemblance to the actual persons living or dead; events; or locales is entirely coincidental.

Dorrance Publishing Co
585 Alpha Drive
Pittsburgh, PA 15238
Visit our website at *www.dorrancebookstore.com*

ISBN: 978-1-6453-0165-3
eISBN: 978-1-6453-0914-7

A Quick Historical Note

Immediately after Grigori Rasputin was assassinated by a group of Czarists in 1916, rumors began circulating that the Mad Monk's prodigious penis had been amputated, most likely by the love-struck (but spurned) Prince Felix Yusupov, but possibly by others. Rasputin's daughter Marie was so incensed by news that a cult had sprung up around her father's detached member that she asked Russian authorities to intervene.

Throughout the twentieth century, the allusive appendage was allegedly spotted in Paris, California, and various Eastern European hotspots. It was consistently described as dried-out and boxed, but Dr. Igor Knyazkin insists the twelve-inch specimen in formaldehyde he has on display in St. Petersburg is the real thing. (For narrative convenience, I have opted for the boxed model.) Contemporary accounts from some witnesses deny that any such mutilation took place, but more than a century later, convincing claims continue to be made for both sides of the argument—it is unlikely we will ever learn the truth.

The seacoast city of Northport does not exist in New Hampshire. All characters are products of my imagination, and all situations fictional. Any resemblance to living people is entirely coincidental.

K. B.

To my sister, Robyn, and my brother, Matt

For Charlie —
My favorite book-
shipper, and a fine
singer —
　　　　Ken
　　　May, 2020

My little girl is singing: "Ah, ah, ah, ah." I do not understand its meaning, but I feel what she wants to say. She wants to say that everything …is not horror, but joy.

The Diary of Vaslav Nijinsky

Chapter One

1

Later, eyewitnesses gave their accounts to the eyewitness news teams, confirming the horrific details of the explosion: the suddenness of the blast, the heat of the fireball, shattered glass, blood, the humanity. Four out of five said it was just like in the movies. Boston television and radio and the *Globe* and the *Herald* all made the bombing their top story for over a week. I was at the very vortex of the innocent bystander whirlpool but failed to merit mention anywhere. I took this in stride, and just as well; if interviewed, I might have said something I'd regret. My father once told me if you're going to do something, do it right. I have heeded his advice and subsequently done very little.

What I was doing at the time of the explosion—the June noon of my thirty-third birthday—was sipping iced tea, seated at a sidewalk table at the River Styx Café on Newbury Street, accepting the fact that I was beginning to dread birthdays. I didn't feel old; it was the annual self-assessment that had become so distasteful. Thirty-three was an attractive age for an ambitious young man on the way up, a parent or provider, an individual of accomplishment. With zero means and prospects, thirty-three was embarrassing. My wife had been dead six years, dead at the age of twenty-two, presumably clear on the fact that life was not fair.

I had a yellow legal pad in front of me on which I was composing an ad, my first, for the personals section of the now-defunct *Boston Journal*:

Single while male, 33. Library book stacker. Seeks female of any age, type, or build for companionship, romance. My dream of being a successful poet has not come true, mostly because I'm not a very good poet, and who gives a shit about poetry anymore anyway. Sometimes even I don't. I have no car and live in one depressing room that's fit only for sleeping or suicide. Deeply in debt, I eke out a miserable living from paycheck to paycheck.

I read this over and considered it too negative. I added:

Have terrific sense of humor.

And then:

Germ-free.

Yes, that should have them breaking down the door.

I didn't bother to mention any physical specifications, being fairly secure in the knowledge that looks-wise, I wasn't about to win any prizes, and I found most women of all shades and types and sizes invariably delightful, but age was becoming tricky. Ross Macdonald wrote that as a man gets older, if he knows what's good for him, the women he likes are getting older, too. Unfortunately, women my age wanted men my age to act their age, which calls into question all achievement, credentials, and material acquisition I had failed to collect on the way to the terminus. Younger women (at least the ones who liked older men) occasionally found my circumstances bohemian, thus romantic, but tended to evolve into very different people every few months.

I tore off the page and crumpled it into a ball and took a sip of my calm and sane drink. People around me were already quaffing fat goblets of red wine and sweating mugs of cold ale with obvious satisfaction, though it was not yet midday. There had been hundreds of mornings I had been drunk well before this hour.

"Can I stiffen that up for you?"

I glanced up to the expectant, confident face of my waitress— tall, busty, blonde hair plaited, *zaftig*. She could have stepped out of a 1920s Berlin bratskellar, save for the piercings and tattoos.

"I'm sorry?"

"Don't be. We got a special on Long Island Iced Tea. You already got the iced tea part. I can just stiffen it up for you."

"Oh, of course. No thanks."

"What's the matter—too early?"

"No. Too late."

This puzzled her; puzzlement turned to irritation, and when she spied my copy of Lewis Carroll's *Through the Looking-Glass*, she decided I was a creep and moved briskly to more conventional nonconformists at other tables. I think she found my accent daunting, as do many in my adopted country. I was born and raised in South Africa, speaking both Afrikaans and English until my arrival here with my parents and brother when I was ten. Nothing has rendered me as much felicity as adopting the English language full-time, but the verbal mark of my past has been slow smoothing away.

I found myself writing a free sentence: "Success is a journey, not a destination." I was writing fortune cookies.

I glanced at my watch just in time to see the second-hand swing northerly in line when the explosion ripped through the interior of the restaurant and smashed its way outward through heavy plate-glass to the sidewalk. Tables, chairs, and debris were hurled like streamers and landed alongside limp and crushed bodies. Screams and horn-blasts were followed by sirens.

I'd lost consciousness for only a moment. I came to on the street (in a loading zone, said the sign, and for once I wasn't loaded) with blood and grit in my mouth, my eardrums feeling as if punctured by knitting needles. I could barely breathe, my older brother from my childhood again kneeling on my chest. I squinted through the smoke. The entire façade of the building had been torn away as if by an angry, giant toddler; the inside of the restaurant in flames, a sheet of shattered glass sparkling the sidewalk. Victims—moving, mangled, dead—lay everywhere as the dazed ambulatory ran and stumbled and bled. Before I faded into unconsciousness again, it occurred to me that I wouldn't have to worry about the check. This one would be on the house—if there'd been a house.

2

My consciousness found its way back in a hospital bed on a fine sensation of floating, disembodied, a few feet about the mattress. I was stoned to the teeth.

I identified the place as Adams Memorial by the distant view of the Charles River and beautiful Back Bay (I had been here while my father was dying; a truly *buena vista*, the old man would say).

Then came a voice: "Hey, hey! Alive after all, eh?"

I was afraid to move my neck, head, or limbs, or to speak or blink; there was a long stretch of silence where I failed to reply or even acknowledge that anyone had spoken. Then the voice asked tentatively, "Aren't you?"

I delicately turned my head as though my neck were fused by blown glass to take in the owner of the voice in the bed next to mine.

He was an enormous man of about sixty. Propped on his gigantic stomach, which rose from his bulk like the dome of the Massachusetts State House, was a tray overflowing with the plates, napkins, and scraps of a happily consumed meal. He could have been the model for Tenniel's Humpty Dumpty: fat, round face like a beach ball split by a wide grin—a little mischievous, possibly insane.

"Yeah," I finally managed to rasp. "Thanks for asking."

"Lucky to be alive, the both of us," he said. "I was there, too. Jus' my luck. I's in Boston only Mondee night and this mawnin' on business, and I gets blowed up." He had a distinct Maine accent, a real down-easter that fairly reeked of clam chowder and seaweed. My head throbbed with more enmity than the thousands of hangovers I had subjected it to. My hangovers were deadly.

"Was it an airplane?" I asked.

"Howzat, fella? Hey, look! We're on the news." He gleefully played the remote, changing the channels on the elevated wall television from four to five to seven to CNN. A bespectacled woman spoke in a monotone intently from the screen:

"Animal rights extremists are claiming responsibility for a bomb blast that ripped through a crowded Newbury Street eatery today, killing at least twelve people and injuring dozens more."

"That's us!" said Humpty.

"You sure?" I asked woozily.

"Sure, I'm sure. What're ya, stupid?"

I thought about that. "No. But thanks for asking."

He flicked a quick, suspicious blink at me, shook his head, and slurped through the straw in his lidded plastic cup. In the quiet after he had finished, I noticed a subtle version of the slurp as an echo in the corner of the room; a bubbling fish-tank sound, but I was distracted from this as a nurse entered, wheeling a cart of medical apparatus in front of her.

"Hey, girly," called the fat man brightly. "Our friend here's survived."

The nurse shot Fats a hypodermic jab of a glance, then sweetly turned her attention to me. She was dressed in the old-English-style uniforms the hospital might have introduced if swallowed up by the Virgin Corporation of Great Britain: white apron over a relatively short blue dress, black stockings, white cap—a true old-fashioned sister. She looked as if she'd stepped out of a black-and-white World War I movie, about to spoon soup to the bunged-up lads two miles back of the Somme. She also looked like a cocktail waitress. I considered how a self-respecting medical practitioner could allow herself to be dolled up in such a way, especially with the nursing shortage; and also that this outfit could prove provocative for cardiac patients; and, that it was suddenly and certainly encouraging to realize that my sex-drive and all essential mechanisms had survived the bombing intact; and that maybe a letter of appreciation to Richard Branson, after all, might be in order along with a rousing chorus of "Rule Brittania." Obviously, I was hallucinating.

"How are you feeling, Mr. Graham?" She sounded like a Londoner. "You're rather banged up a treat—lots of scrapes, bruises, odds and sods—a bit well -n really, but that lot'll heal quickly. Your most serious malady was the pneumothorax."

"The what?"

"Your right lung collapsed, love. Had to perform emergency surgery. We're keeping you inflated right now. Hence the morphine drip in your wrist, oxygen clip up your nose, and breathing-tube in your chest. Be thankful there's nothing stuck up your bum, Bob's yer uncle."

The word *chest* seemed to awaken sleeping sensations, and I became mistily aware of a painful throb under my arm. I lowered my head to see a yellow tube the size of a garden-hose protruding from under my hospital gown and leading to a machine the size of a shoebox that looked to be some sort of pump. Another tube led from this to a tank near the wall, slurping subtly. I pulled the collar of my smock away from my chest and saw that the tube led to a bandaged aperture in the side of my rib-cage. A section of this tube had been tied off with a scissors-like clamp taped to the center of my chest. The shock I felt at the sight of this sent a small amount of saliva down my esophagus, causing me to choke, causing me to spasm forward in a cough, causing me to strike the clamp with my wrist, sending the yellow tube banging against my chest bone from the inside, a painful, disturbing sensation causing an almost simultaneous gasp, gurgle, and groan from the patient.

"Are you all right?" asked the nurse. "Good. And don't touch that. It's keeping your lung inflated. You'll be right as dodgers, don't you worry. You should be back on your feet and out of here in five days."

"You bet!" said Fats. "He's got lousy coverage!"

Nurse primly ignored him with a fixed smile focused on me as she provided water and a dose of Percocet.

I asked, "What happened on Newbury Street, um—Julie?" I squinted my eyes to read her name tag.

"A bomb exploded. The authorities seem to think it was animal rights terrorists, bloody bastards blew the whole place to buggery. Good Lord," she said in a sudden flash of concern. "Were you with anyone?"

I shook my head, slightly, carefully.

"That's as well, then; no more shockos for you, mate. Twelve people were killed, many more seriously injured, but you'll be right as Welsh rain come a fortnight. The police'll be in, I should think. You know, routine." And she winked.

"Yeah, kid," said the Fat Man. "Might be *you* planted the bomb, then sat down for a cup o' Joe!"

Julie smiled again. I was beginning to develop some genuine affection for that smile. I smiled back and asked, "You're English, aren't you?"

She looked politely quizzical, patient to a child's odd inquiry.

"No. Most definitely not. Why?"

Fatigue, injury, pain and morphine were surely collaborating, producing torpor, a pleasant sensation of surrender, and an erotic longing for Nurse Julie in her cocktail number. And now her voice, bouncing and echoing from the public address system of Waterloo Station. "If you need anything, love, just press the buzzer. Anything at all. Even sex."

I attempted to clear my throat, but she had already swished—fetchingly, I assumed, unable to turn and observe—from the room. Morphine. Morphine, of course, was the explanation.

"Bet we're on Fox," said Fats, cranking the volume on the yammering set. "We're famous."

"At last," I muttered, falling back into a drugged sleep.

3

When I awoke, I groggily but urgently put in a call to Kimberly Clark, the only neighbor of mine in my rooming-house with whom I had any sort of acquaintance. She lived across the hall, a chain-smoking and lethargic Amazon who supposedly worked at the local Y (she never seemed to leave the house), but definitely was a stupendous television viewer with a hearing impairment, if one were to judge by the volume of her constantly nattering Sony set. I asked her would she please, please get the pass key from our horrible landlady, Mrs. Fecteau, and once a day feed and water my hamster, Ignatz, whom she would find residing in a large, airy, and scrupulously clean wire cage, complete with wheel, near the window?

"I guess so." The TV set was troubling our conversation.

I ventured that if I weren't imposing on her incredibly gracious selflessness, maybe in addition to the handful of feed from the plastic cookie jar (marked "Feed") near the cage, each day she might also provide the little chubs with a small slice of apple or carrot or dark greens of any kind, which would be greatly appreciated, but of course the main thing was to keep that water bottle full and fresh every day. Okay, Kimberly? This last question brought a moan, which I quickly realized was a reaction to something on the television. She was not listening.

"Kimberly," I said in a raised voice. "You promise me you'll make sure Ignatz is taken care of?"

"Yeah, yeah, I got it. Apples." And she hung up before I could mention changing his woodchips or thank her again for all her help. Fats was buried in several newspapers. I switched on our television and looked at it for a long time.

"There are two officers who'd like to speak to you."

It was Julie, her voice gliding through the velvet curtain of morphine and Percocet that swathed me in the sunny, late afternoon as I stared soulfully at the Muppets on *Sesame Street*, the only thing on seventy-eight channels that I didn't find offensive.

"They're in the corridor. You keen for a chat?"

My voice was carried on molasses. "Sure. Anything to help."

She smiled winningly. "Good show, Pax. Fritzie's in for it the next big push." She winked and strode briskly out. I turned to my rotund roommate.

"Mr.—?"

"Chauncey Alexander MacFarland Jr.'s the name, but you can call me Chaunce. All my friends do, 'cept in the trade. Undertaker, that's the trade. They call me Digger—Digger MacFarland." We both listened to the pause.

"Mr. McFarland?"

"Ayuh?"

"Does Julie sound English to you?"

"How in hell should I know? Never been too far outtuh Yawk County, Maine, 'cept for a coupla morticians conventions in 'Lantic City. Why?"

"Because she speaks with a bloody great goddamned English accent, that's why, and it's weirding me the hell out."

"What is?" came a professional, forced-friendly tone. The cops had arrived.

They both flashed badges at me: the one a big, solid guy, red hair and mustache, a genuinely friendly feel about him; the other, the source of the voice, I wasn't so sure about. She wielded an intense gaze behind oversized frames and an expression that looked to have been hammered in place by years of the sexism served up by the police and military alike to their own. She'd had to prove herself with twice the effort and capability of any man, leaving her with the hard-won halo of the grown-up Margaret from *Dennis the Menace*.

"Oh, this 'n that," said Chaunce.

"Paxton Graham? I'm Special Agent Avery. This is Special Agent Poplin," said the friendly bear with the mustache. "Federal Bureau of Investigation. Pretty banged up, huh? Collapsed lung, she said?"

"I'm on drugs."

"Yeah, we need to ask you about that, too," said Poplin. "What were you doing at the Styx this morning?"

"My day off. It's my birthday."

"Happy Birthday," said Avery.

"Thank you."

"How old are you?" asked Poplin.

"None of your goddamned business," came a small voice from behind Chaunce's wide-open *USA Today*. We all exchanged blank expressions, but the pair of Feds turned to me as if I'd performed a feat of ventriloquism.

"Anyway," said Avery. "What time did you get there?"

"About 11:30. I was supposed to meet a guy who borrowed a tape from me."

"A tape?" Poplin asked quickly. "What kind of tape? A tape of what?"

"An old videotape," I said carefully, concerned the words might slip away from me. "I had loaned this guy a copy of *Valerie and Her Week of Wonders*, which is this rare Czech vampire movie from the 1960s, see, and I was—"

"Yeah, yeah," she interrupted, "but did you see or hear anything suspicious? Anything unusual?"

"No."

"What were you drinking, Paxton?" Avery, sounding as friendly as Jimmy Stewart doing Elwood P. Dowd.

By no means was I trusting my drug-addled senses at this stage, and though fairly blissed on the languid down bedspread of morphine and Percocet, an alarm sounded thickly, miles away through the fog. When you booze heavily five days out of seven and arm wrestle with your tippling on the remaining two, you become self-conscious about your habits. I was trying to quit—again.

"Iced tea," I answered, sounding like Alfalfa Switzer.

"Long Island Iced Tea?" Poplin chimed in from Neptune, brightly, now that she was getting somewhere. "Eighteen kinds of booze?"

"No. Just regular old Lipton or Red Rose with lemon and sugar iced tea that the Queen Mum would drink, for Christ's sake." I had said this, but we all looked at MacFarland and his newspaper again. I coughed.

"Uh huh," Poplin said dubiously, deftly making a note. I decided to change the subject.

"They said on the news it was a bomb."

"That's right," said Avery. "Animal rights activists, if you can believe it."

"Terrorists," said Poplin. "Whatever they want to call themselves, they're terrorists."

"You're telling me," I said, gesturing indignantly to my lung pump.

"Freaks," said Poplin.

"It's the work of the S.L.A.V.," said Avery.

"Slav?" I asked, imagining a group of Russians and Poles in sable hats cuddling koalas.

"It's pronounced *slave*," said Avery. "Stands for the Society for the Liberation of Animal Victims, but it's got that vowel-line thing over the *a* to make it a long sound. Like slave."

"Why did they blow up a restaurant?" I asked.

"They didn't," said Avery. "They targeted the corporate offices of Schraeder Systems above the restaurant. The company owns labs that conduct product safety tests on animals."

"God, that's horrible."

Poplin bored another hole through me with her stare. "Their research saves lives, okay? Children's lives. And these freaks are killing and maiming innocent people over bunnies and swine." She was self-righteousness with a vengeance.

"Take it easy," I said. "I'm one of the maimed innocent here, remember?" She didn't soften in the slightest.

Avery cleared his throat. "The chief reason we're here, Paxton, is because of a pretty bizarre development we thought maybe you could help us with. We've been following these SLAV people for some time. They were too much even for P.E.T.A.—the People for the Ethical Treatment of Animals— so they broke away as a renegade guerrilla group, if you'll pardon the pun."

Avery smiled. I smiled. Poplin didn't.

"Anyway," he continued, "they're most likely behind the kidnapping of Brieanna Crisco, though no one's claimed responsibility yet."

This I knew about. Brieanna Crisco was the twenty-year-old heiress to the Vitapet dog food empire and a Palo Alto coed, and the anonymous kidnappers asked five million for her return. With both parents deceased, the trustees of her $500 million legacy were being positively Gettyesque in refusing to negotiate, despite her hysterical implorations to do so. There was some serious smirking in the media, as Brieanna was a young woman famously spoiled and indulged, whose frequent arrests, public tantrums, suicide attempts, and Marie Antoinette quips about the poor had earned her a rep as one privileged and entitled bitch-on-wheels. The obvious reluctance of the money-handlers to fork over, all things considered, a relatively small sum— coupled with the actual lowering of the price demanded to *four* million—

prompted MSNBC to dub the story "a modern-day 'Ransom of Red Chief,'" a remark later soberly retracted. When the trustees refused to budge, the abductors promised one of Brie's countlessly pierced ears in a giftbox if the dough wasn't coughed up quick. It was now a week past the deadline with no new demands or threats, the criminals apparently trying to maintain a stoic dignity.

"Wow. I didn't know that," I said.

"Of course not," said Poplin. "It's not public knowledge. We believe they're holed up in Canada. The Royal Mounties are working with us."

"Ah. Good."

They both stared at me in expectant silence, like two actors who'd just given me a cue. Finally, Avery spoke. "Your wife, Erika Wikki, was an activist with PETA."

"No, she wasn't. And she's dead."

"Oh, really?" said Poplin, pulling a four-by-six black-and-white photograph from her smart leather binder and tossing it onto my maimed and innocent chest.

It showed my not-so-lately dead Erika's face in sunglasses. Where short, blonde hair should have been was long, black hair; she was smiling and leaning her elbow on the low-slung branch of a weeping willow. This girl wore a tight shirt, pleasantly displaying a pair of delectable boobs. I smiled.

"Why are you smiling?" popped Poplin.

"It's not her."

"Why not?" asked Avery.

"Because for all of her many physical charms – she had a beautiful face, as you can see, I mean, this does sort of *look* like her face, and a lovely pair of legs, nice flat tummy, and an ass about as perfect as I've ever—"

Poplin snapped, "Yes, okay, Jesus, will you just—!"

"She was completely flat-chested!" I blurted, triumphant. "She didn't even wear a bra. I have bigger tits than she did."

Avery picked up the glossy and studied it earnestly, as if for the first time. "Really?"

"Trust me. I remember."

Poplin yanked the picture from Avery's grasp. "You ever hear of cosmetic surgery?"

"Erika wouldn't do that, okay? She was a Grateful Dead fan, for Pete's sake; a groovy, natural vegan who didn't believe in anything as artificial as—"

"And you a chain-smoking lush. How the hell did you two ever hook up?"

I felt she was being rhetorical, not really wanting an answer. "We found fingerprints at the Crisco abduction crime scene and one set matched the prints taken when Erika Wikki was arrested protesting a nuclear power plant with the Clamshell Alliance up in Maine. Her very *alive* fingerprints, your dead wife."

Oh Christ; Oh Jesus. I wanted these Feds very much gone. I wanted to enjoy my languid, drug-fueled drowse, not syllogisms like, *rabbits are blinded for children; your lung has collapsed; therefore, your wife is not dead.* Avery looked embarrassed.

"I know it all sounds ridiculous, Paxton. Like a horror movie, and I know you appreciate horror movies and, you'll probably think this is kind of ghoulish, but—we got permission from your ex-wife's parents—"

"Erika's not my ex-wife. She didn't divorce me. She died."

Pause. "Yes, of course. I'm sorry. We got permission from your ex-wife's—no, shit! Sorry! Your dead wife's … *deceased* wife's parents …" He trailed off, as if confused and drugged himself. Chauncey rustled, then slowly crunched down his newspaper, turning two fat, baleful eyes on us. Avery finished with, "We went up to Maine to have a look at her corpse." He sighed, heavily.

For the first time Poplin looked, in concordance with the now hapless Avery, as though she felt some uneasiness. They stared uneasily.

"And?" I couldn't wait.

"And," she said, "Somebody had—well, they'd broke into the Wikki crypt."

I burst out in a laughing gasp, spluttering, but the sentence that formed in my head could never, ever come out, as the exclamation of alarm was dead-on Tweety Bird from Warner Brothers' Merrie Melodies: *Dey bwoke inna da Wikki kwipt?*

I can only presume I grinned, drugged. It was the drugs. Poplin—God, how I already hated her!—sternly took my imbecilic expression in the face of this ghastly news as sanction to give a vocal crack right across my slack-jawed face. "Her corpse is gone," she said. It worked.

"Oh my God." My lung hurt. My chest hurt. How much more wounded could I possibly—?

"Yeah," she said, smug at my reaction, boiling —and back in black, she was. "So with this photo proof, new breasts or not, fingerprints matching her set from her arrest, and no *habeas corpus*, if you'll excuse the pun… "

What pun? I let it go. We let it go. Avery was with me, clearly an example of that fine American ideal, the decent cop—and likable. (What do Americans say? Everybody hates cops—until you need one.) He looked queasy as she continued. "I'd say it looks possible that Erika never really drowned up there in Bar Harbor, huh?"

I rallied. "I was there. She drowned. The coroner, the autopsy."

She waved this away. "We've looked into it. Seems as convincing as palm trees in Alaska. We don't need you to do our job for us. We do, however, need you to think about where your dead wife might be if she weren't really dead, which we think she isn't. Got any ideas?"

I closed my eyes, trying to reinvigorate the Percocet in my system through an act of will, all the while projecting an aura of Buddhistic calm.

Poplin grew impatient. "So Paxton, you got health insurance? No, of course not. You need a job for that."

"I have a job."

"Not anymore, you don't."

I opened one eye in time to see Avery toss her a reprimanding look, which didn't even scratch.

"Well, listen…" He took a farewell step forward. "You seem a bit fragile at the moment." Poplin snorted (Boris Karloff in *Die, Monster, Die!*). "We'll come back when you're feeling a little more clear-headed. Meanwhile, think about these possibilities. Oh, and if you're released before we see you again, don't leave town without letting us know, okay?" He left a card.

She got off the last barb, over her shoulder on the way out the door: "This is terrorism and homicide now, Paxton."

She said this so emphatically that any observer would have concluded I was the number one suspect. It took only a glance at Chauncey's owl-eyed expression to see that.

4

The drugs and stress kept me on a cycle of insensibility followed by nervousness and dreams worthy of De Quincy. The painkillers wore off with the punctual regularity of a shop steward punching a time clock. As the hour approached, I grew restive, and the dope fiend within awakened with a vengeance. I was learning more about addiction, a subject I thought I knew thoroughly.

This talk of Erika being alive! Morbid, tasteless, uncalled for. I was there when she died, and my grief at having lost her through violence was eclipsed only by the horror that it was my own misbegotten acts that had caused her death. I harbored that flame in the darkest cave of my being, tending the guilt that might light the way towards some form of redemption (this last line may explain why my poetry has been such a smash). This was my cross, with no real atonement achieved in the six years since her passing. (I considered suicide, but only in the sense of a solution; I had no desire to die; I still had plans and hopes which revolved around women, Paris, the Greek Islands, and a small body of poetical legacy, even if it resided mustily on the shelves of libraries; being out of print is not the same as being unpublished. So I considered suicide the way one might consider murder as an alternative to divorce: it solves the immediate problem, but, if you're bedeviled by notions of Catholic sin and damnation, it also opens up a whole can of metaphysical worms. Blowing my brains out would not be worth the headache.)

When I was a child, my mother (elegant, like my father; neither of their sons are) was an associate professor of literature at Emerson College in Boston.

Each year she taught a course on the post-war American "Confessional" poets: Robert Lowell and John Berryman, Sylvia Plath and Anne Sexton, Ted Roethke. She juggled quite a workload of kids, career, a troubled husband, marriage, and mind. Her methods of saving time in a busy schedule showed remarkable flair. When I was still in jammies with feet, she would read me whole chunks of this stuff at bedtime, prepping for her next day's class, on the condition that if I was quiet and behaved, my reward would come in the form of the next chapter of my current Paddington Bear book.

Thus I learned the rhythms and imagery of "Skunk Hour," "Oh Daddy," and "Menstruation" before I'd entered the fifth grade. Even after my mother cracked up for good and was packed off to McLean's hospital (home away from home for so many of her favorites), I harbored resentments through my teen years about her deficiencies, encouraged by therapists to assign the blame for my maladjustment to Mom. Only the chaos and disappointment of my own adulthood provided some understanding and forgiveness towards a woman who I now realize loved me and was truly doing her best from inside the wicker basket of lunacy. This realization, it figures, came long after any opportunity to tell her; she died alone and frightened. If my parents bequeathed to me the germ of a slumbering insanity beyond the relatively banal alcoholism, it had not made itself plain in any serious manifestation. I'd yet to be locked up like Mom and Dad. Yet.

What did emerge was the bequest of my mother's love of verse. The arc of my education might have begun with the post-war Americans (so intriguing, if confusing, to my little mind) but gained its ascent with lifts from Beatrix Potter, Hillaire Belloc, Ogden Nash and Roald Dahl. Rod McKuen (you heard me) built a bridge from the nursery to adolescence, a hand-off to the Beats, and one glance at Gregory Corso told me to go find a voice. I started penning some, if not raw, then at least far-from-cooked efforts that served as filler in coarse and stapled punk sheets that I handed out at places like the Sword in the Stone on Charles Street. One of these, a free verse take by a street drunk on the Eucharist, combining the plight of skid row with the concept of transsubstantiation, was picked up by a few of the more credible coarse and stapled punk sheets and websites in New York and even the West Coast. This caught the attention of Charles Bukowski, who called me long-distance for a praise-filled, boozy chat. I begged the price of a ticket from my father, at the time descending into his last maelstrom, and went out to visit the old souse Bard. I watched every step, and being young, healthy and of fierce tolerance, matched him drink for drink, was sufficiently and genuinely (but not overly) sycophantic, and ventured no opinions on poetry or literature or even art in general that might cause the old bastard offense. He was so pleased with the weekend as he remembered it that he called in a favor at the *Paris Review* and got a few of my poems into an issue. A literary earthquake did not ensue, but led to acceptance in the Gilded Clutch—the Reviews *Kenyon, Evergreen, Black Mountain*, et cetera. By graduation from high school, I was apparently on my way to making a minor name.

> *Thinking of you today, as I floated like a crocodile*
> *In two feet of murk,*
> *I pretended that Chocorua overlooked the Asmat.*
> *The piss-warm water lapped at my vicious jaw,*
> *The dial of my year-earned lake-resistant watch.*
> *A domesticated day turned tropical*
> *On rum, an old World Atlas;*
> *The clerk at Banana Republic*
> *Told me pointedly that the first Panama hats*
> *Were made in Ecuador.*

Thus began my rather long (some said too long) poem, "For Michael Rockefeller, Lost in New Guinea in 1961," which appeared in *The New Yorker* on my twenty-first birthday.

I dined out on the viability of having appeared in its pages for several years. I worked and reworked poems with a vigor and attention to detail that alone convinced me I was the voice of my generation. All the while, my generation was growing up and earning a living. Poetry is no way to earn a living. There was a much-talked-about but never seen book, a first collection. Despite the mounting trail of pieces in obscure rags, Quality Lit journals, and the fat maraschino cherry of *TNY*, as I came to call it (ye Gods), none of the major minor houses were interested. I refused to allow the low-rent operations to publish my book without paying me; I was arrogant.

I supported myself as a clerk at Newbury Street Comics and tutored undergraduates in English and American Literature (who the hell needs a tutor in Lit?).

When I was twenty-two, my father jumped out a fourth-floor window, surviving the fall. He hung on in the hospital for two days, where I held his mangled hand. His final words were, "What the hell's the delay?"

When he died, I came into a modest inheritance.

Chapter Two

1

It was into the tepid gloom of the passing of my mother and father that Erika Wikki stepped blithely, like every step she took in her short, incandescent life. She was certainly enamored of the wretch in a man; she saw me as wretched.

We met at a poetry "slam" (dumb term). She told me upon introduction— with onlookers —that a) I might be possessed of genius, though it was truly second-rate (I could never pry out of her what a second-rate genius was), and b) she was going to marry me.

She was lovely, foot to crown. Godiva smooth and delicious, dimpled knees, small round belly, and, as stressed to the authorities, only a hint, a swelling, of breasts, but who cared? (Not me, always of the opinion that big boobs were one of the most overrated American icons of the post-war era, surely since Hollywood went Hughes Aircraft. I actually preferred the average or small, both seeming friendlier somehow, certainly less demanding; at the same time I was aware that this might be indicative of mild depression). Her true erotic appeal was centered at the *piece de resistance*, a truly callipygian derriere like nobody's business: round, high to the extent that one could play a hand of bridge off it if so inclined, tight but plush with baby fat right round the lower curves and a sensibility that fairly trumpeted *Way to Go!* And best for last, round again (she was a collection of curves, this geometrician's dream), a precious face: full, bright mouth, slight overbite, almond eyes straight from Shirley MacLaine in the *Can-Can* and *Trouble With Harry* period; long bangs over them, and the whole package gift-wrapped by a skin the color of which gave the impression of honey poured from a jar twelve months of the year. She looked good enough to eat, as if biting her would tap a flow of mead to cause ecstatic coronary occlusion in the lucky vampire.

We had been ill-suited from the beginning. She was only minimally interested in poetry, and that of the minimalist variety, rather than the juicily dripping over-ripe fruit I was serving up. Her previous boyfriend had gone out for cigarettes, met an unwashed missionary for the Children of God, and never come back.

There was the matter of the rent.

We found a studio, more like a bedsit, at 7 Grove Street on Beacon Hill: practical fireplace, kitchen view of a brick wall.

One thunderous, lightninged autumn night, a guest told us that seventy-five-year-old Ida Irga had become the fifth victim of the Boston Strangler in August, 1962 in that very room. Erika ate it up. A potential shade made me uneasy, even then.

One snowy winter's morning, I awoke to a distant foghorn permeating the place like O'Neill's sense of doom. I looked down at the sleeping girl next to me and realized I was happy, that she had opened up in me a previously undetected capacity for joy.

She never once, even on the day we were married at the registry office, told me that she loved me.

I discovered with the slow deliberation required to reveal the heart of an artichoke, that at the center of my beloved was a desperately ill young woman. She was given to bouts of mania and depression, cyclical, then all would be well and quiet. For a while.

The wedding marked (typically, given the construct of my generation) the beginning of the end of the relationship. We slogged through five years of discomfort, my addiction trying to keep pace with her mental illness, the toddler of my alcoholism tugging at the sleeve of her insanity.

Breakdowns, hospitals, doctors, pills. Her lifelong interest in the occult assumed a central role at the final disintegration point. She'd spent a bundle devouring everything by or about Aleister Crowley, Israel Regardie, the Golden Dawn. Our apartment she filled with crystals, wands, Tarot decks, totems of an apotropaic or disgusting notion. I was away for two days and she painted all the walls black. She began corresponding with Kenneth Anger; the Samuel Weiser Press sent her catalogs; sodomy with incantations and candles became the staple of our sexual diet, me as dragooned line-cook. When she took to burying her urine in clay jars in moonlit fields and expressed a yen to dig up a corpse and cut off its hand (the *mano morto* being the most highly prized and powered charm), I knew she'd gone round the twist.

She searched everywhere for a straight-razor, found and purchased one, slashed her calves and wrists, bled, was stitched, scarred, and recovered. The doctors were stern with me about the psychiatric help she so clearly needed. There was talk of committing her. She would talk with none other than the High Priestess of the North Shore coven. I tried to ride out the storm and drank.

In the late spring the doctors said a change of scene from the Tomb of Ligeia (as I called the black-walled Grove Street flat) might be helpful. I suggested Bar Harbor, Maine, the provenance of my father's rarely mentioned spirituality, and a tranquil haven in the off-season. She agreed, packing her silk underwear for her own pleasure and her cotton for mine, and a copy of *Naked Lunch*, a book I'd found impossible to read.

We alternated at the wheel of the rental on the nearly five-hour trip up the New England coast. Attempting betterment, I was reading William James's *Varieties of Religious Experience* and tripped over this:

> *The next step into mystical states carries us into a realm that public opinion and ethical philosophy have long since branded as pathological, though private practice and certain lyric strains of poetry seem still to bear witness to its ideality. I refer to the consciousness produced by intoxicants and anesthetics, especially by alcohol. The sway of alcohol over mankind is unques-*

tionably due to its power to stimulate the mystical faculties of human na-
ture, usually crushed to earth by the cold facts and dry criticisms of the
sober hour. Sobriety diminishes, discriminates, and says no; drunkenness
expands, unites and says yes. It is in fact the great exciter of the Yes func-
tion in man. It brings its votary from the chill periphery of things to the
radiant core. It makes him for the moment one with truth. Not through
mere perversity do men run after it. To the poor and unlettered it stands
in the place of symphony concerts and of literature; and it is part of the
deeper mystery and tragedy of life that whiffs and gleams of something
that we immediately recognize as excellent should be vouchsafed to so
many of us only in the fleeting earlier phases of what in its totality is so
degrading a poisoning. The drunken consciousness is one bit of the mystic
consciousness, and our total opinion of it must find its place in our opinion
of that larger whole.

I may as well have tattooed this passage across my back, as I took it for years as an almost mystical license to drink, failing completely to grasp that "so degrading a poisoning" part. I remained pickled.

In Bar Harbor, we checked into the Bluenose Inn and took in the incredible images from the top of Acadia National Park. I was later to view Welsh hills, mountains in Montana, the Russian Steppes, but nonesuch struck me as those in Maine: the land of the Valkyries, the gates to Valhalla—it was unearthly. Erika was impressed, but tired easily. She was hungry—"cranky"—she'd put it, without a hint of self-deprecation.

After sightseeing the first day, we returned to the bed and breakfast for a nap. She surprised me when she initiated gentle, unadorned lovemaking with enthusiasm. We both slept until early evening, showered, and dressed for a dinner at Carmen Verandah, a nifty place with a balcony running all along the second-floor dining rooms.

I drank my usual excessive amount, but she kept pace with me. She usually skipped the cocktails and went straight into the white wine, but she ordered a martini along with mine, then dove into the Frascati, washing down her

Shrimp Diavolo with a waterfall of it, and topping off her chocolate cheesecake with a snifter of Remy. I had equally consumed all these drinks and more, but our routine had been that she, always drinking far less—except when dining at home, when glasses got smashed— would be driving. It was after she swerved returning from the Senorita's room and ordered a second glass of cognac that I grasped she was plastered.

Her mood seemed buoyant; she ate and drank with gusto, as she had not for some time. She engaged me in literary chat. She mentioned several times that she was on a "threshold" to a new life, a new place, really, and that she had me to thank for this. I might have squinted through the blur of my sodden state to consider double or even single meanings of these, in retrospect, unambiguous statements, were it not for the flirtation that appeared midcourse like a premature waiter with an outrageously excessive check. Erika had not flirted with me since the early days of our courtship; never told me I looked attractive; never ran her fingers through the hair that fell on my forehead; never stroked the back of my hand, nor my thigh under the table. All this was now occurring in surreal slow motion. At one point, her full lips wet from her glass, she leaned on toe-tips (shoes discarded) to kiss me full on the mouth to the approving grin and disapproving scowl of an elderly pair of lady and gentleman diners seated nearby.

I was drunk on alcohol, yes, but also life, love, and erotic, romantic abandon, the moment. No excuse. I know, I know.

She gave the impression she had something to say but wished someone else would say it for her. She took off her wedding band and handed it to me. She said, for "safe-keeping." My drunkenness did not, at the time, consider this odd move worth questioning.

After a sweet dessert, she implied there were sweeter meats to be had down south (hers) if we could hightail it to Frenchman Bay to see the moon in full flower. I was concerned about our conditions and lamely suggested first just a nice stroll back to the Inn, lamely suggested secondly a safe slow crawl in the car back to the Inn, then lamely suggested third we find a taxi to drive us to the beach, which did produce from her a snort of contemptuous derision as to how in hell we would fuck in the rear of a cab with the driver at work in the front. Good point. She said she would drive.

As smashed as I was, I calculated that my height and weight would better handle the torrents of booze I had poured into myself than hers would the amount she'd swallowed. I took the keys and hit the ignition. I'd yet to be nailed for driving while under the influence (yet!) and felt the purr of the little rental compact to be a sign of terrific collusion on the part of the car in negotiating the curves of the slim road leading to the sand and surf. I drove endangering our lives and the lives of others like a happy devil, well aware that my speed and condition couldn't possibly handle a situation demanding quick thinking and nimble reflex. A sheep wandering lazily in the road? A van full of nuns rounding the corner, me in the wrong lane? I drove as a menace.

I also became lost. We. I cranked the CD player, blasting Led Zeppelin's ominous "Kashmir" (how she loved it) and used my confusion to fuel the speed of the car, Led Zeppelin by lead foot. She laughed with abandon, ordered me to roll my window up for the cold and sang along with Robert Plant in her high, clear soprano.

I turned to look at her—and took my eyes off the road.

I never saw the bridge coming. I would later examine it from all angles, recreating a chain more than once in other vehicles, the missed signposts (*Slow. Bridge Ahead. Dangerous Curve*) as nothing less than bloody metaphorical. The police concluding I'd taken the twenty-mile-an-hour curve at forty-five.

The thudding impact of hitting the thick wooden guardrail and the sounds of smashed, splintered wood and the cracking windshield I remember as part of a sickening flash as the earth dropped down beneath us and the car fell like a roller coaster the twenty feet to the dark water below, a perfect splash, like jumping into a bright pool on a July afternoon. This sound followed instantly by the rush of cold sea through every channel of the vehicle and the screams—mine, of terror, hers, I swear, of delight— as we sank into what might have been the bottomless depths of the ocean.

In fact, it was ten feet of water to the bottom, and the little rental (a Subaru, I think: how could I forget? I have) settled on the murky bottom of the estuary. As the water rose quickly up my chest, I recalled uncannily from high school physics that the pressure of the interior had to equalize before I could open the doors. I struggled with my seatbelt; it stuck. There is not a single act I have performed in my life with more concentration and determination than attempting to release that seatbelt. The stakes were high. I freed it with an undeclared *Hallelujah thank you Jesus!* and a genuine conviction to devote my remaining life to God's love and work. Erika seemed paralyzed by the rising water and made no movement. I filled my lungs in the last two inches of space beneath the overhead light of the car and descended under water, the interior filled, to unlatch her belt.

We were submerged in the cold shock of saltwater and complete blackness— the light went out instantly. Erika wasn't struggling. I tugged at her belt and her belt released. I pulled her hips up out of the seat, freed her door, and I pushed her from the seat through the door and tumbled over her out of the car.

I ache to declare that I grabbed her waist, her arms, her hair, her ass, and dragged her to the surface with me. Grappled her.

I didn't.

Once free of the death-ensuring safety belts, I kicked upwards, upwards, up, and broke that chill surface, a freaked man fighting for his life.

Rocks, calmly lapped by the sea, were right to hand where I rose up not so much like Poseidon. Reassuringly close, the fear of drowning was neatly removed. I waited for Erika *my Darling, oh my Christ my Darling, please, please, please* to follow.

She didn't.

Later I was assured by cops that my diving back down into the cold, tenebrous drink to find her warranted *heroism*. Make of that what you will. I kicked my way to the submerged car—three attempts—but couldn't find it until I did. I couldn't see; I tried, the salt stinging my eyes to swollen-shut. The passenger door was open, the seat empty. I rose back to the surface, this time as if on wings, and tread water for what seemed a long, long time. Surely she would kick up to me, alive and well, and love me as I loved her, post-traumatic happily ever after.

I don't know how long I waited, but it was long enough to assure me she was not coming back.

I swam slowly to the rocks, dragged myself, dripping and trembling up onto the shore, and clambered and lurched like Victor Frankenstein's sick creation up the hill to the point of impact. There I sat down dejectedly and shivered, waiting.

That's where I was found. I am told, only twelve minutes later, by the police, who had been alerted of the splintered guardrail from a passing clam digger and by the sound of a disturbing howl of despair. I was blanketed, later informed I was in shock, and that she was missing. I knew this.

The police grilled me on the events. I didn't call for a lawyer (I had no lawyer, nor parents, nor influential friends; who would I call? My dentist?) and I didn't lie about any facts easily corroborated by wait-staff at the restaurant. My wife and I had been disgustingly drunk when we'd left. I drove, impaired beyond belief. I lost control of the car, crashed through the guardrail before a bridge … yes, I did. I did. I presumed in those still-drunken moments that those in authority would punish me for my sins.

At 6:07 the next morning, shivering still (a change of clothes from the Inn, coffee, blankets—no matter what, I could not shake the bone-chill, feeling like a take on Macbeth: I would never be warm again—I was informed that Erika's body had been found in ten feet of murky water, five feet from a bank that would have saved her had she been able to reach it. Most likely nitrous narcosis had done it, given the alcohol and cold seawater, said the coroner.

Have I mentioned that Erika couldn't swim?

Despite my admission of complete intoxication while driving—the single ferocious factor in the cause of death—no blood or breath test had been taken from the clearly accountable. Perhaps the investigating authorities concluded that accidentally killing your wife was a heavier rap than they could ever impose.

A hearse-chasing attorney attempted counsel, but was waved away. I had done what was obvious to all. The police infuriated me with their pity and empathy. I was slapped on the back by an official ruling of "death by misadventure," whatever the hell that meant.

I walked. Trembling, shocked, and hung over, I was denied my crucifixion. I had killed the only girl I'd ever loved.

Erika's funeral was held right there in Bar Harbor, at a conveniently available distant branch of her family's mausoleum. I had never known of any family connections for her in my father's favorite retreat; what an odd coincidence. I returned by Greyhound bus to Boston.

Not a single member of Erika's family has spoken to me since the funeral, and I don't blame them. How big of me.

And it is simplistic but true to say that we do not know what we have until it is viciously snatched away. My little sociopath had built a semblance of a life for me. I loved her. Without her, I entered into a false approximation of life, dragging a heavy chain, a far worse drunk.

I knew Erika carried a great deal of pain and never shared it with me. Why? I was supposed to be her husband, but I wasn't. I wanted that pain now, hers—*hers*.

But hers was finished; she was dead. Mine was just beginning. I was twenty-seven, a widower, and a murderer.

Like a Victorian lady suffering from vapors, I can never listen to "Kashmir." Its droning, occult, vaguely Arabic swirls bring me back to a bridge in Bar Harbor that I crossed too fast— failed to cross—because I was too drunk to drive. A reason, not an excuse. I am in no way responsible. I did not want this to happen, I was drunk, but I shall always be damned for being accountable. Can anyone without blood on their hands understand the difference?

A month later, I read Burroughs' *Naked Lunch*, and its giddy horrors spoke to me profoundly from the cold depths of the North Atlantic coast.

I returned alone to the Albert DeSalvo apartment on Grove Street and was awakened by Erika's smell. Though no one ever came to visit, her Miles Davis albums disappeared into thin air. At four in the morning, I heard her giggling in the kitchen.

I was frightened.

I bought a gentle, big-headed, cross-eyed Siamese kitten for company, never bothering to name her. She hissed at unseen shadows, unheard sounds.

I would find her crying, cowering in a corner, then gather up and tuck her under the bed clothes with me, trying to soothe us both, confiding every fear to this simple creature; I was that lonely. She was a tiny, hesitant, awkward housecat, never allowed to leave the apartment.

One afternoon I returned to find the kitten missing—escape impossible through locked door and windows—along with a pair of Erika's underwear I retained as a keepsake.

I tore the place apart in sobbing panic, but both kitten and panties were gone.

I could not make any logical sense of this.

Erika haunted me.

2

Despite a daily drink habit of nearby twenty years (I was my own kind of junkie), my grasp of the insulation of narcotics was poor. When Poplin let slip the news of my being without a situation—jobless, no income, no means of support—what should have been pretty disturbing information bounced off the candy-floss-lined armor of my narcotized state like a ping-pong ball. This information, coupled with the possibility that my dead wife was actually running around blowing things up, including myself, certainly should have been sufficient to set my teeth on edge, but Nurse Julie had warned me that spontaneous pneumothorax was exacerbated if not directly prompted by excessive stress. Therefore, victims should at all costs take it damned easy, and heavy trank was a wicked help with that.

For the five days that I languished in the soft and easy hospital bed, drugs kept me calm and blissed. I felt almost Christ-like in my benign, benevolent forgiveness towards the many real and imagined, right up to the blast, who'd helped me down the path to victimhood, and I was certainly being a good American by reveling in victimization, for this was all the rage in the age of non-accountability and irresponsibility: Anything bad that happened to us was always someone else's fault, never our own, and they must pay. (Several hospital staff inquired as to whom I would be suing; a general question that even children seemed to understand.) I understood this—and a little more about addiction, and the lure of narcotized molasses—and my practical self was closed for nearly a week on account of molasses.

You don't have to take a walk on the wild side, however, to appreciate that the key inconvenience to drug abuse (and this included alcohol) is that an interruption in the flow of substance causes discomfort physical, mental, emotional and spiritual. By the time I was ready to be discharged from Adams Memorial, the prescribed intake had all but ended in complete cessation of the hard stuff, and anxiety was playing havoc with the lingering music of my cherished and greedily protected feeling of great well-being. I was jittery, and the recalled news of my job and Erika Wikki rode in on a wave of dread and fear. Once all depressants had cleared my mind to a raw and fragile condition, I never saw Julie again, and no one would give me more drugs.

Chauncey Alexander MacFarland Jr. had been discharged less than forty-eight hours after admittance. I heard two nurses discuss his aches and pains and malfunctions, all of which, they felt, were unfounded.

One odd note of a punishment element: I was told I must never travel by small plane, hot-air balloon nor scuba dive. This struck me as comically arbitrary ("You must never, under any circumstances, pogo-stick"), but an unlaughing physician said it had to do with pressure. At thirty-three, I'd still held out the hope that I'd rise once more above the Veld by bush-plane, certainly Jacques Cousteau-it at least once in the coral reefs of Key West or Tahiti, and most definitely munch Brie and caviar, if sanely foregoing the Korbel, before my ascent in the romantic basket of a multi-colored balloon. Now, unless I wanted the wet or dry collapse of the organ, no could do. A disappointing pisser.

I was wheeled to the door, my scraped face freshly shaved, my right arm in a sling, with a meager handful of Not-to-Be-Refilled Percocets and deposited on the sidewalk. I squinted into the early summer sun, feeling like a released convict, slipped on my out-of-date prescription sunglasses, and decided to find out about my professional status before taking the drink I desperately needed and had been sternly warned not to mix with the Percs. The stitched wound beneath my arm throbbed.

I grabbed the Green Line and rode the T to Copley Square. Although twelve pounds lighter and pale, I hadn't looked too bad, all things considered, in the mirror that morning. With the confidence of someone who's survived an ordeal and feels deserving of great sympathy, I strode into the Boston Public Library, the cavernous institution that had been my place of employment for nearly a year. I was not a librarian; I stacked books. I took cart after cart of returned items and stacked them on the shelves, eight hours a day, five days a week. I warmed myself with the conceit that at least I was working amongst friends. The books, I mean; the staff ignored me.

I strode purposefully, sling notwithstanding, straight into the offices of Julian Tesseract, my boss. Julian was younger than myself, which rankled me, but not half so much as he was a prissy, overly-groomed, humorless, meticulous lover of administrating. Julian didn't read books much, literature never, and may as a well have been overseeing the maintenance and efficient operation of a cannery. He didn't know F. Scott from Ella and actually flaunted his willful ignorance of literature, smug that in the library sweeps, he was on his way up by a mix of determination, politics, and guile. In the labyrinthian microcosm of the BPL, Julian knew where the guns were hidden.

His secretary ("administrative assistant!") was absent, so I walked through the door to his office without knocking. He was bleeping and blipping schemata on his smartphone with the concentration of a NASA engineer. He glanced at me as I entered, but an actual double-take secured his attention; a forced confection followed.

"Paxton, my God—are you all right? The city blows up, and you're right in the middle of it!" In an awkward, bad actor move, he picked up a crisply folded, apparently unread copy of the *Boston Globe* with the bombing as its big front-page banner. The edition had to be nearly a week old but was apparently intended to serve as a prop; he raised it high, a grinning Harry Truman. "How are you?"

"Well, I'm going to be honest with you, Julian—"

"Why would you be anything else?" he said cheerfully. He had immediately taken charge of this chat.

"Right. Well, to be honest, I'm pretty shaky. My right lung collapsed, I have a stitched and bandaged wound on the side of my chest, and I'm sore and banged up." He gestured for me to sit in the low chair in front of his large desk as he settled into the plush, elevated one behind it. He propped his elbows on the armrests and brought his fingertips together. I settled in carefully.

"You look awful, Paxton."

"Thank you." He frowned. "I mean, thanks for your concern."

"Oh."

"I'm very fuzzy—you know, the drugs they gave me."

"You have to kill the pain, don't you?" He smiled. "Everything in order with your insurance?"

"Seems to be."

"Yeah, they're the best group going. And that's in effect for you even when you're terminal." This took a short second to sink in on both sides of the desk, and he gave a short bark. "From your job, I mean. Now you've got me doing it." He smiled; I smiled.

Smiling, I asked, "Is everything okay with my job, Julian?"

He leaned back in his big chair, fingertips still together. He was really relishing this one.

"Paxton, we have to talk." A steady gaze in silence, waiting.

"We are talking."

A flash of irritation escaped, a crazed gremlin dancing across his face before the Colossus of Control flung it aside, and the Colossus was now all business and Art of War.

"Sure, Paxton. I'll talk and you listen. For the ten months you've been employed here, your work has been exemplary, but the demands of the job of book stacker are relatively narrow, and executing those negligible—let's face it—demands and responsibilities, no matter how proficiently, does not alone constitute a satisfactory job performance. There are other considerations. Like showing up. You frequently don't show up, Paxton. Your absenteeism has been excessive—twelve times in ten months—and don't tell me that's nothing compared with what's acceptable in Europe, because this is Boston, not Stockholm. I had to speak to you about drinking during lunch—"

"And I stopped."

"But there are mornings you've come in stinking like a gin mill. You've maintained that this is due to liquor consumed the night before and not to pre-breakfast boozing, but how can I believe that?"

Breakfast? Was he kidding? "I never drank before work."

"You often smell like a brewery, and that's inappropriate and unacceptable. This is a library, not a saloon. I can't issue another verbal warning or written reprimand." He paused, looked truly sorry for the flicker of an instant, then the sterling conviction of generations of subscription to social Darwinism clouded his features as the presence of a god, and he said: "I'm afraid I'm going to have to let you go."

I couldn't grasp that he was really doing this to the beaten, battered wreck—sling, bandages and all—slumped miserably before him. I couldn't have done it, which is why we occupied our respective positions, he and I, and there we were.

"Julian," I intoned slowly, "if you could just give me another chance."

"I have, Paxton. Several times. Seven, to be precise. On a day you're supposed to be home sick, you're boozing on Newbury Street and get yourself blown up."

"It was iced tea. And it was my birthday."

"Never rains but it pours, huh? Get some help. You're a bright, decent guy and a hell of a book stacker. You also write or something, don't you? But you're a pathetic drunk. Deal with it."

"When do I have to leave?"

"You already have."

"Any severance pay for being a decent guy?"

"Ha! No. I'm not going to pay you to go away. You've got lending privileges for life. You always respected the books, Paxton. Many here will always admire you for that."

I left with no small feeling of dejection. I now squinted into the blazing sun, broke and jobless.

Chapter Three

1

And so to the deferred drink I would take in full knowledge that it was this that had brought me thus: the irony of the alcoholic, drinking to kill the pain caused by the wreckage brought on by the drink. No, defer the drink further. Do one thing of purpose and put it off. Take stock, count dwindling blessings, avoid that greatest abnegation of pride, self-pity, and always look on the bright side. I whistled the Monty Python tune as I attempted to put a smile on my lips and a bounce in my step toward the Copley T stop, but succeeded only in bouncing my slung arm, bandaged head, quavering lung, and enlarged liver, so I stopped that horseshit.

I picked up the Red Line at Park Street and rode the twenty minutes to Wollaston. It was here, a five-minute walk from the filthily un-swim-mable Wollaston Beach (It looked lovely, a present hangover from the Gilded Age, I thought), in the midst of the blue-collared Irish, Italian and (now defining to the area) Chinese (racist natives called Quincy "Quasia") that I rented rooms in a Victorian boarding-house, an authentic Painted Lady, as the landlord would describe it. Two rooms, a single studio that fit me like a loose shirt, with futon and frame, television (no cable, hence no channels), VCR (many videocassettes), CD and DVD player, desk, chair, bureau, and a bathroom with actual bath, and kitchen privileges. It was cheap without a lease.

My landlady, and the owner of the property, was an ancient widow by the name of Minerva Fecteau who invariably introduced herself as Mrs. Edmund Fecteau ("my late husband"), though this man I would nominate for sainthood had been dead for over thirty years. It would be unfeeling to describe her, but I will do it anyway.

I think of nothing so much as a shrunken head never detached from the body. Wrinkled, withered, shriveled, and gnarled beyond all reasonable and admirable vestiges of hard-won time. She stood just under five feet in a corrective boot for a club foot, the platform heel of which was nearly a foot high; she walked now only with the aid of crutches. Her physical infirmities inspired deep empathy and compassion. A personality like an ulcerated sore smashed the empathy and compassion like glass on granite. Minnie was a wraith.

I quietly let myself in through the front door and flicked through a high pile of mail on the hall table when I heard her reedy wheeze emerge from what she called the West Parlor (there was no East). "Mr. Graham!" This was followed by the signature expectoration, clotted gurgle, sniffle and cough. "Mr. Graham!"

I assumed as exaggerated an injured slump and stagger—on top of what was genuine—as I could muster, and gimped down the passage into the tiny parlor.

High-backed chairs and settees were originally well-upholstered and doilie'd, now much unwashed, undusted. Disused roll-top desk, fireplace dead of all practicality. The slow-death ticking of the grandfather clock was the only sound in the stillness. This was indeed a room to die in, and I believe she liked it that way. She stood, stock-still, on boot and crutch, the rheumy eyes the only thing alive in there.

"Your post is here, Mr. Graham," she said, thrusting one arthritically twisted finger straight down upon a stack haphazardly tossed in the center of the coffee table. She then seemed to notice my lack of physical well-being and a sharp thorn of annoyance pricked into her irritated mood. Was I mocking her decrepitude? Were my temporary, young, and healing infirmities a travesty of her permanent, heavy, and life-long burden? She offered an appraisal.

"You look like dog dirt."

The old bat would never say anything even mildly risqué, let alone swear, yet her substitutes for unacceptable language delivered in her pursed and constipated voice somehow came forth obscener than those they replaced. I would have been less offended if she'd simply said I looked like shit.

"I got blown up."

"I know; I read it in the *Herald*."

She reached out a wizened claw trying to find the news, but no paper was in sight. She was angered by this, possibly alarmed, and there seemed nothing for her but to stump about the room to systematically inspect each square foot to locate the damned whereabouts of the godforsaken *Herald*.

"Yes, I saw that, Minnie, thank you. I guess we need to talk about the rent."

This brought her back like a shot, the scent of blood on the water. "That is correct."

"Can we sit down?"

"No."

"I have no job."

She snorted, then sniffed. "A man without a job doesn't want to work. My late husband said that."

"I bet he didn't. Oh, who cares? I owe you two months, but I'm relatively certain I can get you the full amount."

"Relatively certain? Who's left to sponge?"

"Thanks, that's nice. I'll find somebody."

"Mr. Graham. In the thirteen unlucky months that you have tenanted at Wollaston Way, you have incurred many a black mark in my household ledger." And then, bet on it, she crooked the same Finger of Death down to indicate the leather-bound tome placed heavily on the coffee table that had held no coffee since Nixon, the book's edges filigreed by old envelopes, magazine clippings, yellowed newspaper columns, recipes, check stubs, receipts, coupons (so expired and worthless as to warrant full-blown contempt), post-it notes and every other variety of paper garbage to be dragged with her into what she surely viewed as a welcome grave. Across its stained, weathered cover flaked the last of the letters spelling *Household Expenses, 1998.*

She was horribly stooped, so she only had to bend slightly to creak open the thick volume to precisely the page she required (I was impressed). She adjusted the glasses on her beak and read with emphasis and distaste.

"I have on over forty occasions smelled tobacco and other, undefined odors that you claimed to be incense. This is a non-smoking household. On ten occasions your hi-fi has been loud enough to disturb my television viewing in the den. On two dozen occasions you have returned to Wollaston Way in a visibly inebriated state, staggering, swaying, barely able to ford the stairway."

"I haven't had a drink in twelve days."

She regarded me over her specs, feeble defendant that I was:

"Bully for you."

She returned to my stave in the Book of Transgressions. "And finally, you have been late with the rent every month but one and now are two months in arrears."

She dropped the heavy corner shut and damned if I didn't see dust fly. The case was clearly closed; good hanging judge that she was, she indulged in some complimentary comments before passing sentence. She removed her glasses for effect, being blind without them, but still turned her vermillion, sulfurous, and watery gaze in my direction.

"We all have our share of potholes on the road of life; we all step in our share of dog dirt. But you are marching to the wrong drummer, Mr. Graham, and you can't seem to stand on your own two feet. You have really put your foot in it this time. Lost your job? Fired. I shouldn't be surprised. So this is the end of the line. I have to put my foot down. You are a soak and a sponge and what they now call a slack. You are hereby evicted. I give thirty days."

"Now let's be reasonable—" I started, and then she went bananas.

"Soak!"

"Mrs. Fecteau—"

"Sponge!"

"Minnie— "

"Slack!"

I nodded in resignation, scooped up the mail—bills, all, damn them to Hell—and wandered wearily upstairs to my soon-to-be former digs.

I unlocked the door and entered the stale air of my now-former rooms with their faint trace of alcohol, ashtray, and damp wood shavings, and crossed straight to the large wire cage atop an unpainted table in the corner. I found myself smiling as I peered down to where Ignatz made his nest, a comfortable hole dug out of a blanket of pulp with a neat lining of torn newsprint curlicued into a rosy bouquet of a border. And there he was—plumped in the middle of his bed, the world's fattest hamster, and my sole companion.

"Hey, pal. How're you doing?"

He wasn't breathing. I poked a finger through the spokes of the cage to gently prod his corpulence, found him stiff, then unlatched the door, reached into the cage, and grasped his little necrotized body. His eyes were winced, the little mouth a gaping grimace. Dead. There was no food, and the water dispenser was empty. I placed him back in his bed and walked with deliberation through my still-open door to the door of the room opposite.

I knocked. After what sounded like a disgusted pause, I could hear something extricate itself from sagging couch springs in front of the yammering set, forever on and always too loud. This would be my only neighbor of acquaintance, Kimberly Clark, a young woman with a name that sounded like a Playboy Playmate, but was in fact the same as that of an American urinal manufacturer. Both her sensibility and appearance were more in keeping with the latter than the former.

She opened the door with the manner of one who had been comatose for days, dressed in her twenty-four-hour attire for tubing on the sofa—sweatpants, sweat socks, and huge t-shirt. She looked my bandaged, shaking figure up and down with foggy curiosity, scratched her unruly mop, and greeted me with a heart-warming, "Yeah?"

"Hello, Kimberly. You agreed to make sure my hamster had food and water?"

"Huh?" She was without a clue.

"My pet. My hamster?" I wouldn't use his name; I was modulating my rage to a well-timed climax for this exchange.

"Your what?" She too seemed drugged, and dragged on a Marlboro Light 100 as an earnest of her curiosity.

"My hamster. My lovable, cuddly little only-friend-I've-got-left-in-the-world-and-isn't-that-pathetic hamster?"

"Oh, right," she said, now the gist of my request during the telephone call made to her from the hospital one week previous was flooding back. I waited. She slurred, "I couldn't get in."

"What do you mean you couldn't get in?"

"Minnie don't have no key."

"Yes, Minnie do. Of course she has a key. She's got a key to every god-damned lock in this crypt."

She squinted at my reply through her smoke, then waved both away. Minnie said she ain't got it." She was remembering now and nodding with conviction. "Yeah, she don't know where it was."

"Did she look for it?"

"Huh?"

"Did she look for the key? Did you actually witness her *looking* for the misplaced key?"

"No." She looked offended.

"So how did you expect my hamster to survive?"

"That ain't my problem." This was the first thing she'd said with real surety.

"No, you're right. It's my problem. But it was your responsibility to tell me that it's my problem so I could do something about it. If I didn't know you couldn't feed him—you never called the hospital to tell me—and no one else knew you couldn't feed him, how was he supposed to eat? Order Chinese?"

"I don't know nothin' about that. Alls I know is Minnie don't have no key."

"He'd dead. Did you know that?"

There was a momentary flicker, a shift of emotion on an instant, the notion of those most elemental of ideas—life and death—taking hold in the leftover collective unconscious still housed in the base of her brain, and she stole a glance over my shoulder into my dismal room as if she might glimpse some spectral rodent vision hovering in the bad air. Seeing nothing particularly sinister, she turned back to me.

"He ain't alive no more?"

"No, he ain't. And I'm going to make a real Sherlock Holmes leap here that it's because his dinner dish is empty and his water-bottle is dry and both have been like that since I left over a week ago."

She stalled for time by drawing deep on her cigarette, thinking, exhaling the smoke, then poking a new point with the burning tip. "That ain't my business." She sounded pleased and returned the filter to her mouth.

"Yes, it is, shit-wit. You've allowed my pet to die after agreeing to make sure he survived. I'd say that's your business in a big way!"

At my first use of invective, her hostility, which cruised like a dozing manatee just beneath the surface of her stupidity, crashed forth into the open.

"Don't you talk to me like that, ya fuckin' drunk!"

"How could you let a defenseless little animal starve to death? You know what a horrible, painful end that is?"

"It's yer fault! You was dryin' out from drinkin'!"

"Was not, Sasquatch! I got blown up! Don't you read? Look whom I'm asking? Jesus!"

We continued in this vile vein for some moments, the intensity of the exchange covering the compelled drag-stump, drag-stump of Minnie's crutch-booted gait. When she had reached the foot of the stairs, her shrill screech got our attention.

"Be *qui-et*!" Stump, stump with the crutch. I whirled on Fecteau like an injured dervish.

"Why didn't you give your pass-key to this imbecile to feed my hamster?"

She narrowed her thin eyes and hissed, a Harpy from the Foote of the Steppes: "Because we do not allow vermin at Wollaston Way! I will not tolerate infractions. That is why."

Kimberly smirked and narrowed her own ignorant eyes at me, perfectly assured from Fecteau's rationalization for causing the slow death of this poor creature.

Bruised body, crepe lung—delicate and only recently inflated and at-tached—slung arm, cracked head. Any one of these factors was enough to sensibly prevent me from committing the act that came next. Through a rainbow of handicaps, what followed was true fully: I swung my right foot fast and wide and kicked Kimberly in her fat shin. She emitted a high-pitched howl that immediately down-shifted to a guttural groan. Then she was on me like a baboon, all fists and bulk, and unkempt odor. Forty cigarettes a day had done nothing to deplete an energy reserve fueled by dumb instinct. I was immediately alarmed by the pummeling I was getting. I began to drop step by step, crippled and awkward, yelling in protest as the huge harridan flapped above me all the way down the staircase, two steps or more at once, the both of us oblivious to both Minnie being dead in our path and her acute inability to step clear with less than a half-hour's notice. Our hurtling, tumbling, clambering duet knocked her aside like a child-mannequin and she tumbled, big boot and all, to the hardwood (but fake-Persian) carpeted floor. Minnie's banshee soprano stopped Kimberly in her large tracks, and, knowing on which side her jumbo-sized bread was buttered, she stooped to the bones on the earth. I fled through the double doors from the chorus of screams and wails ("Horrible, horrible drunk!") of Wollaston Way.

I squinted up to the same sun that was now warming me, broke, jobless and homeless.

2

So I fled into the sunlight; trembling, frightened, and sore. I needed a drink—that was all there was to it. I needed a drink as so many Western men after a terrifying turn or close one do. I think of the company of Gable, Cooper, Bogart, Faulkner and Hemingway; no, scratch those last two; they were uncontrollable lushes, like me. No, I mean Raymond Chandler, who keeps a bottle in his desk and has learned to knock his shots back neat. A shot, yes, I needed a shot— maybe bonded rye. I didn't know what the hell bonded rye was, but it sounded perfect. I gimped my way down the street to the Hope Street Grill, the local public house, an establishment I avoided on general principle unless in dire need of liquor (which tended to happen, on average, twice a week). The Hope Street (called, you guessed it, the Hopeless) was an old-fashioned, Irish-American, blue-collar, white, working stiff, racist, sexist, homophobic saloon. A gimlet eye was cast on outsiders or newcomers, at least for the first decade, so I drank alone and stared silently, having the good sense from experience (I had spent some brief time working in an auto-parts factory) to not bring with me any reading matter. (Chuckling over a witticism in a spangly issue of *Vanity Fair* or whistling at the prose in a passage from Proust definitely flew the freak flag up the pole.) Desperate drunks require desperate measures, the measure of a shot, to put a fine point on it, and as I did not keep fifths and pints in my lodgings through any dependable system, I would be forced to make the pilgrimage up Hope Street.

I adjusted to a John Wayne gait and ambled in past the two neon Bud signs and was blasted by cool air-conditioning carrying the twin scents of food (Piggy's quahogs—revolting industrial stuffed clams, the only edibles offered to qualify for a liquor license) and stale beer. An announcer called a Red Sox game from the very loud television (pandemic malaise of the times), and a white-haired, florid-faced old rummy named Billy McCarthy wheezed phlegmy sighs over his boiler-maker. What a dump—and a fine place to get fucked up.

I ordered a Jack Daniel's on the rocks (I had a bar tab), sat on a corner barstool, and got down to the business of extracting a serious plan from the encroaching swamp of my troublesome circumstance.

I hadn't once called to follow up with the ghastly Kimberly or the execrable Fecteau on Ignatz's well-being. I'd spent a week in a comfortable bed, meals wheeled right to me, getting off on narcotics and not giving a damn about the filthy old world beyond Room 323 of Adams Memorial, not a second thought to the one living being that depended on me for anything, in this case the sustainment of his very life. I groused that at my age I should enjoy the trappings of an adult—home, family, career—yet I had proven in one afternoon that I was unfit to handle even mediocre work, pay the expected hire on a hovel, or take responsibility for the care and feeding of a hamster. Sasquatch and Bigboot hadn't killed Ignatz; I had. He must have thought I'd abandoned him, and I had done that; I was not worthy to care for the poor little guy, goddamn zero that I was, and where the *hell* was the drink I ordered?

"Paxy fella, well knock me ovah with a featha!" came a friendly voice in this unfriendly surrounding. I turned to witness the splendid sight of my moon-faced, planet-sized recent acquaintance, resplendent in a perfectly-tailored suit, matching tie and handkerchief, and handsome walking stick— Chauncey Alexander MacFarland, Jr.— "Digger" to his friends. The few hopeless patrons at this hour stared in astonishment at the likes of which they'd never seen in there before.

"Chaunce," I started in amazement.

"'Digger," he corrected.

"What the hell are you doing here?"

"Looking for you, my young souse. I was comin' up the street in my cah towards your address when I seen you perambulatin' with difficulty into this establishment." He looked around with distaste.

"I just ordered. Why don't you join me?" I glanced up the rail at the barkeep, who, far from having made the supreme effort to fill a tumbler with shaved ice and one-and-a-half inches of bourbon, was now leaning into a salacious conversation with a tight-attired tootsie sporting two-inch square-tipped fingernails. He didn't give a damn about my drink.

"I got a better idea," said Chauncey slyly. "You come'n be my guest fuh lunch at someplace more apropos to my proposition."

"Proposition?"

"Ho, yuss ..." And he took my good arm, flashed the Tenniel smile, and gently tugged me from the dank and fetid cocoon of the hopeless Hope Street Grill.

It was lunchtime, and the high noon sun (the same that had witnessed me blasted into the air above Newbury Street six days earlier) was starting to warm me up a little.

Chauncey's chauffeured, vintage masterpiece of an automobile had to be seen to be believed: his 1954 crème-colored Bentley Continental ("R Type," he said with a wink, "known as a 'Flyin' Spur'") smoothly carried us on the Southeast Expressway into the heart of Boston. Soon we were ten miles north and fifty stories above Wollaston Way, in the Top of the Hub restaurant at the pinnacle of the city's tallest skyscraper, the Prudential Tower.

For many years the joke had gone that one dined at the Top of the Hub not for the food but for the view, a panoramic picture of all of Boston, its harbor, and the Charles River. The scene was impressive both day and night. But the old standby had changed hands, the décor had been upgraded to swank, and the jewel in the crown was now—surprise—the menu itself.

The *maitre'd* extended a warm personal greeting to Chauncey, and though his suggestion to lunch here had been seemingly spontaneous, it now seemed as if we were expected. We were shown to a fine corner table. As he settled his bulk into the chair opposite mine, Chauncey said, "Swell romantic, ain't it? And you're stuck with me. Tough luck, fella." True enough, but he was paying.

The waiter was there in a trice, and given the desperation of my craving, I was slightly astonished to hear myself ordering a tonic water well-zested with lime.

"Just a reminder that Schweppes contains quinine, sir," our waiter helpfully informed me.

"Ayuh," said Chaunce to the waiter. "He knows. Done his military service in Rangoon. That quinine watah'll do ya good there, Pax. Look a tad malarial this mawnin'." Chaunce chuckled and the waiter laughed along with him, bursting with the joy and certainty of an impressive tip at the end of the prandial road.

The abstention was two-fold: I realized I was very hungry and wanted to savor the delights of the *pate* and *chaudfroid* and cucumber-dill soup and lobster salad offered up by this rare luncheon. One Chivas on the rocks or Beefeater martini straight up with an olive would be followed by at least two more, and then I'd be off and awash, the food lost on a sea of white wine, then ignored altogether. Alcohol killed my appetite, kicked my stomach, and said, *to Hell, let's get pissed*, and many an evening of fine and costly dining had been totaled by my hell-bent-for-leather boozing.

I was also intrigued by Chauncey's pointed mention of a proposition. My tonic came, as did his stinger, and he put his fingertips together, elbows on arm-rests, as Julian had done earlier in the day. "How's things?"

"Well …" I began, gazing out across the promise of the skyline. "I'm down to my last forty-one bucks, in precarious health, and today I lost my job, my home, and my hamster died."

He stared at me only briefly. "Jeezum Crow, that's tough. But like they says, Paxton, ever' cloud's got a silver linin'. My *pahtickulah* proposition provides you with an income and a place to live. Sorry 'bout the hamstah, but I can help ya 'mmediately with all the rest. Now tell me this is *not* your lucky day!"

"It's not?"

"No, no, it *is*, it is. How ya feel 'bout relocatin'?"

"Where to?"

"Northport, New Hampshire, just up the coast."

"I know the place. Why?"

"On account o' Wicker Madness."

"I'm sorry?" I thought this might be a continuation of the malarial humor.

"You heard right. Wicker Madness. One of my five wicker and rattan furniture outlets— Northport, Peabody, Salem, Dedham and Danvers. Hadn't ya evah heard my commercials on the radio?"

"I only listen to NPR."

"Snob."

"I thought you were an undertaker."

"I'm diversified, Paxton, but I'm also in a jam. My shop up there was bein' run by these two German kids, Dolf and Irmgard, nice blond kids, real efficient, kept great books 'n' inventory, good steady sales, and the place so clean ya could eat offa the floor. Everything was just jakey till three days ago"

"What happened?"

"After I got blowed up with you and was recuperatin', lying next to you as useless as a single order o' smelts, they ups and takes off, abandons the place—*vamoose, amscray,* no *sayonara* or nothin'."

"Why?"

"Shoulda seen it comin'. Seems Dolf, when he ain't out girlin' was gettin' a little too chummy with Hildegard, Irmgard's twin sister. She was livin' there helpin' out with the store and whatnot, which's fine by me long as them visas is square, and it sure as shit seemed fine by Irmgard, as she's the gormy cuss what got her sister over here from Dusseldorf in the first place. Clearly that plan didn't include Hilda getting' knocked up a stump by Dolf and Dolf wantin' to set up housekeeping in some sorta *menage a* threesome. Anyway, Irm refused—can't say's I blame her—and Dolf and Hilda took off for Branson, Missouri 'cause her friend's cousin works for some old singer out there and Irm's lit out after 'em. She mailed the key, *auf wiedersehen,* and me left high 'n' dry with a three-thousand-a-month store front, and who's mindin' the store? Nobody, that's who."

He paused to look at me for a moment, then said, "It ain't gonna pay for itself." When I still didn't respond, he tried, "That's where *you* fits in."

I stayed with the poker-face but was instantly smitten, appropriately Germanic. I'd visited Northport a few times— a quiet, scenic little harbor town off the beaten track.

"How tough is it to run the shop?" I asked with the steely, unwavering gaze of a hitman weighing a contract. Chauncey smiled.

"T'ain't in the least. Perfect little set-up for somebody convalescin' like yourself. Like me, for that matter," he said with mild irritation. "No heavy liftin', all the pieces in the place're just floor models—ya order it all. Customer falls in love with the Nantucket set, you close the deal, set's delivered to their door in three weeks. No fuss, no bother, the stuff sells itself. And when you ain't waitin' on customers, there's all that t'rific down time to read and write your whozit."

"How much?

"Five hundred a week, plus ten percent commission, but here's the clincher: 'bove the shop there's a cozy one bedroom with a view o' Northport Harbor. That I'd throw in lease-free and complimentary. You live overhead with no overhead."

I asked, "Why me, Chauncey?"

"'Digger'…aw, Lawdsakes …" He looked embarrassed. "You jus' seem like a decent kinda fella, and it didn't' take no genius to figger from yuh conversation with them cops that you's down on yuh luck. I been there too, you know. And heck, know when ya travelin' and yuh make bonds, strike up fast friendships with each other? Guess getting' blowed up together's kinda the same thing. Like we survived a shipwreck, eh?"

I thought about that for a nice, reflective moment. "I thought you said in the hospital that you never traveled."

He flushed, chuckled, looked sheepish. "Didn't say I *nevah* traveled. Jus' said not much. I done my shay-uh. So come on, Paxton. Ya only have ta commit for the summah, then if ya likes it, stay. Whatdya say?"

"Does the French Foreign Legion still exist?"

"Huh? Aw—you and yer kiddin'—no, seriously."

Given all the facts, what the hell else could I say other than, "I'll take it"?

He was delighted, and happy to pay for our outrageous lunch, which included steaks, oysters, and caviar, finished off with fresh raspberries in caramel.

A curious thing happened during the meal, however, or didn't happen. I never ordered a real drink, even after consuming all I wanted of the excellent cuisine—not even a good glass of wine. I could have downed at least a snifter of cognac, and Chauncey even suggested a bottle of champagne to seal our deal, and I didn't demur; but nor did I press the point when he failed to remember the suggestion after polishing off three *crèmes de menthe* with dessert. And it was clearly forgetfulness, I thought. Clearly, as he reached for a check that read like the bill for the Bunker Hill Monument.

3

I spent much of that evening humming, "What a Difference a Day Makes," as I had forgotten most of the words. Chauncey was so eager to have the shop staffed and reopened for business that he refused to allow my loose ends to impede the alacrity of getting me ensconced in Wicker Madness. I mentioned my concern about returning to Wollaston Way to collect my things, what with back-rent due and the inevitable confrontation with Medusa Minnie and Gorgon Kimberly, which could lead, in this day and age, to assault charges from both. Not to worry, said Chaunce, and with dispatch he would arrange for a team of Mayflower movers to pack up my books, posters, and CDs, and place them in Back Bay Storage, then package and mail my clothes, toiletries, and notebooks via UPS. (I asked Chaunce to see to it that Ignatz was given the decent burial he deserved in the little park near the Southern Artery cemetery (I'd often take him there for washed dandelion leaves) but remain uncertain whether this was carried out. When I let it subtly slip, repeatedly, that I teetered on the razor-blade-edge of complete penury, I was advanced my first week's salary in cash, peeled from a thick wad held fast by a gold-coin money-clip and, lacking a car ("Natch," said Chaunce good-naturedly), a one-way bus ticket to Northport along with the keys to the shop and the flat. I was deposited directly from a post-luncheon stroll through the Common Gardens (Bentley crawling close by in case of sudden and unassailable exhaustion) to South Station to board a C&J bus. I had time to have a drink in Clarke's, the station tavern, but didn't. By late afternoon I was standing in front of Wicker Madness. It had all happened so damned fast.

4

Northport, New Hampshire is a classic example of the recent evolution undergone by many a New England seaport community, with all its hideous implications. Founded a year after the Pilgrims apocryphally stood on Plymouth

Rock and found the view acceptable, Northport stood as solemn witness to and participant in the events leading up to 1776. Washington, Franklin, and Hancock had all done much sleeping in Northport. One of the signers of the Declaration was a native; hell raking John Paul Jones drank and wenched here. By World War II, the vast and deep harbor was home to a naval shipyard whose war-effort boast was production and completion of one submarine per month. In the 50's and 60's, the place was a blue-collar town with no pretensions and a rich historical heritage mostly ignored by its citizenry.

A native son might say, "'T'was those from away wrought the change," first for the better, then for the worse. The 1970's felt the first rumblings of the impending renaissance. The sleepy harborside town of 18,000 was discovered by painters, broke folkies, and poets who came for the sea air, the cheap rent, and the light. As their influence made itself plain in a decade, the privileged wealthy—most blessed with an abundance of leisure time and choice of address—followed in their wake.

Change became the rage. Hosker Park by the Sea began hosting a summer festival. Chowder fests and chili fests and fiesta days and a behemoth, commercialized Market Square Day were all inaugurated within five years. The local flea-pit, the Colonial, began showing Fassbinder films. Finally, the apotheosis of the transmigration of the town that had lost its soul came when Teddy's Lunch—a greasy spoon on the square where you could grab a slab of pie, a cup of coffee and a pack of Luckies—was transmogrified into Café Brioche, a pastel eatery where one could drop by for a tarragon kale-and-spinach salad before appreciating the touring Peruvian dance troupe appearing at the restored Music Hall (formerly the Colonial).

By the end of the century, emigrants from Boston, New York, and Philadelphia were pouring in, and the independently owned shops had mostly been squeezed out to make way for the Starbucks and Gaps and Banana Republics. That most ironic group of the dispossessed—those dispossessed by having stayed put—could no longer afford to live and work in their own community and had to move elsewhere. Taking their place was a thundering herd of out-of-towners, a hoard escaping the filthy cities on a mission to gentrify the ramshackle neighborhoods of this unbearably quaint place with the money and imagination sorely lacked by the original occupants, thus skyrocketing the shop and home values, taxes, and rents. Dot-coms and high-tech were now the order of the day, money as the last great American frontier. Large and tall Hilton Gardens and Sheraton Towers blocked the view of the river. You would be hard-pressed to find a native born in Northport today who didn't earn an annual bundle. Struggling artists create the initial attraction, and are then displaced by the rich, who find it all so grandly appealing.

The town's geography was more attractive than its recent history. Located across the Pipsissewa River from Kittery, Maine, Northport commenced the Granite State's thirteen miles of coastline. The streets and lanes were carved out through a tangle of 17th and 18th Century sensibility that had not imagined the automobile. Privateer mansions with widows' walks were uneasy neighbors to saltboxes and capes, which in turn looked down on utilitarian monstrosities thrown up in the rush of the Industrial Revolution. Last and least were the interchangeable housing developments and suburban tracts for gracious living. Old Yankee pride and yupped-up money.

Wicker Madness was located in a four-story brick building on Congress Street, two blocks from the center of town, and a five-minute walk from the bus station. I walked the five minutes with a single plastic bag from Rite Aid, having used some of my advance to purchase toothbrush, toothpaste, and shaving necessities until the meager possessions of my life arrived in a brown truck. I unlocked the heavy door, made my way as instructed to the security system keypad, and tapped in the five-digit code to deactivate the alarm.

I found the light switch (the only windows being at the façade of the building, and these cast a mean light, the shop being deep and rectangular) and the illuminated room gladdened my heart: track lighting, exposed brick, beautiful teak floor, real potted plants in panicked need of water, ceiling fans above, and an array of woven furniture pieces, sets, and suites, all crammed haphazardly into the show space. It was like a sturdy home in Port-au-Prince with twelve living rooms and no walls. The "business" area of the set-up consisted of a huge wicker wing-backed chair in front of a rattan desk with a telephone, answering machine, and large calculator, all artfully concealed from view by two tall Japanese *shoti* screens.

Chauncey had explained that the archway at the rear of the shop led to the stairs to the apartment above; the side-door near the entrance gave onto a lobby and staircase for the rest of the building, which housed offices, the whole place owned by Chauncey. I switched the lights off from the back and was about to lock both doors (it was the magic hour for June, now near seven o'-clock and closing time) and check out the upstairs, when I heard the bell on the door announce that someone had entered the shop.

I had to cross through the field of furniture to get a closer look. She was young, late teens or early twenties, with large, liquid eyes that were spooky in the half-light of the strange room. She was dressed in a short-sleeved, blue silk shirt and a pleated, white cotton skirt, short enough to display to mid-thigh a perfect pair of brown legs. Her polished and pedicured feet were wrapped in a pair of white doeskin sandals, one ankle clasped by a gold chain. A belt matched the sandals. Standing stock-still with her big eyes staring straight at me, hands folded demurely in front of her, she could have stepped off an Edward Gorey calendar.

"I'm afraid we're not—I'm—not—open."

She stared.

"The shop's closed. I'm sorry; I just got here."

"From where?" she asked.

"From Boston," I replied, an *if it's any of your business* lift at the end.

"Oh. That's interesting."

I didn't agree that my one-hour move over the state line was even remotely intriguing, but what did strike me as terrifically interesting was the clear beauty of her face as she stepped into the yellow pool of light thrown from a tall wicker-shaded lamp. The large eyes that appeared so ghostly from a few yards now registered a soft, inviting gaze, which might appear to the cynical as a "come hither" look, but to me arrived as pure and lovely. Her hair looked as soft to the touch as the different fabrics of her clothes, and even the skin of her face and neck seemed to radiate a warm invitation to caress. I was dumbstruck.

"Is it?" I responded, now meek, and taken aback; no instinct could form a coherent philosophy yet. My gaze had actually locked into hers, captured. She smiled self-consciously (or was it the satisfaction of a point already gained?), glanced away, then back in an alluring manner so charming I wouldn't have been surprised if she'd flipped open a handfan and started singing Gilbert & Sullivan. I had just joined the ranks of the deluded. If I was not on that instant in love, I had cracked its foot-thick frozen casement with a fire-ax.

"Yes, I think so," her voice tinkled musically, "and you will too, if you stick around here long enough."

"Just for the summer, I think," I said dreamily, a Victorian vicar enthralled by a vampire. If she noticed my somnambulistic gaze and imbecilic half-smile, she showed no sign, but began a gambol around the shop with a subtle sway that would have turned Mae West malevolent. She put down the battered Signet paperback she was carrying—Ian Fleming's *Thunderball*.

"That's awesome. I just came in for a hand-mirror and I know exactly where it is. Do you mind? I won't take a sec."

I watched her drift through the maze of furnishings. "Here it is!" She lifted a blond-wicker, long-handled mirror from a coffee-table. "I'm off to a birthday party, and this is my gift. It's twenty dollars." She drew a crisp, folded twenty from where it had been tucked out of sight between her breasts. She proffered this, then giggled at my expression. "Sorry. I don't have any pockets or a purse. Would you gift-wrap it for me?" I willed the enchantment from my psyche like a man knocking water from his ear and admitted I had no idea where any gift-wrap might be, if in fact any existed. She smiled, turned, and nearly walking on tip-toes in a proud parody of a schoolgirl, opened a cabinet to reveal wrapping, boxes, ribbons, tape, and scissors.

"Well!" I said, delighted by her and her late afternoon magic. "Isn't that something. You've been here before?"

She moved a stack of fabric swatch-books and laid the wrapping materials on a large table under a hanging lamp and pulled the chain to illuminate the space. I now had to concentrate on not making a botch-up of wrapping her gift.

"Sure," she said. "My friend Hildy worked here. Oh my God, would it be rude or hurt your feelings or anything if I wrapped it myself?"

A true Tinkerbelle. I may have been blushing as her resourcefulness was certainly warming up my features, I could feel it. She smiled again, the wryest dance of coquetry about her lips, dropped her eyes; I melted. She switched on a stereo I hadn't seen and something I recognized as Chopin filled the air. Although I was doing absolutely nothing but watching her—her hands, with their perfectly manicured white nails, graceful as she pulled the ribbon from its spool, her perfect curve as she bent forward—I felt no self-consciousness about it, nor, apparently, did she. As she ruffled the ribbon into a bow with the scissor-blade as a final touch, she spoke—low, quiet, a touch of the curt.

"I know who you are, you know."

I stayed quiet, not completely convinced I had heard correctly, much less the meaning.

"And," she added. "Oh my God, I knew you before you were who you are now. We've met."

Perhaps she spoke of reincarnation. The soft play of the light in the shop; the thick, muggy air beyond the windows; her beauty, the very tantalization of her presence—it was all getting a little heady.

"What's your name?" I asked.

She picked up her wrapped gift and admired her work. "There. That looks awesome, doesn't it?"

"Very nice." I hadn't taken my eyes off her.

"If I tell you my name that'll give it away."

"What?"

"The game. You don't remember me, do you?"

"My God...I'm sure I would have...I doubt I could forget you." *My God* was right. I was talking like the soppiest sap to ever gee-whiz in a Dick Powell musical. She laughed in light appreciation, powers at full strength.

"I look a little different, so I'm not really being fair. Six years ago, at your wife's funeral."

I held a baffling image of this creature floating gently above the congregation, iridescent.

"I was twelve. You gave me your copy of Maurice Sendak's *Chicken Soup With Rice*."

Now I remembered. That kid, the daughter of a cousin of Erika's.

"Hayley," I said without exclamation, almost reverent, as if invoking a mystical name.

"The very same." She smiled. I felt like hugging her.

"What are you doing here?"

She ignored this, but looked genuinely pleased. "I never forgot how nice you were. I was too young to understand what you must've been going through."

"So was I."

"Sorry." And she looked at me, sweetly, and I had the sensation that I was in the presence of a rare flower, and why I should clasp so strongly to so slender a stem I cannot explain, Oh my God. She asked, "Did you know I live in Northport?"

"No."

"We moved down from Presque Isle four years ago when my father got his job. I graduate from Northport High in two weeks."

"Congratulations."

"Do you remember me?"

The gathering after the funeral service had been held at the home of one of the distant Bar Harbor relatives, a large, impressive house not far from the Rockefeller summer "cottage." I remembered the atmosphere of a vigil of mourning turning quickly to a social event with many of the island's most famous inhabitants in attendance. The funeral had been held in the afternoon rather than the morning to accommodate some late arrivals, and as the reception stretched into the late evening, a chill sea air descended upon the house, and late summer that it was, the outside lamps and indoor candles began to flicker and even fires were lit to crackle beautifully in several rooms. I had retired to one of these rooms, a masculine den with leather chairs and a mounted moose head, and helped myself to the decanter of what turned out to be good Scotch (I kept my imbibing low-profile the day of the funeral, considering the cloud of suspicion regarding my inebriety the night of the accident, which lowered over my head). I settled into a plush loveseat with a glass of the single malt and stared at a Vermeer reproduction and the flickering fire and felt a little like Barry Lyndon toward the end of his life. "Fur Elise" drifted in from somewhere. I glanced up from the hypnotic flames in calm surprise to see a phantom had appeared at my elbow. It was the very Hayley from the present, but a smaller model with bigger eyes, a child of Walter Keane and Mark Ryden. She was a twelve that could have passed for six. I was not pleased to see her. She wore a thick, padded, floor-length robe belted around the middle and slippers, and carried both a stuffed version of my old childhood chum Paddington Bear, complete with "Please look after this" note attached, and a book.

"Hello," she offered.

"I don't think so."

Clear, child-like question: "Your wife died?"

Cynical, childish response: "Tell me about it."

The poor thing looked puzzled, bit her lower lip, fidgeted momentarily, then with a barely perceptible nod of her curl-tousled little head—the decision had been made—she asked if she could sit with me while climbing up onto the sofa, taking no chances. Could one be possessed of curmudgeonliness at twenty-seven? I had never liked children and never given them a moment's notice except to object to the culture's mawkish tendency to grossly sentimentalize them. My nephews, my older brother's two kids, had been growing up without any kindness or attention from their uncle, probably to the relief of my brother. Swallowing a mouthful of the smoky whisky brought on an intrigue; I decided to attempt kindness and attention with the moppet as guinea pig.

"Hey, kid—what's the book?"

She beamed as if I'd inquired as expected and presented for my approval a hardcover edition of *Charlotte's Web* by E.B. White. I felt a sharp pang.

"I love this book," I said.

"It has a sad ending."

"I know," I said, flipping the pages to look again at Garth Williams' sublime illustrations. "My fourth grade teacher read this book to my class. I expected a happy ending like all the other children's books I'd known. And then Charlotte died. I couldn't believe it! I guess that was my first real grasp of mortality, you know?"

"Uh huh," she nodded, adjusting Paddington and reaching over to show me a picture of Templeton the Rat. I was talking to this child, my co-initiate in mortality, little more than a stuffed animal herself, as if she were in secondary education. I continued. "Have you read *Stuart Little*?"

She nodded vigorously. "I love that book—and this one too—just like you."

"That one ends sadly, too."

She nodded gravely. I leaned closer to her, to make my point, like Henry Kissinger with President Thieu. "I mean, think about it. Nothing is working out in Stuart's life. His ideas, his projects, his romance—it all turns to crap. He feels like he's a burden to his family, so what does he do? At the end he just drives off alone, destination unknown, as if to spare everyone the burden of him. Christ, that's depressing."

She nodded again. "It is." She paused. "You talk different. I never heard anyone talk like you."

"I'm from Johannesburg. You know where that is?" Of course she didn't; I hadn't met an American yet who'd know where that was. *Africa, isn't it?* Very good: narrowed it down to a continent.

"Um ... the nation of South Africa." I was impressed.

"That's right—um, as you put it—what's your name?"

"Hayley."

"Like the comet?" This brought forth a burst of the girlish laughter I would hear again six years hence.

"Course not—that's *Halley's* comet," she said, rolling those big eyes heavenward as if exchanging an exasperated glance with the famous celestial body. "I'm named after the actress, Hayley Mills."

"Oh, yeah, Walt Disney. I always liked her."

"My favorite is *That Darn Cat*."

"You ever see *The Moon-Spinners?*"

She hadn't see that one. And so we talked like two old critics. She said all the candlelight reminded her of Christmas; she didn't remember ever meeting Erika. I finished my fishbowl of Scotch and filled another. At times, steered by me, the chat would take on a bitter, fatalistic flavor, and she would purse her lips, frown, furrow her brow, and you would swear a spittoon had appeared between us, but after a respectful moment of glum rumination, she would toss up a topic like a tennis ball and be off and running on Dahl, Belloc, or dear old Lewis Carroll. I was completely at ease—feeling restful, even—with this wind-up doll. I had quickly developed a large respect and affection for her—me, who had never kept no poppets—but to what goddamned end? I didn't even like kids.

I pulled from my pocket the pocket-sized Sendak and handed it to her.

She thanked me profusely, said her mother might be wondering where she'd got to. She slid from the sofa, touched her feet to the floor, said goodbye, and stepped to the door, then spun decisively, came back, and wrapped her arms around my shoulders and hugged me, brushing her cool lips across my cheek. I was startled by her gesture, but had no chance to react before we both felt the foreboding presence that had entered the room, Grendel's shadow descending across the floor. A chill touch had vanquished the warmth of that small room.

"Hayley!" The snap of a thousand icicles.

This tiny kid seized, threw herself backward, and stood swaying at comic attention, trying to keep her balance. The tall, stern woman radiated fury, her intense focus flitting from one of us to the other and back again, like an overwrought performance in a silent melodrama.

"Mother." A meek voice redolent with dysfunctional relativism. The unhappy, unhealthy vibe in the delivery of that appellation could level brick. And the woman was livid.

"Where have you been? Did you know that your father and I have been looking everywhere for you? Did you know that we intend to leave very, very early for Montreal tomorrow morning, and that's a very, very long drive and you need to get to bed?"

"Have you ever actually driven a standard?" I asked Hayley.

Though the features of her face remained blank, Hayley's suppressed reaction bulged her eyes out as she regarded me like a mini, feminized White Rabbit. The mother glared at me with suspicion, distaste, maybe hatred, and spun the kid like a top to march her out of the room, tossing me a rather toneless, "You have our deepest sympathy for your loss."

Hayley looked too embarrassed, disappointed, and distraught to manage any kind of farewell. The Mother, Sharon Glass, was a distant cousin to Erika, a psychologist and lacrosse coach at a private girls' school. Erika disliked her, so never spoke to her (or perhaps it was the other way 'round), so I never liked her, and now my dislike for her took on whole new realms consonant with this latest exchange.

"The kid's an eccentric little dope," I thought. "Tough luck she's saddled with a creep for a mother, but we all have our lacrosse to bear," but a glimpse of Sharon's rich potential for Dickensian villainy stoked a reluctant affection for the little slob.

"So you do remember me," she was saying now. "You look a little lost."

"Of course I remember. You were wonderful. A real precocious little poetry freak."

"Still am. Not precocious, but—still a poetry freak."

I put her straight to the test. "Like who?"

"Oh, everything by everybody, but I guess my top ten greatest hits list would hafta have Shakespeare and Shelley and Yeats," she ticked them off on her fingers, "and Hopkins, Lawrence, Thomas, Eliot, Lowell, Sexton, Plath, Berryman, Hughes, and Larkin."

I was stunned. "I couldn't have put together a more perfect list myself. Any new stuff?"

"Sure. I just read this poem in an old *New Yorker* about this guy Michael Rockefeller who disappeared in New Guinea in 1961 that I thought was a minor masterpiece."

She smiled, letting the meltdown begin. I was so delighted and touched and flattered, I'm surprised I didn't' guffaw like Goofy in a Disney cartoon. A lachrymose, "Aw shucks," was dangerously close to apparent in my eyes, if not exactly tumbling from my lips. I was speechless, though the idea of scooping this now-grown little doll up in my arms and carrying her off for the rest of our time on earth to keep— be it crumbling castle, windmill or tower, an abandoned lighthouse, or shack-on-stilts in the Everglades—and simply love her every which way, did occur to me.

"Have you seen the upstairs?" she asked. "You *are* staying in the apartment upstairs, aren't you?"

She stepped smoothly to the archway, and with a quick flick of her wrist, simultaneously turned off the shop lights and turned on the stairway's. She regarded me once like Dracula's daughter ("This way"), but she did not, in fact, say anything as she turned, and I followed her ascent.

She opened the door at the top of the landing and turned on a lamp to illuminate a pleasantly and tastefully furnished apartment. It made Wollaston Way look like something out of Nelson Algren. It was a charming loft set-up with a raised ceiling and canopy bed, queen-sized, ersatz Edwardian by way of Levitz. As she opened windows to let in the evening air, I wandered over to the bed, inspected the apparently working fireplace, and felt somewhat humbled by the comfort of the space that I could now call, at least for a while, my own. I felt a sudden and great sense of gratitude toward Chauncey.

Hayley then recited:

"Stirring in our marriage bed,
Creeping from my fusty socks,
to hollow warm against my head,
to breathe asthmatic in my ear,
the Siamese girls curl up, embrace
the only lovers here."

This was the opening stanza of my poem, "The Half-Mad Clock," which had appeared in an issue of *Juxtapoz* Magazine when Hayley would have been, I quickly calculated, about seven. Once she saw she had my astonished, rapt attention, she continued:

> "My ankles twist me back to bed,
> Feet cut on broken promises.
> For when you've parceled off your heart
> to have it tossed upon the sea,
> you cannot get it back again;
> it's gone, you see; it's gone, you see.

> "The clock stops always, starts again,
> Paid off, proceeds, our auctioned life,
> Rousing me from cats and keep
> To never die from lack of sleep.
> And you, my wife, should praise the dawn
> From well-earned rooms, not that you've gone."

She paused for a long moment when she'd finished; she was facing away from me.

"You wrote that before you were married, and she was alive."

She returned her head, and her face appeared over her shoulder to gaze at me and smile. I crossed the room, drinking in its cedar smell, with no conscious intent, but found myself taking that lovely face in both my hands, and with no further words, her face was coming close to mine, her eyes closing, her lips parting, as though in full acquiescence to the demand that I kiss her, and we kissed, two mouths met in serenity, *eros* achieved, stimulus to commitment, sensual, aflame, the real McCoy.

She danced me to the bed to her hummed rhythm of "The Merry Widow Waltz." When we reached it, still locked in a warm kiss, bumping the frame, a puff of sweet-scented breath expelled into my mouth from her giggle. In the terms of the hipster and the travel agent both, we were halfway there. We descended onto down-filled quilts, quickly sank. Could I get the light, she asked?

Below, a car moved slowly down Congress Street, playing Jimi Hendrix. The feather-tipped strands of "Little Wing" flew in through an open window.

Chapter Four

1

If the sweets and salts now passed my way (or fairly plopped into my lap) were unearned and undeserved, then just as unjust were the events to follow, circumstances so bizarre that in the days to come I frequently expected to wake up with a shriek in a cold, seal-skin slick of sweat to discover with relief that the whole Byzantine fiasco had simply been a monstrous dream. It was a nightmare, all right—a waking one.

We did not make love that first evening. Had I attempted any seductive maneuver more daring than the relatively chaste caress of her luscious backside, there lurked the danger of appearing a randy vulgarian trying to make as much as I might—the realm of the fumbling college-boy. With so much inner swooning and heart-shaped anticipating already clouding up the room, I settled on the better part of patience. She was like a sunning butterfly I was afraid I'd startle. Had she been more aggressive with me, say, thrusting eager hands down my trousers or hiking up her skirt with the crude words of an adult-video actress ("Give it to me, baby") I would have been put off. Salubrious adult-video enthusiasm was always to be approved—but not on the first date— and this didn't even qualify as a date, what with no bread broken or bottle broached. She was, instead, every inch a class act.

If you are a man distinguished by fine looks or wealth or power (and I'm only guessing here), the very value of the commodity you possess can be tragically bent as the instrument of your downfall. I had nothing to worry about. All I owned in this June twilight was what I had not lately come to think of as my mere ability to create, my small talent as a poet. That was all. Toss onto the sunset swirl of the Northport canopied bed a spectral nymph of dewy eyes and limbs and charms who knew my "work" (ha!) as a nineteenth century Etonian knew his Milton, the wet temptations of flattery, vanity, and gratitude grew fierce in me like a phalanx of demons bed-intentioned. The kiss and all else following confirmed what I'd intuited when she'd crossed the shop threshold, and perhaps (and best not think on it) in the embryonic fluid of that first unsealed meeting six years earlier? I believed I was already in love with her.

And why the hell not? She was beautiful and sexy, with a taste and scent that delivered the crucial percentage of love. She was charming and funny and cheerful and sweet, romanticism and eroticism oozing off her like butterscotch off a sundae. She was intelligent, a reader (the Bond novel, sure, but also plowing her way through *Middlemarch*, for the love of Mike) who knew and loved good poetry, and well above all, she knew and loved my stuff, *ergo*, she knew and loved me. She was a bounteous gift to a man who had been thankful for the unconditional devotion of a hamster.

As I said, that first time Hayley served as guide up the staircase, we did not make love, but off her came the bouquet of two dozen tea-roses. She was sitting on a potential burst of promise.

But it was a bad time—a climate, as they called it in the courts of Salem, Massachusetts, and the hearings of Senator McCarthy—and an illogical one. The sexual conservatism of the 1950's produced a culture that reflected that era's sensibility. The ideals of the permissive '60's and prurient '70's were mirrored in the aesthetic of the times. Now, in my times, we had a culture as salacious and scatological as that of Aristophanes, yet a society whose mandarins condemned real sex in real life, a demonization of the ugliest stripe, and it would get worse: this was the forecast. The black thunderheads and ominous winds gave me no pause as I skipped and whistled swinging a picnic-hamper into the eye of the storm. I could have been a drummer-boy with Napoleon's army marching happily into the Russian winter of 1812. I was that clueless.

2

From that first night we were inseparable, and life was timed on the construct of a Swiss watch. Hayley had graduation practice, forms to be signed, last meetings and functions, but she was free in the late afternoons and evenings. I ran the shop as the shepherd or lighthouse keeper I had always yearned to be. Most customers were browsing tourists with no intention to buy; they appraised my wicker world with vague interest and moved on. Chauncey advised that two sales of a major set per week would qualify as success. He was correct that the caney stuff sold itself. All buyers were women (sheep husbands in tow), who knew what they wanted before they walked through the door. Barely had I glanced up from *Lolita* and the deal was closed. The only noteworthy moment of that first week occurred when a grubby hoyden of ten contravened my suggestion she take her dripping ice cream cone the fuck out of the shop. She summoned her mother from the sidewalk; I denied everything but was not believed. A lawsuit was threatened. The dash of retail.

But I was in a dream state between visits from my girl. The film series at the Music Hall changed its program daily, affording me the chance to play the cineaste and squire her to screenings of *Lawrence of Arabia*, *Dr. Zhivago* and *Ryan's Daughter*, whetting an appetite for epics reciprocated when she was able to drag me to ("You are so not serious you've never seen it, Oh my God,") *Titanic*.

We watched a muggy open-air production of *A Midsummer Night's Dream* in Hosker Park, took in jazz in "arts spaces" and lingered over long meals by candlelight. I hooked her on raw oysters; my aversion to mousse and cheesecake and all things confected challenged her; many females would have bristled when I said only women found chocolate exciting; she drew her sword and described a grin:

"I'll give you a sweet tooth yet," a true Cheshire Puss.

This was not a rejuvenation or a rebirth, no renaissance so much as habilitation in the first place. I was celebrating, and it felt fantastic. My happiness was so unexpected, inexplicable, and indescribable, I won't attempt to describe it, but will settle for the joke about the most notorious curser in the town, a fellow known far and wide for the putrescence of his filthy language, the streams of obscene invective served up whenever life afforded the right moments, and they were many. One day he was carting his wares to market up a steep hill when the tailboard of the cart let go, sending the contents crashing to the bottom of the incline in utter ruin. A crowd gathered to await the apocalyptic outburst sure to follow. Instead, the man gazed dolefully on the sight and said: "I cannot do justice to this situation."

I was joyous. Bubbling on the froth of good clean fun and adolescent dates, I was living the happy late childhood that had never been, a lovesick swain fallen hard. I had been a daily drinker from the age of eighteen, scarcely drawing a sober breath since. It's said when a drunk at last puts down the drink, he'll find himself (in emotional development at least) right back at the age he was when first he lifted the glass. I did the math: Hayley and I were actually peers.

But what of my reluctance to advance our relationships beyond the tactile appreciation of her skin surface, lips to toes? Was I not possessed of lechery? This weighed heavily on the carnal instincts, but wasn't discussed; it never seemed to cross her mind. It was she who initiated that first kiss, she who took my hand strolling up the glistening moonlit beach at Pirate's Cove, she who slung an affectionate arm around my waist in a summer throng. She attended me more attention than any high school girlfriend I might have had and as much (no, more) as my departed wife. I felt whole, at peace, healthy, and positive as any mother's hopes, dating the girl next door.

(Had her parents discovered our relationship, they would have gone absolutely ape. The tracks of our clandestine assignations, including the occasional overnighter—sharing the four-poster bed, but clasped in unconsummated devotion—were covered by an elaborate network of exaggerations, obfuscations, distortions, and outright lies provided by Hayley's bosom bunny buddies, and a salutatorian on a scholarship to Dartmouth gave scant cause for suspicion to a father steeped in lucrative business dealing and a mother burrowing away in the septic cavities of child psychology.)

And I was not drinking. I was afraid to examine that one too closely, like an unread contract already signed. I had nary touched a drop since before the explosion, but carried with me still the lingering afterglow of the death-like paralysis of that last harrowed hangover. But this cessation was not so unusual. At least three or four times a year I would stop long enough to feel well again (meaning the discontinuation of constant nausea, the triumph of keeping food down, the evaporation of paranoia and groundless terror; farewell to shakes, tremors and sweats, hello B-complex, steady hands, regular meals, and a reliable sense of well-being), get the body fit and act like a normal human being until I inevitably tore myself down again.

It was different this time. When an addict gives up his currency, a substitute must be found in which to channel the impulse toward excess, just as energy must transfer itself to a new form when the old becomes untenable (not for this reason alone did I believe in the probability of a life after this one). Since arriving in Northport—as clear evidence for a case of geographical cure as needed, and meeting Hayley, simultaneous events—I had experienced no desire nor even temptation to drink. My mistrust of this disinclination sprang from the knowledge that any cause for celebration was as good a reason to guzzle as bad news or the mundane daily grind.

I had been a heavy drinker for fifteen years. James's "degrading poison" had possibly leached away my talent, my sense of the sound, and my integrity (integrity, finally, being the most sacred; if you could fake that, you had it made). Booze had also become my chief reason for getting up in the morning. How could my unapologetic and fiercely determined thirst be so quickly slaked by this juicy Northport peach? It didn't add up. I didn't care; I was floating on a pink cloud raining pennies. It crossed my thoughts that maybe I should check out a meeting of Alcoholics Anonymous. I had heard they were pros. Later, later.

I was now fresh and fit and rested in the morning, clear-eyed, clear-minded, and bursting with a sense of health and a desire to be productive. All in ten days. Amazing what recuperative powers the human body can command. Since leaving the hospital, I was experiencing a sensation of renewal, the new lease on life one hears about. I had not dared a cigarette, and the wrestling match I'd endured with my smokes caused considerable rue. All the while I knocked Kimberly's bowling alley puffing, I should have footnoted the hypocrisy that my own consumption over the last year had risen to some thirty Silk Cuts a day, cigarettes I could ill afford in health or pocket. The nicotine intoxication alone was enough to bestow a daily sense of unease, but hyperventilating during panic attacks (also daily) induced by severer blackouts and coughing fits in the hot spray of the shower each morning surely taxed my lung capacity. I had come clean to my doctors. Why lie? I was given the professional information that I was alcoholic and should not drink.

Now, if I drank, I would surely smoke, and I should not smoke, as my lung would collapse again, and the painful sensation under my right arm and the memory of the chest-tube inserted bitingly between my ribs both gave me the willies. And by probability, there was a good chance of death by alcoholic misadventure: I had passed out with many a lit cigarette, burning pillows, carpets, floors and fingers, but not yet the house down. Not yet also the fall down the stairs, nor the William Holden head-gash, the Dennis Wilson drowning, the Jackson Pollack car crash (if I had a car), or the Malcolm Lowry overdose. The list of *Yets* was near endless. I had to quit and stay. My ferocious oral fixation was more than compensated by Hayley's throbbing delights, and she was right—I had developed a sweet tooth, and who would not be satisfied by such a lovely sugar substitute? Perhaps I was finally growing up.

3

Morning the tonic,
Gulped gratefully bedside
From the water glass.

A feeble haiku, but it was the first thing I'd written in over a year, and I stared at the three simple lines with something close to pride. I was sober, in love, and writing again. Good God, a miracle! I had turned from a pickle back into a cucumber, as my darling bud put it one morning.

Now—what was to become the notorious Night in Question: the evening of Saturday, June 14, was balmy. I remember thinking of that word as I closed the shop for the night to thrill over the still-novel idea that life was, in fact, worth living. Then the temperature turned cold, even for a New England June, an ominous portent for the horrors to come.

Fact: I took Hayley to Goldi's, the only authentic New York delicatessen in New Hampshire. I took sloppy delight as a Dutch/Polish Catholic convert by way of the Dutch Reform Church in introducing her maiden but half-Jewish palate (her mother's side, yet the woman was a blatant anti-Semite) to the joyous sweets and sours of deli, which she'd honest-to-God never had, but for which she was now riding a galloping enthusiasm. There is no sight to behold more enjoyable and luxuriant than a lovely, mannered woman with a savage appetite. We dined on cold borscht with sour cream, pickled herring in wine sauce, gefilte fish, cheese blintzes, and a dozen half-sour pickles washed down with iced celery soda.

Next: We attended Bergman's *Smiles of a Summer Night* at the Screening Room in nearby Newburyport, me enjoying the plummy fairy tale for the sixth time, Hayley labeling it "elegantly horny," following the remark with a glance that caused me a warm purr of delight.

Fact: After the film, we proceeded to the Newburyport apartment of one Maurice Micklewhite, Hayley's drama teacher who'd promised to loan her a videotape of a college commencement speech delivered by Kurt Vonnegut. Since Hayley, as class salutatorian, was expected to speak at the graduation ceremony, he'd strongly urged her to watch the tape for tonal inspiration. The governor of New Hampshire, a self-made woman of considerable accomplishment, would be giving the keynote address. Utterly devoid of humor and imagination, the governor's speech was expected to be lethal, and Micklewhite wanted the remaining addresses to be lighthearted, and to please. He'd forgotten to hand it off to her; no matter. Though in Provincetown for the weekend with his boyfriend, Hayley was welcome to let herself in to his flat using a key provided by Chip, a trusted neighbor famous for his indecently short cutoffs.

We arrived at the apartment, took the key from slow but friendly Chip (who posed as if loitering in a bus terminal), and let ourselves in. The videotape was waiting with a friendly note on a table near the door. Directed lighting in one corner illuminated a wall-sized and magnificent shrine to Barbra Streisand. It took approximately sixty seconds to enter the apartment, collect the tape, pocket the note, *salaam* before Streisand, step back outside, lock the door, and return the key. We got into Hayley's new car (an uncalled-for graduation present from the rich paternal grandparents, a sporty silver Ford ZX-2) and drove the twenty miles back to Northport.

I believe we must have overdosed on the erotic vibes of the film, the night, the chill sea breezes. She'd been driving her new car fast and recklessly, but that night insisted I take the wheel. I avoided driving at all times, both voluntarily (who would I kill next?) and involuntarily (I had no license), but she pressed the issue as if some measure of her femininity was predicated on my taking the wheel.

I reluctantly agreed, she snuggled in close as I drove, and whispered somewhat hotly in my ear that she was covered till morning by a concatenation of lies, and that she was also "in heat." I was to carry her over the threshold and up the stairs over Wicker Madness for some rite concocted in the festival of her head.

This I did, with an ease that surprised us both, Hayley being quite light, true, but me suffering from a lately-diagnosed touch of scoliosis (though I had always maintained a rule of thumb to never be sexually involved with a woman I could not physically lift – I was that messed up).

The night air was crisp, and she insisted I build a fire with the cord she'd had delivered by Baptists. She produced cold bottles of ginger beer and fat, saran-wrapped brownies, baked herself, heavily hashished. We sat in front of the fire, ate the brownies, drank the Jamaican Brew ("Nonalcoholic 'cause you're not," she declaimed with the arrogance of a young miss) and listened to Ravel's *Bolero*, of all cornball, predictable choices. I'd opted for a new CD of Berg's *Lulu*, but she insisted on *Bolero*, she'd heard it was sexy (unobservant as usual, I missed she was warming up; in my defense, I'd been in the wake of her erotic charge on a daily basis and had grown numb to subtle implications), and I countered that only the Blake Edwards movie that introduced the piece to a generation of zipperheads stressed the hackneyed idea of screwing to it (not that I presaged that it was screwing she had in mind. How about Scriabin's *Poem of Ecstasy*? Now there's a rumpypumpy sort of—).

"No, no, no! *Bolero*, goddammit!" All right, already.

Its leisurely rat-a-tat filled the room. The hash was kicking in, I was not used to it, and I had an uncertain, hallucinatory compulsion to urinate without any actual physical need, which resulted in an hour of quiet contemplation in the lav (actually, I imagine, about fifteen minutes).

When I emerged at last I was met by a sight that could have been lifted from the pages of *Playboy* between 1963-1966, and for a brief moment I believed I was hallucinating before I came to terms with my grips: Hayley lay on her stomach on what appeared to be an honest-to-Christ polar bear rug angled neatly in front of the hearth, unclothed save for a pair of white panties with pink ruffles on the butt. Both legs swung up at the knees behind her, ankles crossed in white ankle-socks, pink-ribboned, her eyes sparkling in the firelight. Surely I moaned.

My own knees almost gave way beneath me, but I managed to glide across the room into this vision, which I drank in as parched earth rain. The room turned ultramarine as I smoothed the hot palm of my hand down her back to the plush moon of her bottom. As I conducted a tactile comparison of the satin of her back with the silk of her upper thighs, I nuzzled and kissed her neck and cheeks and lips, and the musk and dew of her flesh and mouth were sufficient to induce a screaming attack of hysteria right then and there. Instead, at the precise moment when I felt my whole temporal being merging into her, she bade me carry her to the canopied bed as an impromptu Heathcliff in a spinner-rack bodice-ripper.

"You should love me while you may," she whispered.

I obliged (I may even have nodded, tumescent white zombie), and as she sank into the deep down-quilt, her cool hands were between my open shirt and back, and she was disrobing me under the direction of Douglas Sirk. She kissed me with an ardor I'd only read about, and as my hand explored the puffy, white-cotton wedge between her thighs, she said, softly sibilant: "I left those on so you could take them off."

I had to quell the iced adrenalin—hash be damned—spreading through my chest like mercury with the racing heart of an adolescent (mine, not hers) and find the will not to end this beginning with a *grand mal* seizure.

Suffice to say the angels and nightingales both were giving voice full-throttle to accompany the most delectable tryst I had ever known.

But if angels sang, somewhere the devil glowered through a rictus, fully erect: "Go Fuck Thyself."

I could not have imagined the transport afforded by a more considerate or experienced lover—surely based on her acumen, I must have been her hundredth lay...

The next morning, however, there was blood on the sheets.

Chapter Five

1

Two days later I was seated at a wicker table in the big Sydney Greenstreet fan-back chair, dawdling over a Dante imitation (yup) when she breezed in at noon, the hem of her thin summer frock lifted lightly like dandelion fluff by an actual breeze as she entered. My love felt like a big huge tank.

"You're early."

"Too early? You still writing? I can come back."

"Unthinkable."

She sat down next to me, pressed against my seated form, arm around my neck, free hand in my hair; my arm around her waist, free hand up her skirt. She kissed me, explained how she'd slipped her uncle's 1935 polar bear rug out of, then back into, the den of his waterfront condo without a hitch. Hayley knew where the key was hidden.

"You know," she said, "I was thinking that in the grand scheme of things, first marriages don't really count."

We smiled, my sylph and I.

"They let us out of graduation practice early," she said, sounding tired. "It was kinda hot on the field. They sorta lost interest. Besides, we can all walk in step to the music, which is kinda all they care about, that we sorta look good. We look awesome. So do you." She kissed me again.

I said, "From listening to you, I'd kinda never know this girl read, like, Ezra Pound, sorta kinda."

She thumped me hard, kissed me harder, told me I shouldn't talk since I talked, with my accent, like an Amish farmer reciting Shakespeare—an unjust remark, but clever enough to allow me to overlook its cruelty. She reported with lubricity the need to piss, "Like an Arabian racehorse," and exited upstairs, leaving her canvas beach bag behind.

This sack served as catch-all for her pens, notebook, Big Red cinnamon-flavored chewing gum, lip gloss, toothbrush, ATM card, credit cards, fake ID, Kleenex, tampons, condoms, sunglasses, sunblock, and cell phone. Today protruding from its unclasped maw were trade copies of *The Plumed Serpent* and Ted Hughes's *Crow*. The minx. I'd only just mentioned that here was a book I cherished, and here it was, picked up—I could see from the complimentary bookmark— from the local antiquarian bookshop. As I flipped through it with pedagogical approval, a sheet of typescript fell out. On one side read:

Peach

…Somebody's pound of flesh rendered up …
Why the groove?
Why the lovely, bivalve roundnesses?
Why the ripple down the sphere?
Why the suggestion of incision?
…Here, you can have my peachstone …

D.H. Lawrence

And on the other side, neatly typed:

Rigorous logic leads clearly to the realization that fascism provides a gut-level attraction that communism and socialism lack. Fascism is built on aggression rather than ideals—aggression against an aggressive world.

The pressures and confusions and castrations of our sick society are vanquished and

It ended.

What the hell? Was my cuddly poetry-lover penning manifestoes for jack-booted brownshirts?

She came back. I held up the sheet with a pleasant, nonthreatening smile that probably overdid it.

"What's this?"

She stopped dead, but neither face nor eyes betrayed a hint. Finally, a pliant smile.

"It was in the book when I bought it. Weird, isn't it?"

She plopped her warm weight heavily onto my lap, adroitly squirmed to evenly position my startled cock between her lovely, plump cheeks, and put her head on my shoulder.

"Seems to be pro-fascist," I said.

"Well, duh."

"This paper doesn't look old; this was typed on a computer, so we can rule out a Mussolini supporter. Do neo-Nazis read poetry?"

"Could your apartheid pals in grade school?" She considered this a cruel shot; she'd done some research since we'd met and would flaunt her political knowledge of my childhood under Botha.

Before I could answer, her nose was on my neck and curiosity over the note was supplanted by more pressing matters. I got up and put the "Out to Lunch" sign on the door and locked it.

"But you're not eating," she giggled.

"That's what you think."

2

The next day (bringing the total number of days since our seminal congress to three) brought a fresh Hell, swift and stern, with Laurel & Hardy timing. It was half-past three: Hayley would be along within the hour. I flipped open that morning's unread edition of the *Northport Herald*, the town's daily. One of the four front-page banner headlines read: NHS TEACHER SUSPENDED OVER ALLEGATIONS OF SEXUAL MISCONDUCT.

I skimmed the article: Maurice Micklewhite, 48-year-old drama instructor at Northport Senior High School…allegedly furnished his Newburyport apartment for sexual purposes to graduating eighteen-year-old female … and a thirty-three-year-old *high school librarian*.

My name was not mentioned, nor was Hayley's.

I was stupid with shock, having recognized her, I, him, but unable to make any sense of what I read. His apartment for sexual purposes? High school librarian? A photograph of the hapless Maurice stared back at me pop-eyed from the page, equally dumbfounded.

The shop's landline was ringing. My greeting was met with a gulping, sniffling, incoherent garble of tear-choked spluttering. It took a few moments for me to realize it was Hayley.

"Slow down. Get a grip!"

Well, it was all there: Her mother had tumbled to the suspicion that something was up, her daughter frequently, it turned out, not being where she was supposed to be when she said she would. Alibis were investigated and alibiing confederates, pressured, cracked and sang the roof off about our assignations, one of two unsteady feet still in their childhoods.

(Several years back, a young Tech Ed. at a high school one quaint New England village over from Northport, had taken a sixteen-year-old male student as lover, then convinced him and his teenage pals to kill her young husband for insurance money. Although the police knew it was premeditated murder and not botched burglary—so poor was the planning and execution of the crime—

they had zilch for clues or leads until teenage pal friends confiding in friends confiding in friends ("Don't' tell anyone!" each teenager demanded of each subsequent teenager) formed a chain of information that wound its way to the cops and hanged Ms. Murderess, inspiring a book and motion picture. There's a lesson here, kids: Teenagers cannot not keep their mouths shut. Ever).

I then learned that Sharon, Hayley's mad monk of a mother, had sped straight to Hayley's journal. My bowels took a long drop down an elevator shaft.

"You keep a journal?"

Sniff. "Yeah."

"Since when?"

"Oh, a long time. Ten years. Since I was eight."

That long. "Just," I started hopefully. "Like an, 'ate a boiled egg today' type of journal?"

"No." There was a long pause. "A detailed journal. All the details. That's why I had a lock on it."

"You mean," I asked pointlessly, "One of those adolescent, girly, cloth-covered daily dear diaries with the flower-pattern and the little lock and key?"

"Snoopy and Woodstock, actually!" she snapped back. (I later learned this was not true; her blank book was an elegant blue. She was hurt, offended, and angry in the twinkle of my put-down. Impressive, in retrospect.) "If you must know."

"Then how could she read it if it was locked?" I heard myself yelling.

"She pried the lock off with a screwdriver!" she yelled back.

"What?! Your mother, the MSW child psychologist, ripped the lock off her daughter's diary? That's sick!"

My declaration was followed by a blast of blubs and gurgles climaxed by all-out keening. I tried to calm her since it was crucial we collude here, but was ignored (no more confidence as to who knows best like that of an impendent high school graduate), but I did catch the words *schoolboard* and *lawsuit* and *police* before a stentorian male voice boomed on from another line.

"Is that you, you son-of-a-bitch?" it asked.

"Yes."

"Do you know who this is?"

"Taylor Swift?"

"Stop calling my daughter, you freak!"

Hayley, sounding frightfully childlike: "I called *him*, Daddy."

"You fucking pedophile!"

Pedophile? She's eighteen! And in that instant, I gleaned this particular score, a cultural stereotype with razor canines. Hayley was the only child, a dressed-up doll. I had seen daddy's favorite snapshot of her in an album she'd insisted I appreciate, and there she was, a precious and squeezable toddling two, one idle hand resting on the powerful and protective shoulder of Frank (his name—*perfect*) as she stood toddled behind him on the breakers at Rye Beach, New Hampshire. He, mustached, brush-cut, mirrored Saigon shades, the smirk of Special Ops, the assassin he'd probably been wherever Over There was at any given time during his military career, retired young, now in heavy and profitable contracting. He'd prayed for a boy, but if he wasn't blessed, he would be all that he could be to this little bundle from a cruel but just Almighty, and tear off the testicles of the first male who gave her a sidelong glance. She was now and forever Daddy's Girl.

She hardly ever mentioned him. Why? For fear I'd be jealous of a father only a decade my senior? Strange Electra territory only Hayley understood, probably by the age of six. Long before, I'd heard it said that a thirteen-year-old girl has more in common with a thirty-year old woman than she does with a thirteen-year-old boy, and had failed to understand the remark. Now I knew—and given half the chance, this brute would kill me. The intelligence from his daughter that Frank was bullied and flummoxed by his wife honed his fury lethal, a bull gelt by his cow.

"Well, you can damn well *stop* calling him!"

"Yes, Daddy."

And there it was: my accomplished intellectual on her way to the Ivy League, but caught by Papa Bear, dwarfed to Goldilocks in back-flap pajamas, spineless. Our capable Alice, so British and sensible with Mad Hatters, would have slapped her. I myself could have spanked her, had the urge not segued so depressingly to the erotic.

Frank resumed with, "And another thing—" as Hayley took up a new chorus of wailing.

I didn't wait for the other thing, but hung up as Agent Janis Poplin marched through the shop door with an uneasy jingle of the bell.

"Oh, for Christ's sake."

"That's right, Paxton, it's me. You just can't seem to stay out of the papers, can you?"

"I wasn't in the papers last time."

"Don't quibble. Bad news dogs you like a stray."

"That's pretty good."

"Oh, shut up."

She leaned over my wicker waving the day's *Herald*. "You're in trouble, Paxton, and I don't just mean this," jabbing one nail-bitten-to-the-quick finger into Micklewhite's startled face, the poor apple. I suddenly knew I was scared, and she knew it, too. She straightened up, ballsy-proud.

"We need to talk." She sat across from me at the rattan table, produced a white, not yellow, legal pad from her briefcase and told me to close the shop while she conducted her "interview."

I picked up the "Out to Lunch" sign, then chose the simpler "Closed" one, grabbed a black-felt marker and added, "On Account of Molasses," hung it on the door and turned the lock.

"You weren't supposed to leave town without telling us, Paxton."

"I was offered an opportunity and took it, and in the rush of moving—how did you know I was here?"

"I'm a professional, Paxton. I detect. I wondered about that accent of yours. South Africa, huh? Quite the political hotspot. We're getting a rundown on your activities while you were there."

"My cricket bats?"

She squinted. "What the hell is that supposed to mean?"

"I left Johannesburg when I was ten, you jackass." I would now be ballsy as well.

"You're not telling us everything, Paxton. It doesn't make any sense that you're at the cafe when the bomb goes off—"

"I could have been killed— "

"And your wife who's supposed to be dead is in on it, and this MacFarland character is there—"

"He could have been killed—"

"Aw, he was barely scratched, and now you're working for him up here and he's off having tea in New York with the Crisco attorneys."

My mind was reeling. The explosion. Chauncey with the Criscos? The heiress-supposedly-kidnapped-by-Erika's-group-of-animal-rights-nuts Criscos? My activities in South Africa?

"And the lab tested positive those were Erika's fingerprints you found?"

She blinked. "Huh?"

"The fingerprints," I repeated. "You said those were a match for Erika, the fingerprints you found at the Crisco abduction scene?"

She narrowed, "What the hell are you talking about?"

"You said," I said impatiently, "that you found Erika's very-much alive fingerprints where Brieanna Crisco was kidnapped—that they matched her arrest with the Clamshell Alliance protesters?"

"The what? When the hell did I say that?"

"When you saw me in the hospital!"

She shook her little head rapidly, eyes closed. "You were drugged. I never said a goddamned thing about any fingerprints. Don't play games, Paxton. The proof that she's alive I'm going to get from *you*."

I sighed. She grinned.

"So, Paxton. What does the little girl have to do with all this?"

"Nothing." The old cold sweat—the first since stopping the booze—began to creep its petty pace up my spine. I said, "This is unreal."

"Doesn't have to be, Paxton. No charges have been filed over the child, and I doubt they will be. I can help you, I promise." She looked indulgent. "Nobody likes a cop until you need one, you know?"

"I've heard."

"You're talking to a cop. Means you're either a victim or a perpetrator."

"I'm thinking I'm neither."

She took up pen and pad. "Okay, a few questions. Take it easy. You're all sweaty."

"You going to make a note of that?"

"Now, then. When did you first have sexual intercourse with Hayley Glass?"

"Oh, please—"

"Okay, sorry—you're right. Bad start." She thought for a moment, ballpoint between her teeth. "You're a raging alcoholic, right?"

"I think I need a lawyer."

"No, you don't. But it will help this investigation if—"

"Which one? The SLAV freaks, my wife's missing corpse, my sex life?"

"Cooperate now, and it'll go easier on you later."

"What'll go easier? Have I committed a crime? Did I break any law?"

No. The age of consent in New Hampshire is sixteen. That's for the innocent party. But if the adult party—"

"If both parties are sixteen, then aren't both consenting adults? And innocent?"

"Unless the older party is some kind of authority figure with coercive influence over the child."

"What child? You said consenting adult!"

Didn't miss a beat. "Like a priest or a coach or a high school librarian. Then it's age eighteen."

"But I'm none of those things."

"You were a librarian at a high school." She was referring to my six months as a paraprofessional at North Quincy High (MA), before I was hired by the Boston Public Library.

"So what? That was over two years ago. I didn't even know Hayley then, and even if I'd been her damned soccer coach, she's still eighteen, which still makes it legal even if that were the case, which it isn't, so where's the logic?"

She shook her head emphatically. "You don't understand today's climate."

More climatology. "Hayley was, is, eighteen, and it didn't happen when I was her authority figure, which I wasn't, and she is, was, eighteen when it did happen, when I wasn't her authority figure, correct?"

"Huh?"

"The sex!"

"Did you furnish drugs to her? Did you perform oral or anal sex upon her?"

I should have been sharp and focused, coursing verve to aggression, but I wasn't; I was numb and defeated, as limp as I'd been in the hospital bed when this twat had first grilled me about Erika and the bombing. I felt defeated already, and I had not yet begun to fight. I stood up.

"I'm not talking anal with you or anybody, Sweetheart. This is bullshit. I got three points for you. One: I don't know anything about terrorists or the bombing in Boston. Two: my wife is dead. Three: I'm not breaking any laws in my relations with Hayley, so it's nobody's goddamn business. And finally, why don't you *fuck off*, okay? Oh! I'm sorry! That's four points."

She calmly replaced the cap on her pen and gathered her things. "That doesn't bother me," she said. "I hear that every day. Big talk, Paxton, but you look scared. You look like you're about to cry. And you don't have a smart-ass response to why MacFarland's palling around with the Criscos, do you?"

She stepped very close, almost nose-to-nose. "And I still say this is all connected. You might be able to run, Paxton, but you can't hide. And I am about to become your worst nightmare."

She clacked out across the pegged-wood floor, and I yelled, "*Become?*" before she was gone. A pretty lame last word, I admit.

3

In the days that followed, I went out as infrequently as possible. I had eight cans of Campbell's chicken noodle soup and Chinese take-away. The phone rang incessantly; I took no calls. Manchester's Channel Nine and the *Northport Herald* finally mentioned me by name (along with Micklewhite; but not Hayley—evidently a legal adult, but not a grown-up) as the "high school librarian," having carnal knowledge of a small girl student in my charge, no doubt inspiring visions of sweaty abominations conducted beneath her hiked cheerleader's skirt across a desk in a darkened classroom.

Harley's parents forbade her to contact me, and tried for a restraining order, which was denied. Mother Glass, the mad monk, hired an attorney who left a profusion of messages, which I also ignored. He seemed mildly unhinged.

I consulted a cuff-linked attorney from the Yellow Pages ("Sex Offenses? Call Us First!") who informed me I didn't really need representation, as I hadn't broken any law, but perhaps I would be sued for depravity or rape, as one can sue anyone for anything in these litigious United Stated ("It's the climate"). I did not grumble or bitch about America; if I didn't like it, I could always go back to South Africa. No thanks). If I would like to reassure myself with his cuff-links, a retainer of one thousand dollars would be required.

I skulked out in wraparound shades on Saturday to attend the Rite of Reconciliation at St. Bartholomew's. I had not been to confession in years, so spared the priest a cumulative account of interim transgressions—this would have taken days and horrified us both—but stuck to the recent problem.

Bless him, his Irish accent, and Holy Mother Church: he said, unabashed through the grill, that there was nothing wrong with the age difference between myself and the young lady (he certainly would have recognized the scenarios from the newspaper coverage, day in and out, this being a slow period for juicy stories). No, no; a perfectly good candidate for matrimony and fruitful multiplying. What was, of course, the grievous sin here, *sure 'n' 'tis*, was the fornication of two not joined in the Holy Wedlock, ya young, sinful, bastard. Ten Hail Mary's and make a decent woman of her in ordinary, or at least advent time.

The urge to drink was fierce. I prayed for a visit, note, or call from my beloved—some forbearance of this misery. I received instead an anonymous letter from one claiming to be privy to the local branch of the NEA, the teacher's union representing Micklewhite, and that he was being framed.

School Superintendent Rebecca Schrechlich had been quite the trollop in her day, sleeping her way through a collection of hedged bets and stockpiled favors with a succession of personnel, one of these a former principal of the high school. He had spurned her, then been arrested for drunk driving. She had fired him and exploited the story in the media. He committed suicide. Another colleague/lover left her for the more tempting attractions of—Maurice Micklewhite. The spurner moved on, but Maurice lingered whilst Schrechlich sharpened her knife. Hell hath no fury like a woman scorned, but whoa nelly! if she's dumped for a queer.

The letter went on to say this mess could have ended as a private family matter had Schrechlich guts or sense but was a "wicked poltroon" terrified of even a frivolous lawsuit from the lunatic Glasses, and was herself as crazy as a rat in a drain-pipe. A rich read, that nameless note.

4

The Northport Senior High School commencement was conducted under a pall of unease. The graduating class jubilantly tossed their mortarboards into the air at its conclusion. One spun freakishly into the crowd of spectators, slicing open the cheek of a seven-year-old girl, blood spilled, stitches required. This was taken as "deft symbolism to inflame community outrage (this from a column by one Mickey Frost, who declaimed that sexual predators like myself—he mentioned that I'd met the still anonymous Hayley when she was twelve, pushing the inference, I had fiendishly "targeted the child" for the better part of a decade, then ravished her in Micklewhite's flat—should not be allowed within ten miles of a schoolyard. The facts—of no importance to Frost—had been twisted for breathtakingly inaccurate editorial nitwittedness), thus leading mob psychology to the conclusion that the NHS graduation was ruined and a waif maimed because homo subvert helped pedo pervert defile and debauch.

Hayley delivered her speech (with the Vonnegut quote, genesis of all catastrophe!) and was sent proudly into the world.

The next day another letter arrived at the shop in Hayley's loopy penmanship, though for this brief note she dispensed with the hearts, smiley faces, and multiple exclamation points she usually employed for punctuation. In its entirety:

Paxton:

We can never see each other again. I trusted you as a mentor and role model and you violated that trust by seducing me. I am a child and you are an adult. You have despoiled me. I will forever be scarred by your selfish betrayal. Do not ever try to contact me, or my parents will take legal action.

My best,
Hayley Glass

I did not believe she had written this tripe. It had *The Manchurian Candidate* wackiness of the mother smeared all over it, but it depressed and sickened me that she could be coerced to pen this steaming pile of horseshit in her own hand.

The sun was already sinking over the ridge of the buildings across Congress Street, lowering the shop and my mood into dimness. The classical station from Boston I was tuned to played a Chopin nocturne, and I burst into tears like an eighteen-year-old girl.

She had said she loved me. She had treated me with respect and fondness. She had made love to me. She had been proprietorial, jealous, and petty regarding my attention to her beautiful, lyric faults. How could the mind-washing of parents she held largely in contempt compel her to do this?

I was feeling pretty whelmed, a state I'd been advised to avoid on doctor's orders. The notion crossed my Raskolnikov mind to clean out the till of its few thousand dollars (I hadn't made a deposit in days) and flee the town; I was *depravare non grata*.

But that would be immoral: Old Chaunce had aided me in my time of need, and I would be paying him back by ripping him off. Both conscience and karma could not handle that kind of overdraft. That was the ethical part.

The practical part puzzled where I would go. My brother Tobias (these names my mother chose!) was a successful developer in Hawaii with a rich wife who hated my guts. On the last occasion we'd spoken, he'd told me his tolerance for me had worn thin. I still owed him three thousand dollars. That was it for family. And friends? Like the rest of my clan, I had no flair for friendship. Our fault.

If this was loss, it was not like Erika, the loss of death. This was betrayal and abandonment, fevering a brain with the heat that the givens of trust and love and loyalty were all mere clattering din, tinny, cheap, and false.

Bitterness had its fangs locked deep, poisoning my psyche; I was more poisoned than I'd been on a three-week, round-the-clock binge of alcohol and nicotine, when my breath, urine, and skin reeked of the filthy deposits. If already polluted, you join the army of the doomed and snork your way with liquor to slow death, a suicide, with no "pale-but-true, there gleamed the light of other days": no other days, just darkness, bats, and, "Mr. Graham will have his breakfast at the bar." The title of my tavern-mornings memoir: *What the Hell Are You Looking At?*

But this was different. I could not calmly step off the boat into the irreversible jungle of brain-damage. The twaddlement of this much injustice was goading me.

For the second time in under a month, I was sunk. Which was worse? Homeless and penniless in Boston, or an employed and boarded pariah in Northport? What a choice!

So I cried. Not for myself—I was not played out yet, but true, destiny was spanning its bridges ahead of me. Not for Hayley—she would land on her two entitled, lovely feet. I cried for something nurtured by us both that had died. Panicked by the spectre of drinking, that night I fought the tears, the urge and the fear, before drowning, a dry drunk, into sleep.

Chapter Six

1

The next morning came the doldrums of a Thursday, and I was drinking a Dunkin' Donuts iced coffee the size of an oil drum when Chauncey's planetary bulk blocked the late-morning sunburst through the door, which, being a cool day, was propped open.

"'Lo there, young fella," he said breezily, doffing the hat more for the jaunty effect, I think, than true manner. The silver-handled stick was again to hand, and the ensemble today consisted of off-white flannels, starched shirt, blue double-breasted blazer with gold buttons, and straw Panama hat. The breast pocket handkerchief and the band of the hat were of the same color-splashed cloth. The mountainous gent looked sharp, fat, and sassy, nobody's idea of a State o' Maine undertaker.

I rose cautiously to his, "Don' git up." He crashed into a rattan loveseat to the audible splintering of woven wood. He plucked the fluted handkerchief from his pocket, mopped his face, then stuffed it back, leaving it trailing. He puffed, sighed, and looked around the shop as though it were all new to him, then fixed his gaze on me. He raised one thick finger in pronouncement.

"We ah ow-ah choices."

I mulled this over. He smiled, then said, "Jean-Paul Sartre. French philosophah fella, 1905-1980."

"Ah. We are our choices."

"You betcha. But no point cryin' ovah split milk, despite this monstrous depravity—the publicity, I mean—blowin' fit ta make a rabbit cry. She's legal, though how you could be so cussed stupid to dilly with a eighteen-year-old in this bass-ackwards age is beyond me. Still, don't make no damn's-odds, and willing snizz don't grow on trees, so's ya got m'empathy if not m'approval."

"Thank you."

"No sweat," he said perspiring heavily. "How's business? I'm thinkin' mebbe allis publicity mightn't be too good for you right about now, naw fo' the shop. Them doctors said you's s'posed to avoid stress, right? Well, bein' on display here as a sexual menace is no way to go about it, what with things all jizzicked up."

"You're firing me?"

"'Cous I'm not firin' you. Don't be so spleeny. Got another opportunity faw ya." He leaned forward conspiratorially from the third chin up, droplets streaming cheek and nose. "Need ya ta make a delivery faw me."

He began speaking in a low, *sotto voce* stage tone, though the shop was empty. "I need ya to delivah a very impawtant package containin' a very costly curiosity 'bout this big." He held his open palms a foot from each other. "To a Mistuh Saeed Kureishi."

"A what?"

"A Mistuh Saeed Kureishi—don't interrupt. Like it sounds: Sah-eed Kur-ay-shee. Pakistani fella, in Rangeley, Maine."

"Where's that?"

"Coupla three hours. You kin stay ovah night under an assumed name."

"Why would I do that?"

"So's not ta'tract attention, ya dummy. See, this curiosity, I didn't come by it zackly by the book. It's somethin' of a collectah's item, and this Mistuh Kureishi, he's a collectah willin' ta pay top dollah."

"It's hot, you mean," I said. "Stolen."

Chaunce waved away the semantic wisps with the nimble flutter of five fat fingers. "No need talkin' legal. I just can't take a chance strollin' into Rangeley. I'm a mite easy to spot, with this paticklah item tucked under my arm.

Customs got a tip it passed through Logan Airpawt. People are watchin' me, and they're watchin' Mistuh Kureishi. Not very nice people."

"Why me?" I again found myself asking. "I'm not zackly—I'm not exactly low profile of late, am I? The feds think my dead wife's blowing up bunny killers, they've been here to see me, and now I'm the Boston Baby Raper, and the Feds told me you've having lunch with the Criscos, whose kidnapped daughter is being held captive by a group that my dead wife allegedly blows up bunny killers with, and you think I'm a good choice for delivering hot property?"

He continued smiling, as if he'd heard none of my argument. "Whadya think?"

"With all due respect and gratitude, Chauncey, I think it's a profound piece of dumbfuckery. If they're connecting you to Crisco and me to Crisco and you and me to Kureishi—what is this thing, anyway? Some manuscript or amulet or something?"

At this point the great man placed both meaty palms on either arms of the chair and with concentrated effort lifted his bulk from its woody confines and propelled it unsteadily onto both feet and stick. Gaining ballast, he strolled quick-step with graceful little flicks of the walking-stick to the door, which he closed and locked, placed the "molasses" sign—after glancing at it and shooting a double-take at me—in the window. He retraced the route back, but this time settled into a wider seat adjacent to his rapt audience of one. He continued in an attitude of intense secrecy and earnestness.

"Not quite. You evah heah of a fella name o' Rasputin?"

Of course.

And I told Chauncey all I knew: Grigori Efimovich Rasputin, friend and spiritual advisor to Nicholas and Alexandra, the last Czar and Czarina of the Russian Empire, a holy man with reputedly supernatural powers. He had a wild, unkempt, even repulsive appearance and smell, piercing eyes and a prodigious appetite for women and drink; but he was also terribly charismatic, genuinely psychic, and possessed of an inexplicable healing gift that won him favor with the royal couple because of his ministrations to their only son, who suffered from hemophilia. A group of aristocrats decided that Rasputin had too much influence over the weak and ineffectual royals, so they plotted to assassinate him. Legend has it that in 1916, his enemies lured him to a midnight party where they fed him wine and cake with enough poison to kill an elephant, yet he showed no sign of the slightest discomfort. So they shot him—twice—but he still managed to escape. They pursued him, beating him and crushing his skull, but he didn't actually, finally, succumb until they had bound his hands and drowned him in an icy canal.

"Ayuh," said Chauncey. "That's 'bout right." And then Chauncey proceeded to tell me portions of the story that I had never read in any book.

It seems that Prince Felix Yusupov, one of the aristocrats, allegedly had a romantic yen for Rasputin, but the attraction was not mutual. In an unbalanced and passionate fit, Yusupov emasculated the mystic before his body was dumped in the drink. The preserved sexual member of the monk had spent most of the last century changing hands in the four corners of the world ever since. And now it was, at least temporarily, in the ample hands of Digger MacFarland.

"Oh my God."

"Ayuh," he winked.

"How the hell did you end up with it?"

The wink again, the finger raised to one side of the nose, "Don't ask."

"Listen, Mr. MacFarland—"

"Ya gotta staht callin' me Diggah."

"I'm really rather concerned now. That hologram Poplin seems to think— "

"Don't you worry none 'bout her."

"I am worried. I don't trust what she's up to with this crazy idea that Erika's alive. She thinks I have some connection to the bombing! Terrorists have Brieanna Crisco and Poplin's saying that you've been meeting with Crisco family; she's trying to tie Hayley into all of this and now you want me to deliver a petrified …" I trailed off, I admit.

"Prick," he finished, helpfully.

"I wasn't going to say that. You want me to transport this thing illegally to a Pakistani?" I paused to let the full effect of this scenario sink in for the both of us. "Do you see how I might be reticent?"

Chauncey mopped his brow and jowls again, then folded his hands, smiled.

"Now listen ta me, Paxton. I like you. You're a nice fella. Can't say as I 'prove of the filly, but yaw awright. You still seein' her?" I shook my head. He nodded. "Good thing. You needs get outta Nawthpawt 'fore the school board and parents gets preemptive and hangs you from your petard and you end up like ah friend Rasputin heah."

He gave a chuckle, rose from his seat and squeezed a path through the tightly-placed displays to the framed Nora DeBolt print on the wall near the business nook (DeBolt was the only artist Chauncey allowed on the premises, so high was his estimation of her bucolic watercolors). He produced with a flourish a plastic cardkey and swiped it across the underside of the frame. There was a metallic sound of pressurized release. The frame swung open to reveal a small safe. Chaunce shot one cuff and twirled the dial with zeal. The tumblers fell; he swung open the door and took from the interior its sole item: a mahogany box a foot long and a half-a-foot wide. He slammed shut the safe and refastened its false front.

He fell back onto the woven wood with such deliberate lack of care, I thought the settee would split. This was no way to treat your wicker. He placed the box with reverence on the table before us.

"Well…that's it," he said, re-mopping his moon-face. After catching his breath, he turned to me impatiently. "Well, dontcha wanna see it?"

I looked at him, then hesitantly leaned forward and opened the lid. The box was lined in powder-blue velvet and served as an elegant casket for what looked to be a withered, blackened and rotten banana.

"Holy cow."

"It's a beaut, ain't it?" asked Chauncey. "I mean, as fah as these things go…"

Circumfused with disbelief, yet I felt the undeniable sensation of some kind of awe in the presence of the penis of such an infamous figure, reputedly of supernatural powers. I was impressed, but skeptical.

"What does this Pakistani guy want with it?"

"Told ya, he's a collectah," Chauncey replied without a trace of humor, as if we were appraising a commemorative spoon. "But that's not important.

It gets complicated. Mistuh Kureishi won't deal with the actual sellah, since he's in the slammah and no-can-do. Nevah you mind who, so the sellah in th' slammah, who shall remain 'nonymous, has enlisted his old buddy Diggah. This was in a lockah at Logan Airpawt. We're talkin' 'bout a hundred thousand dollahs. And yours truly's gettin' a piss-pot full faw his troubles." He winked again.

"You're like James Bond or something," I said drily.

"No suh, I ain't. That's where you comes in. All ya gotta do is bring this up to Rangeley and collect the scratch. Place called Khartoum, seven o'clock tomorrah night."

"It sounds weird and illegal."

"I'll pay you three thousand, half up front." He pulled a fat manila envelope from his inside pocket. "Hope ya don't mind fifties."

"Is this dangerous? Like, I could get shot through the forehead?"

Chauncey looked affronted. "Mistuh Kureishi is a respectable businessman, like me. No horsefeathers."

"What does this have to do with Brieanna Crisco's kidnapping?"

"Absolutely naught. Criscos been good family friends to the MacFarlands since the robbah baron days. I lunches with 'em whenevah they git ta Boston. Good people. Shame 'bout Brieanna, fishy little doxy. But don't trouble yawself with that." He waved the pay packet as invocation, and grinned so drippingly with intent, I felt I was being swayed by some courtesan of darkness.

I don't recall any logical progression of thought arriving at my agreement. I do remember Chauncey puffing his way up the narrow staircase, without an inch to spare, to watch me as I packed and slipped the mahogany box and manila packet (having transferred two hundred to my wallet) into my well-worn leather shoulder-bag, and promised to be on the first bus in the morning from Northport to Rangeley. He reminded me in his best avuncular manner that he was continuing to provide, in good faith, a steady means of my support.

2

Anyone who has bargained with addiction can attest to the ease of quitting as compared to the bitch of sustained abstinence. Abstinence without a sound plan of recovery—a series of replacements for the habit, a new attitude, a support system, a spiritual awakening, or at least a deadly resolve—has no chance of success. I had not crossed the threshold of the halls of Alcoholics Anonymous. I had not checked myself into rehab or hospital in a syncope of acceptance. I was not on my knees praying for grace at the dawn of each day. I should have tried it.

I had tried, instead, to purchase my redemption at the altar of love and sex, to rise like some faux Phoenix from the ashes of my immolation in Hayley, and this had been no sound plan. Bet your heart on the whims and caprice of a young woman (teenager, teenager, what the hell difference did it make now?) still mastered by parents crazy, as Chauncey put it, as shithouse rats, and what do you get? Again, to quote Chauncey, *absolutely naught.*

Chauncey left with the benefaction of telling me I could close the shop and take the rest of the day off. He didn't seem to care too much about the wicker business, not, presumably, when there was money to be made in more colorful endeavors. And he rightly assumed I needed time to prepare for my new career as courier of a desiccated appendage—a strange calling, but a lucrative one. So I left "Closed On Account of Molasses" on the door, locked it, and set off to the muggy, pre-noon penumbra of Northport's waterfront.

It would be untrue to say that I did not wrestle with my conscience and do battle with temptation for over three-quarters of an hour; both had me by the essentials. I felt like a man in an arm-wrestling contest, taking on a duo in turns. I might beat back the Devil only to have God as Higher Power lose vital ground. I needed time to prepare. After nearly an hour of slow-motion circling the winding streets of that picturesque burg, I found myself saying to Hell, and crossing the dark and cool outset of the State Street Saloon.

I kissed away over twenty days of sobriety with a Scotch on the rocks. After three of these, I talked friendly to a gap-toothed, unshaven troll named Sully on the barstool next to me and bummed an unfiltered Pall Mall from him, easing the smoke down guiltily into my still-healing and surely outraged lung. I ordered a boilermaker. When Sully ran out of smokes, his company became intolerable, and I sauntered across to the Oar House (picking up a pack of Silk Cuts at Federal Cigar on the way) for a few of their fabled Bloody Marys.

At this point, haze plays havoc with recollection. I attempted pleasant chat with a handsome couple at the bar, but the husband abruptly halted my Thin Man imitation to inform me that he wanted to talk to his wife and his wife only, did I get that? The bartender asked loudly if I was driving. I paid the bill and left.

Next stop, right up the street, was the Dolphin Striker, which I called the Porpoise Whacker, ha!, to the utter lack of amusement of the barkeep, who, after serving me a Beefeater martini straight up with an olive and watching me attempt to raise the glass to my mouth, shut me off.

I returned to the State Street, where I had earlier noted that slurred speech and an unsteady gait seemed no hindrance to service. I drank three draft Buds with two whiskey shots, accepting one from a gigantic biker resembling Haystack Calhoun, named Tiny. Or perhaps it was three shots. Eventually I was roused by a new server who chided me for falling asleep on the bar. She didn't seem to know where or even who Tiny was (a hallucinated two-ton sprite?) and suggested that perhaps it was best for me, her patrons, and the establishment if I left.

There is an unfocused Polaroid in my memory of stepping from the dark cool of the saloon into blasted light and a heated broth that swirled the hair around my forehead. I last remember fancying I was Jacob Marley's ghost in damnation—then nothing. A total blackout. I couldn't have been served anywhere else; at this point my thick tongue and slit-eyed gaze were beyond the subtleties of ordering a drink. I do recall having difficulty placing one foot after the other in an effort at progressing up the sidewalk. I lurched on independent legs, a marionette whose puppet-master is loaded. Loaded puppet-master, loaded puppet.

3

I came to in what appeared to be a villa in Tuscany, judging from the view from the open windows (and I mean open; there were no panes of glass, just large fenestrations in the stonework of the walls) of rolling verdant—then golden—fields and hillocks, an exquisite landscape. My four-post bed had been thoughtfully moved from Northport to the vast, breezy room. It must have been breezy, as the tapestries on the walls wafted regally. Crimson rays burst from the sun, but I could not determine its direction. East or West—was it rising or setting?

"We have just lived through the Hour of the Wolf," came a voice, and I realized that I was no longer looking at the room and at my bed, but I was in the bed, naked with a heavy down comforter drawn over me.

The voice issued forth from an enormous cat, the size and chocolate color of a grown Newfoundland dog, seated in the middle of the stone floor on an elaborately-patterned carpet. It possessed huge eyes, a Cheshire Cat, something out of Bulgakov—and what? In reminder, it rocked its eyes back and forth in horizontal ticking, flicked its thick tail rhythmically back and forth, mouth open and grinning, tongue lolling.

"Remind you of anything?" it asked cheerfully. The voice was male.

Yes. The clock in Dr. Shattuck's cold office, my pediatrician when I was a kid, you Cheshire Puss. This was telepathy, surely, as I hadn't said a work, but the cat nodded.

"Correct! But, who, pray, was your pediatrician when you were no longer a child?" It stretched lazily across the carpet and yawned. "You had better get going. It's past six."

Six o'clock! I'm late for the play? I need to get into make-up and costume and check my props before the house opens and—

"Six a.m." it said patiently. "Don't embarrass yourself again by waking up the stage manager. You haven't' slept through your call, Joe. It's morning."

Joe?

"The fat boy. Narcoleptic." He signed. "*Pickwick*, you illiterate."

I was greatly relieved and asked the cat if I might hug him.

"God robbed poets of their minds that they might be made expressions of His own. Are you so terribly bitter that you are a failure as a poet?" He was ignoring my question, changing the subject, but I could play at cat-and-mouse.

What was the question?

"Have you no pride?"

Of course. I have pride and ego, in that I take pains so that people know that I understand my accomplishments have been modest—hardly Poundian. Once that given has been set, I'm free to thrive in that context.

"Only the dead luxuriate."

I was now down on all fours next to the enormous feline.

"You're perorating all over the carpet," he said.

I stroked his back and behind his ears, and he began to purr with the fury of our lawn mower back in South Africa, one hundred years before.

"You never left," *she* said in a seductive, female voice. I had a sense of Hayley inside this rich, furred costume. Where was the zipper? I must find it!

She spoke again, the accented Krazy Kat: "Dontcha luv me no more, Ignatz, ma l'il dollink?"

I embraced her, tearful, but she flipped me onto my back as the carpet on the floor became the mattress on the bed, this enormous, ridiculous, Princess-and-the-Pea four-poster, and the cat crept slowly up my body and settled heavily on my chest, gleaming yellow eyes and white teeth inches from my face, but changing from a kitschy benignity to something sinister, tempting and seductive in a matter that stirred the loins and promised the deliverance of a blanketing, viscous, angry shudder, but the hint of castration, emasculation, the sweet of the orgasm cut clean by the cutting of the genitals by a razor-slash, to form a thick paste of blood and sugar, Good God, what a horror! The cat was crushing my chest, ponderous on my erection, and my desire was steeped in dread.

I closed my eyes, felt her breath on my mouth and the ice-water splash of terror straight to my heart in a fatal, cardiac arrest and rueful climax, when a familiar voice tinkled, *"Good morning."*

4

I felt her breath on my mouth and opened my eyes. I smelled a scent from a face too close to make out, though I recognized the tune of her hum as, "A Sleepin' Bee," and then soft, full lips I knew.

Warm weight pinned all my limbs. The crapulence of the binge had me paralytic; I couldn't even flinch.

I was in bed in my transient's home.

"I said *Good Morning*."

I cracked my parched palate, a mouthful of chalk: "Izzzt?"

She laughed and her spasm jerked up and back, bounced the mattress, and brought her into focus: Hayley, stretched full atop me.

"You see," she said with enthusiasm. "It's stuff like that—at a time like this—that makes you so awesome. I love you to bits and pieces." This last gross preciousness delivered with a kiss active to my passive, but vanity beat carnality to the punch, and it dawned that goats had been pissing in my mouth as I slept, and my breath could stop a clock.

"Gaw Godawf breff," I said, voice guttural, raw, stained.

"I love you so much, Paxton," she said.

I stared her down on the off-chance I was still out. Nope. She continued, "But yes, I'd say the Irish fumes are considerable," yet she smiled indulgently, rolling aside. I reached for a glass of tepid, day-old bedside water, rinsed my mouth, swallowed, and fell back with a sickly grimace. She climbed back on top.

"How are you, my darling?" Her pelvis pressed down on mine and she sighed, as if the move had been independent of her will. My hands, independent of my will, cupped her buttocks, rooting to their love for the bottom, the fell last root of things. As gratifying as this was, my confoundedness conspired with the sour sensation in mouth and throat, a pounding in the right temple and the demand of a queasy, stagnant pool collecting in my food-deprived yet greed-filled stomach to propel me out of bed straight into oblivion. Explanations must wait. I went with David Niven.

"Darling," I clipped, "I'm sorry. I'm so happy to see you, and I know we've lots to talk about, but if I don't get up and into the bathroom immediately, we're both going to be ever so much grossed out—excuse me."

She was up and off me in a flash, pulling back the bedclothes (how had I managed to crawl under them in my drunken state?). She was loving in the clearing of a path, solicitous, devoted again.

The shrunken, myopic Churchill of my present self mumbled *skullduggery's afoot*, best get to the bottom of this, and God, how I'd missed her bottom, but first things first. I swayed vertical, feet on the floorboards, then a sailor's roll to the head, noticing, incidentally, that I was wearing green silk pajamas. I plucked the fine cloth from my front and glanced to Hayley, posing on the bed for a boudoir photographer, chin on hand propped on elbow, the tip of one little finger (lickin' good!) tucked between the tiny teeth of an impish smile. I scurried through the door and locked it behind me.

"A few moments, my love!" I called, Cary Grant now.

"All the time in the world, my sweet!" she called back. Hell, we could do this all day.

I tossed the toothbrush from its opaque, paste-smudged cup (came with the joint) to the floor, filled it with cold water from the tap, and as tablets of Alka-Seltzer bubbled merrily away, ran a torrent of hot water from the shower. I had to proceed without pause to a sane place before any consideration of my sick condition. Almost thirty days (let's call it) without a hangover, not much, but still I was shockingly out of practice. I rehydrated at length under the long, hot shower (*The Long, Hot Shower* – good Faulknerian title, must remember that, wouldn't), reached to the toilet-tank top for the fizzing bromide, drank it down in one gulp, dared the cold tap for thirty seconds of heart-stopping shock (an old girlfriend named Lexi swore by this treatment every morning; she's now an entertainment lawyer), screamed, then toweled off to discover I was sweating again, alcoholic sweat; the loins leaching out once more, welcome back, Lush, Lush, and Swine. I reached the mirror pretending I was calm, but the shaving-foam in my palm showed tremor. Forget shaving or risk a blood bath. I glanced up at a cheerful digital clock that announced it was ten o'clock. Good show, except the clock was as unfamiliar and novel as the silk jammies.

Now bemused to the unbrushed teeth, I spied the bathroom wicker waste-basket, lined by plastic-bag and abrim with ice and a triumvirate of pilsner bottles of Miller High-Life. Without a second's pause I pried off the cap of one bottle, and gulped it in five deep drafts, then downed a second, accompanied by much Falstaffian belching.

By the third, with doses of aspirin, B-complex and Visine, the sweating and trembling had ceased. I thrilled on the minor scale that I did not have to resort to the analeptic swig of cold cider vinegar, straight from the bottle from the fridge—*uksuss*, the phonetic Russian. The third bottle ensured safe shaving and would grudgingly allow a breakfast of dyspeptic bursts.

I emerged from the steamy room, heard Hayley repaired to the kitchen. I donned fresh socks, shorts, black t-shirt and jeans. While dressing, I glanced around the bedroom to see if anything else had been added in my absence, and how long had I been absent?

Equilibrium restored, I was uncertain which approach to take this morning, impulses of fear, curiosity, delight, anger, and embarrassment all pushing and shoving like a crowd of shoppers at an old Filene's basement sale. I must compose one fine opening statement before entering . . .

It was hopeless. I forged on, a prairie oyster ready to clam up in panic.

I hadn't taken in her attire, which gives an indication of my stupid-with-shock state. No one should have missed the cotton tank-top with the lace edging and the white denim shorts, her fresh tan glowing, her be-jeaned rump as nexus to the whole, and I found rancor teetering on the tightrope of love and hate (that saintly, satanic team): yep, there was my honeypot.

My honeypot was scrambling eggs. Bagels, lox-spread, a Silex of coffee, and sliced canteloupe all in exquisite presentation. She spoke first.

"Now, I know you're under the weather, but there's more beer in the fridge and I thought just something light—I've made these moist and fluffy, the way you like them—and Tabasco."

The delightful homemaker who had betrayed and abandoned me.

"Yes, of course, sensational," I said, drifting to the icebox to uncap my fourth beer of the morning. I was now feeling pretty good. The comfort irrigating my grateful cells brought fresh assurance and even the desire to cock a snook.

"Now, tell me," I began carefully, the cheery domestic setting spinning the fantasy that we were a young married couple (well, she was young, anyway) at Sunday morning brunch, in love. "What are you doing here, and how did I get here, and what does this all mean? These questions are to be taken literally, mind you, not as some existential musings." She giggled. "So what gives?"

"Well may you ask," she replied, licking her thumb after slathering a sliced bagel with salmon cream cheese, then proceeding to bite into this with gusto but no pause in her speed, butter knife in hand.

"My pal Alessandra called me about eight o'clock last night and said she saw you passed out in a doorway on Marcy Street," she explained, biting, chewing, continuing full-mouthed and somewhat unclearly, "Say she first thought you pray sick or unconscious, then she saw the boll blackbree brand you were—"—swallow—"cradling—that the word?" Bite, chew. "'N she knew you akshy dead drunk."

Blackberry brandy? Yuck and shudder. Wonder where I got that.

"'Absy stinkin', she say, akshy."

"How kind."

"Yeah, she bi' uvacunt," she said, and swallowed, and was articulate. "Anyway, Alessandra called me on her cell and told me where you were and she and me and her boyfriend, Belsen—"

"Who?"

"Huh?"

"Did you say *Belsen*? Like the death camp?"

"The what?"

"Nothing."

"Yeah, well, the three of us got you into my car and back here, thank Christ you didn't lose your keys. You never woke up or threw up, thank Christ again, and boy, were Lessa and Belsy scared you'd puke on them, but I told them how you never throw up."

"No cops?"

"No cops."

She took a dainty nibble and turned her large eyes on me, forlorn concern playing on her loveliness. "Let's eat."

I was surprised how hungry I was. The hops and malt had worked their magic. After consuming most of the plate of eggs and two bagels with "smooshed fish," as she put it, three cups of coffee, orange juice, and half a melon, I polished off the last two Millers and felt very well indeed. The elasticity that would fail in time.

I arranged my chair to face her at the angled table, the corner of the kitchen drenched by sunlight she called "the breakfast nook." I swigged the remaining glug of pilsner as she reached across the table and took my hand.

"Why was I wearing silk pajamas?"

"I love you, Paxton."

"Me, who violated your trust by seducing you? I am a child and you are an adult. I relied on you to behave decently and responsibly and you didn't. I will forever be hurt by your selfish betrayal.'" I was sickened that I could recite this verbatim.

"You didn't really believe any of that?"

"Whose pajamas are those?"

"I don't believe you! Jesus, Paxton! I just took for granted you knew that that ridiculous letter was from my nutty parents! They made me write it! I mean *they* actually wrote it; I just copied it out!" She punched my arm, hard.

"Ouch!" She stopped, shaken.

"I just copied it out.... My God, I just assumed you knew....I'm....I'm *speechless.*"

And she was. Her mouth pulled a couple of koi maneuvers to speak, then the head shook, and the lips closed tersely, the silent sobs beginning. Then, finally, "How could you think that?"

So I was a bastard. A stupid, self-centered beast of little faith. Her actions had been clear and unambiguous from the moment we'd met; she had behaved devotedly, affectionately, passionately. It had not been an act; certainly no eighteen-year-old fluffernutter was that good an actor. How could I think that, indeed?

I dropped to my knees on the floor in front of her, and taking both of her hands said, "Hayley. I don't know why I believed it. I must have been crazy. I'm so in love with you, and I thought I'd lost you—and lost love is something I know a little bit about—and all this insanity with cops and lawyers and reporters." I laid my face on her bare upper thigh.

"I'm so sorry. Can you forgive me?"

There was a long silence, neither of us moved, and I was getting the unsettling feeling that no, she could not. My admission of an utter lack of faith in her had torn the tender fabric uniting us, smashed the glass unicorn of our romance onto the stone floor of fate, and let slip the hounds of love, and when in *hell* was she going to say something?

She lifted my chin in her small hand, bade me stand up, and led me for what seemed a countless time (but was, in fact, the tenth) to the canopied bed. Nothing like an after-breakfast tryst.

Afterwards, she fell straight into an untroubled slumber, her back to me, her warm form spooned into the curve of my body, my arms around her, my face nuzzled into the nape of her neck. A cool, stormy breeze played the thin curtain of the bedroom, and thunder rolled boastfully in approach. I was so content. Yet as I drowsed, I dreamt again of the chamber in the villa in Tuscany. Now she was there with me.

We were making love, both of us kneeling as I penetrated her from behind, a replay of everything that had just occurred in the waking state, but pleasure turned to fear when I realized we were not alone.

Grigori Rasputin and Erika Wikki stood in a corner of the chamber, watching us. Hayley took no notice, just moaned softly with each thrust of her hips. I said nothing, but was embarrassed and alarmed. Then a third figure came into view, a man dressed in the uniform of a British officer. I recognized him as Charles George "Chinese" Gordon, the nut who had done nothing to avoid the siege and massacre at Khartoum in 1885.

He saluted me: "Well done, old man."

He removed Chauncey's mahogany box from under his arm and handed it to Rasputin.

"You'll be wanting this," he said drily.

Rasputin held the box in front of him toward Erika, who, after a glance at me, opened it and removed—not the contents I expected—but a huge, glittering, Eastern dagger. She grinned at me malevolently, and all three of them slowly approached . . .

Chapter Seven

1

I awoke to the clear-headed feel of refreshment and an erection to find her head propped on one elbow next to me. She beamed a bright smile.

"You old slyboots. Knew just how to get into my pants, didn't you?"

"I think it was the other way round. Are you always this beautiful? And always so glad to see me?"

"I'd say you were the one glad to see *me.*"

She kissed me without removing her head from her hand.

"Paxton, remember when you talked about a consensus in America, fueled by the media? That whole corporate/puritanical complex that tried to convince us that sex is simply an adjunct to what's truly essential—either as an expression of matrimonial love and procreation, which is sanctifying it, or as some salacious entertainment, which is demonizing it?"

"I said that?"

"It's the Madonna/Whore concept, and it denies sex its very essence—its daily renewal of the life-force."

"You sound like the nutty general in *Dr. Strangelove.*"

"I'm serious, Paxton. There are certain things that society permits us to think about but forbids us to do. I'm a young woman, right? A legal adult. But look what happened with this whole mess. Society stops me from making my own decisions, satisfying my needs, tells me that 'good girls' don't sleep around. Our permissive society allows the proliferation of erotic images in movies, television, commercials, advertisements—which excite us—but forbids us to seek actual sexual satisfaction, and calls this pseudo-pornography *culture* to boot."

I considered all this while she waited for a response, staring at me intently with those big eyes.

"Yeah, I know," I said.

"Oh, Paxton!" she said in a burst of excitement, jumping naked from the bed with a bounce and scurrying to her bag. She trounced back onto the mattress with a clutch of pamphlets and a well-thumbed paperback. "Look. I've discovered the most awesome genius ever— Wilhelm Reich."

I plumped up the fat feather pillow behind me to examine the reading matter. The brochures were titled, "Synopsis of the Function of the Orgasm," "Critique of Ether," "God and Devil," "Nanterrein Tract, 1967," and the book, *The Quest For Wilhelm Reich* by Colin Wilson.

"Isn't he the guy who had people sit in a box?"

"Yes—yes! You've heard of him?"

"Vaguely."

"He was the most amazing man, so way wicked ahead of his time. And just like Jesus and Galileo, misunderstood and prosecuted."

"Christ-like, huh?"

"Well, only in that he had awesome ideas and got nailed for them." She yawned, having utterly missed her outrageous pun.

"That's terrific," I said pulling her with enthusiasm to me and palming one lovely soft, firm, breast. I kissed her, her breast sleepily woke up and brought forth a morning bud, but Hayley had other, less tactile ideas.

"No, Paxton, listen, I'm serious—"

"So am I—"

"No, listen to me—listen!" She slipped from my arms and took my schoolboy face at sober attention.

"Reich's theories have changed my life."

Oh, God.

"It's not just the function of the orgasm, which is central, of course." I bit my tongue as she grabbed the pamphlet, flipped, skimmed, and read: "'We demand sexual freedom without regard to established laws and moral precepts. We demand freedom to live free of guilt according to our desires and aspirations. We demand the right to realize our sexuality. This right has been taken away. The young must take their fate into their own hands if they want to put a stop to the misery about which they talk so much. We do not ask for our rights; we fight for them.'"

I think she expected applause. Her eyes burned with the flame of new fanaticism.

"I'm with you," I said, attempting a nuzzle. "Let's—"

"But it's not just sex, Paxton. Sex is a bridge to an understanding of our character armor, the roots of anxiety, vegeto-therapy, psychoanalysis, Marx!" She actually beamed.

"Marx? Are you kidding?"

"No."

"Hayley, Karl Marx went out with overalls and brown rice."

"What's that supposed to mean?"

"He had one laudable theory, communism. A noble experiment that didn't work. The Soviet Union, the Eastern Bloc—all gone. Cuba's on the ropes, China now reveres authoritarian capitalist pigs. It didn't work. It doesn't work. It goes against the grain of all the human nature you're going on about."

She thought about that, biting her lip.

"Well, okay," she said, conciliatory. "I don't know anything about that, but maybe you're right. All I know is that Reich's awesome, and I'm now a dedicated Reichian and all that goes with it."

"Good girl." I actually patted her head, then froze in horror at the move. "I have some news!" I said, furiously changing the subject.

"What?" She slid back atop me, snuggly again with all sociopolitical concerns resolved.

"I got a job. Another one from Chauncey. He wants me to deliver a package to some little town up in Maine."

"A package? A package of what?"

I went to the closet for the mahogany box and brought it to her like a sampler of chocolates.

"You're gonna love this."

I lifted the lid. "Now what do you think of that?"

She stared. "It's a big rotten banana."

"No, it is not."

"Then what is it?"

"Do you know who Rasputin was?"

"Yeah. He was a chef or something."

"No, but close." I proceeded to deliver a brief but colorful digest of Grigori Rasputin's remarkable career, ending with the inept efforts of the Russian assassins to actually get him to die. When I had finished, she looked nonplussed.

"So, what? That's him?"

"No. That's his penis."

She screamed and slammed the lid shut, startling the hell out of me. Then she froze, and whispered: "You're not serious!"

"I am."

"Where did you get it?"

I told her the bizarre details as best I understood them, stressing the crucial factor of my getting three thousand bucks. She considered the whole bizarre deal for some time.

"How long're you going to be gone?"

"Just overnight. Chauncey doesn't want me to manage the shop anymore. He says he's concerned about my emotional state, but I think he's worried about publicity. If he doesn't offer me a job washing his Bentley when I get back, I don't know what I'm going to do. There's no affordable rent in Northport for a Barnes and Noble sales associate. I have to go someplace where the livin' is easy."

"And the cotton is high."

She thinks Rasputin's a chef, but she can quote the Gershwins with aplomb. I had such a crush on this girl, there were moments I felt that if things fell apart and the center did not hold, I would have to actually crush her.

"Well, that's an interesting coincidence," she said. "'Cause it just so happens I need to get out of here, too. My parents are out of their tree, school's out, no summer job. I've got nearly eight thousand in the bank, and my car. Why don't I come with you?"

"You mean run away from home?"

"I'm eighteen! Is that running away from home?"

"In your house, thirty-three would be running away from home."

"Then I guess I am," she said. "With you, my May-December lover."

2

I packed as Hayley cleaned the already immaculate apartment. I then called Chauncey and left a message with his service that Operation Russian Cock was under way. I put a sign on the door: "Closed by Order of Trotsky." By mid-afternoon we were on the Maine Turnpike, heading North.

3

Her spoiled-brat car handled well, windows down, her hair in the summer wind, her designer shades, the whole psychic ensemble could have been cruising off Route 66 in the 20th Century year of the same number. She was driving, negotiating the wheel with the one free finger of a hand busy with a dripping white nectarine. The other mitt twirled the stereo trying to find "something good." She was sick of her collection, and NPR, jazz, and classical were unacceptable ("For Christ's sake, Paxton, *we're on a road trip*") and the tunes had to be just right. She settled on something by Madonna that had charted long before her birth. I was tolerant.

This freshly minted Marxist/Reichian axis rankled. She detected as much and observed that I was a perfect example of Vogt's "Right Man"—always knowing what was best for everyone in his orbit. I added Vogt, whoever he was, to my list of disliked individuals.

"You probably got my whole future mapped out for me, right, darling?" she said, rubbing her wet, bitten fruit against my cheek. "Marriage?"

I wiped the nectarine gunk. Marriage? Not quite. So now she had political implications. Very commendable. Change the world. Save the whales. Save the bunnies. Blow hell out of bystanders like Erika and SLAV. First in the air. But good God, Marx? Workers of the world unite? That was as dead and useless as vacuum-packed Lenin in Red Square. I had grown up in the shadow of Botha and de Klerk, and my parents had worked against the injustice of that time. Fascism, totalitarianism, communism, military regimes: all evil. I had lived through its lingering memory and had no patience for empathic political dilettantism.

And Wilhelm Reich, Lord love a duck! What connection did his babble have to the "fascism provides a gut-level attraction" nonsense I had found in her possession? Marx and Reich! Hayley was young; if it weren't' them, it might be Hesse or Gibran or Ayn Rand charging her battery as if she alone had discovered them for the world. So it was nothing, really—nothing.

She tossed the gooey pit of the fruit onto the highway, licking her fingers, wiping her hands on her bare thighs (the hem of the short summer skirt I insisted she change into danced happily beneath the line of her crotch), and sang loudly with the radio.

I snapped the volume off.

"Hey!" she snapped back.

"Where'd you get all that Marx and Reich crap anyway?"

She regarded me sidelong with her too-cool-for-school confidence grooving like a supermodel.

"My friend Malcolm."

"Malcolm? Who's Malcolm? High school kid?"

"No. He's older. Older than me. Not as old as you."

"Thanks a lot." She squeezed my thigh, leaving nectarine-stains. If she went for my hair, so help me—"

"He's like a brother to me, a mentor. A brotherly mentor. I met him at a protest rally at Costco."

I released my safety belt to twist in the seat and face her.

"A protest for what?"

"Animal rights. To prevent the abuse, torture and exploitation of— "

"And this Malcom's a full-time activist for animal rights?"

"For a whole slew o' stuff. Animals, clean water, theatre."

"Theatre?"

"Oh my God, yes. He's awesome."

We shot through a long underpass, and as we emerged from the darkness I felt a change in the air, the temperature dropping. I waited, the only sound the roar of the wind whipping at seventy miles, for a dour narrator to lean forward from the backseat and explain that I had, in fact, just entered the Fucked-Up Zone. She turned on the volume. I snapped it off a second time.

"Hey!"

"Why didn't you tell me you have a friend Malcolm who's older and— how old?"

"He's twenty-five."

"—Interested in Reich and rights and all that bullshit."

"It's not bullshit! And why didn't you tell me you're still married and your wife's a terrorist?"

"What?!"

"You heard me." She was quite calm and collected.

I, on the other hand, trilled a rising, shrill sound like a seagull.

"I'm not married. My wife is dead, dead! Drowned. This terrorist thing is completely deranged. That crazy FBI freak Poplin even wanted to know if we—"

She smiled, unnerving me further. "We....?"

I said, "She won't let go of this fantasy about Erika being alive. *Jy if 'n dumkoph!*"

"What?"

"Nothing."

"What'd you say?

" I was swearing in Afrikaans. Not about you," I added quickly.

She turned to me with feigned sympathy, pouty lips, hand back on my thigh. "You really feel like you killed her?"

"Oh, baby," I melted. "I dunno. Sometimes I just—wait a second! Why in hell would you say that? Pull the car over, Hayley!"

"Here?"

"Pull the car over, damnit, NOW!"

"Okay, okay, calm down."

She started laughing—inappropriately, I felt—but maneuvered skillfully onto a perfectly-timed rest stop exit ramp and sailed across an empty car park to bring the sleek vehicle to rest under a thatch of pines. She yanked her glasses off with a flourish and stared at me mock-earnest.

"Go on."

"I could spank you."

"Later, sweetheart. Baby's gotta drive. I'm waiting."

"All right," I began. "Let's start with how do you now about Erika allegedly not being dead and my supposed guilt feelings, huh? Start there."

"Poplin told me all about it. She grilled me a couple times."

"About what?"

"What the hell do you think, Paxton? The Northport city attorney was working for the school board and they were all pissing themselves over a lawsuit from my parents, and nutcase Superintendent Schrechlich kept talking about statutory rape, even after they explained to her what that was. The fact that I'm a legal adult seemed lost on everybody. Everybody except *you*." She winked.

"What'd she ask you?"

She signed, suddenly bored with the topic. "Well, she seemed particularly interested in why you preferred butt-fucking to blow jobs."

Oh, Christ. Poplin! How I hated her!

"What did she say about Erika?"

She gave the question what looked to be considerable thought. "Why didn't you tell me about getting blown up? And now this idea she's not dead and she was involved in blowing you up—ironic, huh?"

"Apt, I'd say."

"Would you ever get back together with her?"

"She'd dead!"

"But what if she isn't?"

"Hayley, for Christ's sake, I've been doing this with professionals."

She seemed to respect this. She said, "Since we're coming clean about everything, I guess I should tell you some stuff, too."

"You're sleeping with Malcolm?"

I sounded weak, hating Poplin and Schrechlich and Hayley's parents and myself. What a flair I had for chaos! It was the booze. I knew in that ghastly moment, sitting with her in the auto under the trees, an honest-to-Christ epiphany. My life was a mess because I was an alcoholic, and if I was a great glamorous writer, which I wasn't, then I'd be Delmore Schwartz convulsing in a Times Square hotel or Hart Crane jumping into the mouth of a shark. I knew it in every fiber of my being. *Duh*, she would have said, if able to read my thoughts. Perhaps she did. She took my face in her hand, and looking me straight in the eye, commanded no nonsense:

"I am sleeping with *you*." She let her gaze linger, then kissed me with tenderness.

"Then what is it?" I asked.

"We're going to the same place."

"I know. Rangeley."

"No, *mein Schlaf*. I mean I'm going to Rangeley to see Malcolm and my friends—who happen to be the same people you're delivering your package to." She grinned.

"How is that possible?"

"Because Chauncey Alexander MacFarland Jr., is selling that cock to a Pakistani who's promised us a cut—for the money. I mean—for hooking him up in the first place, but there's now every indication, as Malcolm says, that your boss is gonna double-cross us."

She was sounding like a *noir* broad from a pulp fiction paperback. I found it very sexy, actually.

"Paxton, we need your help."

"We?"

"My group. SLAV."

Perfect. I was back in the hospital, hallucinating again. This whole concentric cycle was just gonna keep a-rollin', beginning and ending, probably, with my not-so-late wife.

"Now, hear me out, Paxton. I know there's some crazy stuff that looks really bad here, but you've got to believe me. We had no idea you were going to be at the River Styx; that was just a coincidence, and I had no idea you were gonna wind up smack in the middle of all this. I mean, Chauncey doesn't know I'm with them, and he doesn't know I'm with you now. That was part of the smoke-screen of not seeing you for the last few weeks, just in case he got suspicious."

"Your parents are in on this, too?"

"No. That was real. My parents hate your guts and wish you were dead."

"Oh, good. At least that's sincere."

"But me ditching you like that—we were afraid Chauncey might get wise."

Get wise. I was with Peggy Cummins in *Gun Crazy.* I needed to clear my head. I wanted to dive into cold water (unfortunate metaphor) to unravel this web of confusion and what was looking disagreeably like deceit. I gently—as light as my uncertain touch could bring to bear—stroked her forearm and implored her.

"Please—Hayley, just start at the beginning. Slowly and simply."

"Okay." She peeled the wrappers off three sticks of Big Red and wadding the gum into her mouth, tossed the paper and foil onto the floor of the car. She settled in as if about to synopsize the past week's episodes of her favorite soap opera.

"SLAV is dedicated to the immediate overthrow of any government that allows the torture and vivisection of helpless animals in the name of cosmetic murder—not just the U.S." She looked around the rest stop like a spy under a lamp post and dropped her voice a tone.

"Our leader, Dora Shannon, was doing business with Mr. Kureishi when she found out Chauncey had gotten hold of Rasputin's cock through some connection in Tel Aviv. She hooked the two of them up and has acted as go-between for the transaction, so she just wants a cut—like ten percent of the money being exchanged. SLAV really needs fast cash."

"So you knew all along about this revolting item? You were faking all that shock?"

She shook her head. "No, I was not. That was real. I only knew that Chauncey might be using you to make the exchange, and I had to keep an eye on you."

"So you were using me, too."

"Oh, stop it, Paxton. Don't confuse things. We're trying to protect you. Dora got word that Chauncey doesn't dig cutting us in on any of the money he's getting from Saeed, so he was going to charge Saeed extra, but Saeed said he wouldn't pay it, and that's when Chauncey allegedly said, 'Why not 'liminate the middleman?' That being us."

I was confused. "Let's skip over this part."

She sighed. "So obviously Chauncey is using you to deliver this to Kureishi, and I was recruited through Malcolm to keep an eye on you."

"That's all? That's the only reason we're involved?"

"Oh, of course not, you idiot!" She was suddenly angry. "I fell in love with you! You think I been planning to set you up since I was twelve years old? Jesus, what kinda girl d'ya think I am?"

I feebly tried to rub her arm again, but she slapped my hand away. I asked, "Why was Chauncey at the River Styx with me that day?"

She still looked sore, but rallied to the espionage.

"We can't figure that one out," she said. "*Is a puzzlement.*" She gave a little devilish smirk. "Question is, why's he trusting *you* with all the loot?"

I shrugged. "Guess 'cause we got blowed up together. It's sort of a bond."

She put her hand on the back of my neck. "Malcolm says if we pull this off, Chauncey'll get his money, Mr. Kureishi will get his cock, and we'll get what's coming to us fair and square, and nobody'll get hurt. Safe as milk, Malcolm says."

And she kissed me. I listened to the rush of the strong breeze through the trees around us with closed eyes as her cinnamon-scented lips and tongue explored my mouth. I thought of Michelangelo Antonioni listening to hundreds of recordings of wind rushing through trees before selecting the perfect choice for *Blow Up*. I thought about the fact that the amputated sex organ of a man who once held sway over the last captains of the Russian Empire was traveling in this very car. I wondered where I had heard "safe as milk" before. I thought about Hayley, kissing me now with so much warmth—both in temperature and abstract—and why she was so impressed with this Malcolm.

I didn't like any of it. In movies, whenever anyone about to commit a crime says nobody'll get hurt, somebody always does. If ever I was living in a film, this was it. But I tried to push all tumbling, troubling thoughts out of my head and concentrate on the sound of the breeze and the feel of the girl.

4

We were not so driven by passion to make love at a highway rest stop. On we drove.

Or I drove on this stretch, to afford Hayley the change to bask in the sun, stick her toes over the side of the passenger door and display a severe deficit of attention from channel to channel on the stereo.

"Go faster, will ya Paxton?"

I would not. I hadn't explained that my driver's license had been revoked some time back for multiple convictions of drunk driving and I had never bothered to attempt to reclaim the privilege, opportunities to slip behind the wheel in Boston being few.

"No, pumpkin. I think not. Speeding is against the law. Don't want to attract the attention of a Maine state trooper, now do we?"

She chewed this over along with her ever-freshened wad of Big Red. "No, I guess not," she agreed. "Good thinking."

For years I had prided myself on my ability to face the day with a hangover, even a bad one (what a drinking friend of my father's named Jan Cremer Gats used to call a "wangdanger"), and rise to the challenge. Medicating myself became a ritual—the order and regularity of the steps serving as some totem against mortality—and a race: How soon could I beat the devil of my physically unwell state and rise from the smoldering, crapulous ashes of the fires from the night before? Self-destruction galloped through my family (with the exception of my brother, who, on closer inspection, was also destroying himself by denying any drop of the Dionysian in his frightened, ordered life). I seemed to Calvinistically enjoy the punishments and sorrows of the morning after as much as the joys and highs of the revel itself. I courted physical, mental, and spiritual disarray like a minion of Masoch. The true slow suicide of the coward. I didn't have the guts to swan-dive off a roof like my old man. I chose my poison drink by drink for drink's sake. Perhaps it was brain-damage time, but most definitely I was doing myself in.

I had told myself, with wounded pride and what little self-respect remained, that something in me had died in Bar Harbor along with Erika. But now I was certain that I was slowly killing off whatever else held on. I was a slave to it; the booze was not operating as both balm and bane, and as I drove the car up the Maine Turnpike, I knew in every filament of my being that I was an alcoholic; determined, unapologetic, a drunk. My favorite line from playwright Simon Gray: "I don't have a drinking problem. I drink heavily every night. I'm used to it again. There's no problem."

I certainly was that man. But before this day, the sense of dread and unease had never been so acute, never inching me quite so close to the abyss of all-out panic and breakdown. The six-pack of pilsner had calmed thrashed nerves in the late morning, the bromides and unguents for the devils of the belly and the demons of the mind had done quick work, but now disease was creeping its spider's crawl to an irrational notion of seizure. I had never seen my knuckles so white as they gripped the wheel, and though I focused intense concentration on the road in an attempt at distracting a calliope brain, I knew a growing sense of panic that only more alcohol could quell. Should I tell Hayley this truth, that I was so enslaved to the juice that I couldn't get through a pleasant afternoon's drive without a repeated fix? How humiliating. Steady on. One could but try, thoroughly ashamed.

She kept spinning around in her seat, buckling and unbuckling her belt, twisting to gape in every direction. At first, the silky sight of her purple bikini pants glimpsed beneath the ascent of her skirt as she turned was heartwarming; then an odd mixture of resignation and foreboding seemed to sweep over me like a great bird. No, more like a pterodactyl. Who was I kidding? This kid and myself? When we weren't kissing, screwing, or discussing ephemera, what sort of connection could we hope for? Neither of us saw life as the other did. True, this might still be the case if we were of the same age, but it was hugely unlikely that we could bridge the chasm of experiential sensibility that yawned, bored, between us. I could count on one hand May/Decrepit romances that had worked: Charlie Chaplin and Oona O'Neill, of course, Bogart and Bacall, John and Bo Derek. Who else? Then there were the disasters of Rolling Stone Bill Wyman and his thirteen-year-old Mandy, J.D. Salinger and Joyce Maynard, and other train wrecks.

As I glanced again at the lavender underwear and she burst a pink bubble across her nose and had to peel it off her glasses with, "Oh, fuck, me, man," and angrily cranked the offal discharging from the speakers, a tapestry of medieval images swayed from the castle-kept walls of my romantic ivory tower: I saw slayings, eviscerations and writhing on impaled fundaments, all witnessed by Dark Ages faces of Mona Lisa serenity. This was a cautionary tale being spun. I knew in that moment what had to be done: Stop drinking; rehab; ditch Hayley. To hell with this half-ass Robert Ludlum shit. Have Haley drop me at the nearest bus station (or better yet, Amtrak had reactivated the old Boston & Maine line—train keep a-rollin' indeed!), toss her Rasputin's filthy member and *Dasvadanya*, darling.

What immaculateness of purpose! What a sense of joy washed over me!

Chapter Eight

1

Now, despite the unease brought by the public scandal and excoriation, love found, love rejected and lost, love regained, I was pleased by my sudden calm.

"Hey, look!" she chirped as a sign swept above us: "Exit 11—Glass and New Gloucester! Now that' a good omen, isn't it?"

She flipped open her *Cosmopolitan* with a nod.

Two hours later, we had left civilization behind. There was scant evidence of population as dusk approached and long shadows descended over endless high trees. The zinging of insects was starkly underscored when the car came to its few occasional halts.

"You know what you are?" Hayley asked. I glanced over at her, her brows furrowed in concentration on the glossy page inches from her nose.

"I can't wait."

"You're an *ephebophile*."

"What the hell's an— "

"Ephebophile? Funny you should ask." She cleared her throat. "It says here it's someone sexually attracted to young women between the ages of eighteen and twenty." She put the magazine on her lap and grinned at me.

"Well. Isn't that something."

"It's all here in cold, hard print."

"Why do you look so pleased?"

"I'm happy for you," she said. "At least you're not a pedophile."

"Was there any doubt?"

"I get mixed up. You know—my parents."

"And it stops at twenty, this lust? I couldn't possibly be with a woman, oh—say— twenty-one?"

"Nope. They turn into pumpkins on their twenty-first birthdays right in the middle of the unnatural act. And you're left fucking some squash."

She laughed, and I glimpsed, for a second, the presence of a small flash of evil. I should gallop to my Hail Marys and my rosary beads. Sade wrote that slavery begins with the fear of death; self-pity could not be far behind its ghastly haunches.

Finally Rangeley's Exit 12 loomed up after nearly four hours of travel. We had arrived.

I turned the car onto Main Street and immediately the Rangeley Inn and Pub loomed up from its sharp crest on the right, where Chauncey had made the reservation. I parked the car on the street and stopped Hayley before she could leap.

"Hang on."

"What?"

"Will this fit?" I unbuttoned the breast-pocket of my shirt and extracted Erika's gold wedding band. She looked tickled.

"Are you proposing to me, Paxton?" she giggled.

"It's a wedding ring. Just see if it fits, will you?"

She daintily held out her right hand for me to slip it on.

"It's worn on the left."

I handed it to her. She smirked and slipped it on. She held her hand out and angled her head, admiring the ring like a freshly engaged lass.

"It fits perfect."

I said, "Just in case the community standards up here in Hicksville ain't as liberal as back down South. French Catholics."

"You really think they would let us check in if they thought we weren't hitched?"

"I really don't think anybody's going to believe for a second that you're my wife, but they can't rightly argue, can they?"

She smiled then, very oddly, as though satisfied with something, then kissed me suddenly, clutching me hard and close, her hot, bubble-gum breath puffing with glee. It was a disorienting moment, sending erotic charges straight through me, along with something fixed and portentous, attached to omens, signs and the mystical weight of Rasputin and Reich up here at what felt like the end of the earth.

In control, she kissed me, deftly licked my lower lip, kissed me again, and said, "Let's go check in, Mr. Graham."

The drill, apparently, was to answer something like, "Certainly, Mrs. Graham," but I would let some more potent third party provide that flummery for her.

We had no difficulty at the front desk. All concerns were dispelled when the prissy, pampered tub ahead of us collected his key. He was put out with the clerk—a goatee'd and bow-tied gentleman with an English accent, a pair of half-spectacles precariously resting on the tip of a hawk nose. Evidently Tubby wanted a room facing East (religion?), and Tubby was used to getting what he wanted, and Uncle Onslow had stipulated when booking, you see. Both clerk and customer raised their voices, playing to their audience of two. Finally, fat fingers snatched the key, and the castrato snapped, "Your name?"

"Alan Lee," the clerk snapped back. "Alan B. Lee!"

"We shall see about this!" minced the man with either a very bad toupee or extremely viscous hair oil. Then, turning an odd beat, he stated to Mr. Lee warmly, "We're heading to Digby, you know," and winked, as one letting another in on a secret. He waddled off in his white loafers. Mr. Lee considered us with gravity before asking, "Where the fuck is Digby?"

We were home free, Poe and cousin Virginia Clemm, and the mood swung uphill.

We took supper in the pub, and Hayley, feeling daring as a newlywed, ordered a glass of Chardonnay with her chicken from the meek mouse who waited on us. The mouse noted the ring and served her. At the power of betrothment will few women sneer.

2

We had settled into the clean and pleasant cocoon of the Inn.

I took a shower. She announced that nothing would be lovelier than a long soak in a hot tub. While she did that, I was silent and relaxed on the big bed, reading Stephen King's *Salem's Lot*. She had presented me before we left with a paperback copy, declaiming that if I were such a fan of Hammer Films and all things vampiric and *Grand Guignol*, then I most definitely must dip into this modern American masterpiece. I condescendingly and carelessly read the first twenty pages and was astonished to find myself hooked. What's worse, I was embarrassed. What a literary snob I was, never bothering to read King on the theory that if that many readers adored him enough to regularly place his books at the top of the bestseller lists, then he was clearly of inferior quality, this buster of blocks (the Big Mac—as I think he himself once put it—of the world of letters). It was well-written, thoughtful—and frightening.

She emerged wrapped in a huge towel, and set out and lit several small candles she'd packed for the trip. She turned down the lights in the room and sent a smile of silvery delight in my direction, then returned to the bathroom.

As the sound of the final glugging of the bathwater down the drain echoed off the tiles, she clicked off the last light and came dressed in what I had once remarked was my all-time Number One Winner in the Outfit Worn by a Pretty Girl category—a white t-shirt and a pair of brief panties.

She skipped across the carpet and bounced her lithe little body onto the bed next to me; then, the bounce settled, kissed me almost chastely on the cheek, her wet hair smelling of strawberry-scented shampoo, her lips and limbs a marvelous buffet of warm and cool, toweled but moist.

"Anybody die yet?" she asked, indicating the book.

"Just horrible old Hubie Marsten."

"It gets better—and worse."

She stared at me with deliberateness in the soothing, flickering candlelight, the three warm glows of her, me, and the room. I lifted the tail of her shirt, stole a glimpse of her baby-blue bikinis, and asked, "Those for me?"

She smiled. "No, for the night clerk. He's eighty-six and comes on duty at midnight." She winked. Then she took the book from my hands, gently pushed me backward onto the pillows, and sat astride my midsection, her bottom just brushing the drowsy erection that had roused itself. She kissed my face, neck, opened my shirt, her delicious hair smothering my nose.

"I love you," I said.

She nodded as if I had complimented her shoes and spun around, and—her knees pushing to arch her back—pressed that gift-wrapped mound softly against my mouth. She tossed over her shoulder an impish smile of sheer decadent abandonment. My succubus then languidly closed her eyes, exhaled deeply, and moved herself backward with a contented squirm. In a spirit of sexual equity, she began to stroke me through my jeans, unbuttoning the top button....

When something truly amiss—wrong, improper—seemed to enter the room like a phantom. How could this be? My young lover was undulating over my cock. I was so pleased; all sensory input was being collected for a lifetime of memory; the moment luxuriated in itself as though carefully rehearsed—perhaps it had been, and perhaps that was the problem. She slowly inched her knickers down over her rump. I had an inch from my ecstatic nose, the smooth cleft of a dewy and compliant Georgia peach—and I was conflicted.

"Are you sleeping with Malcolm?" I asked, which startled me probably more than her, though I had the feeling I was addressing her vagina.

A disgusted sigh. "Paxton—"

"I'm serious."

"Oh, for Pete's sake!"

She pulled herself from me with a violent jerk, saying, "You really know how to wreck the moment!"

She stood on the mattress, pulling the wisp of cotton to her hips with defiance. I was staring at her crotch and repeated, "Are you?"

She grabbed the paperback and threw it at my head, a direct hit that smarted considerably. She jumped off the bed.

And it was if, as she landed, she transformed into an entity I had not encountered beyond the glimmer of the moment before we checked in, like watching a vampire metamorphose from human to bat to mist and back again.

"Yes! Yes! I'm sleeping with him because I love him, and he's everything that you could have been but aren't. We fuck all the time. Happy?"

"Not really." I rubbed my forehead, but there was a worse hurt than that. "What do you mean, he's everything I'm not?"

She looked tired at that. "Oh, let's face it, Paxton. You're a nice guy, but you're a drunk, a zero, and a loser. Any talent you might have had got drowned in the booze, and your ship sailed long ago. Hell, you don't even write anymore. You're thirty-three, scared, desperate, and addicted. Just because you've gone one whole day without a snort doesn't mean shit. And you're in love with me—a girl almost half your age. Doesn't that strike you as pathetic?" She stared at me challengingly.

"Gee, Hayley. I was actually feeling pretty hopeful of late. And I didn't think that loving someone could ever be pathetic, as long as there was always—respect?"

She looked pitying now. "Well, there you are," she said matter-of-factly.

"I had no idea you could be so cruel." Oh, boy, was that the wrong thing to say.

"You wouldn't," she started venomously. "Your sob-sister friendship's all well and good for talking things out like a couple of girls—and maybe a pity-fuck—but when I'm looking for the real thing, sensitivity don't enter into it, if you'll pardon the pun. I can't sit down on sensitivity."

"But I love you." I played right into her hands.

She placed those hands on her hips and her feet apart.

"I'm going to quote Malcolm here—a better poet and a better man than you—because you need to hear it. He says that love is the most insidious instrument of social repression. And you're repressing me. And I hate you for that. Do you understand? I hate you!"

I jumped from the bed, glimpsed her startled expression as I grabbed her arm and slapped her, not very hard. She lashed out, pummeling my face, head, arms and chest with bruising punches, but it was no match for the fury I had harnessed in the heat of her speech, and I barely flinched under the blows as I swept her from her feet and tossed her roughly onto the bed. Before she could even gain any bearing, I was on her, tearing the thin fabric from her hips.

The implications of the instantaneous erection troubled me, but only for an instant. Somehow, I corralled her energized counter-assault at the same time I loosed my unbuttoned pants.

She may have been moist from the hot bath, but even the prelude of her orchestrated foreplay had not lubriciously prepared her. She was not ready; the quick, sharp penetration was painful for me—her yelping made it clear that it wasn't pleasant for her, either.

I thrust like some thug in an alley, pure anger and resentment fueling an act that had little to do with sex and nothing to do with love—rank hostility and aggression. She continued to kick and beat and yell (but not scream) as I wrestled with her flailing wrists and repositioned myself for easier entry. After only a minute of this new assault, I felt a warm flood envelope my loins, she moved, and the rest was easy.

She ceased struggling and abandoned the fight to painful impulse, and—her eyes closed—began caressing my neck. Her total attainment of control wrecked my anger, inspiring me to withdraw, flip her over, and using her own lush fluid as lubricant, surprise her elegant rectum, but she was panting and murmuring now, my face was settled into the hollow of her neck, my mouth hungry, and I was amazed to realize we were about to climax together, simultaneous orgasm something having never happened to me before (or her, I discovered later). She thrashed in a plateau that propelled her to wrap her legs around me and pull me in as deeply as she could. We had no condom, a precaution we both viewed with solemn sobriety; but she held me in place, both our bodies at the end nearly motionless. I almost had to bite my tongue to keep from whispering the three words again. We came like a preplanned explosion. The whole thing was diabolical.

I expected another beating, or a sustained wail that would bring pounding on the walls and porters scurrying to the door. But no. Our heavy, sweaty panting settled into a slow, synchronized rhythm—and we fell asleep, me still inside her.

Later, I made a barely perceptible move to withdraw, but she breathed a small coo of objection and tightened the scissors-grip of her legs around me. Perhaps her sex wanted mine as a trophy: if this had been ravishment, then the power she sat on had triumphed, deflating me to uselessness.

At some point I extricated myself from her embrace to extinguish the candles and maneuver us both under the bed-clothes; and she, too, must have risen, for in the morning she was snoring in my arms, my palm caressing one plump cheek of her bottom beneath the waistband of a fresh pair of briefs.

3

We slept late, despite the early hour of our retirement the previous night, the exertions of mutual scorn and physical assault capped by sexual deliverance apparently a great stimulus to the spell of Morpheus.

And evidently appetite. We both awoke famished, but neither felt like breakfast, despite the return of healthy morning hunger now that my stomach was free of the sauce. (My stomach and body, yes, but that was the easy part. It was the death-grip that the obsession, the phenomenon of craving, had on the psyche that was so cunning, baffling, and powerful. Amen.) We checked out and went for an early lunch.

We left the car where it was parked and strolled up the sunny Main Street to the Red Onion Restaurant. Halfway there, she nonchalantly took my hand.

During the leisurely meal of sandwiches and iced coffee, there hung a resigned civility between us: not much conversation, but mercifully, the stretches of silence were not uncomfortable. We behaved as if used to one another, and for a moment, that seemed a happy thought. But she had said the night before that she hated me, and I knew that at the least, I was growing weary of her.

After lunch, we drove the three miles out of town in the eerie quiet that can accompany hot, sun-blasted country noons. We reached Dodge Pond Road, dust-devils swirling behind the car as we rambled past a large sign proclaiming, "Orgonon". Hayley had me stop the car.

"So this is where it all happened," she said reverently.

As it happened, this was merely the visitors' center, the actual Where It All Happened being a drive up the hill. I clarified; she sulked all the way up.

Neither of us were disappointed when we reached the top. The museum was impressive. A stone laboratory placed evenly on the peak, with a gorgeous view of the dense surrounding forest. It was easy to understand what drew Reich here in the first place – or anyone.

I pulled my knapsack over my shoulder, the mahogany box zipped securely inside. We parked the car and strolled around the grounds.

"He arrived in 1942," said Hayley, "Purchasing over two hundred acres of land. Look at it; it must be worth millions now."

"Yeah. He probably paid something like three hundred dollars for it."

She ignored me. The gift shop sold the collected works in hardcover and paperbound editions, as well as commemorative videotapes, even clothing. It had the feel of an arcade for intellectuals.

We were ushered, along with two women and a little girl (the only other visitors that hot day) into an annex room beneath the observatory to watch a short video survey on the life and work of Wilhelm Reich. We then enjoyed a brief tour of the compound, followed by permission to roam freely but not touch anything.

It was all so lovingly preserved: the Great Man's library, equipment, microscopes, even his white lab coat. The museum boasted several of his huge "cloud busters," apparatuses designed to remove DOR (deadly orgone energy) from the atmosphere. He had allegedly once made it rain in the town of Ellsworth.

We were on the second floor of the laboratory, when my attention was distracted from Reich's personal library by Hayley's voice growing loud:

"So you're—what—from Cuba?"

"No," replied an impatient, woman's voice, "I'm from Puerto Rico, but *I'm Cuban*."

"So what does that make you—Sorta Rican?"

I wheeled around. She was standing next to one of the women accompanying our "tour." The both of them were in front of a display detailing the sexual build, plateau, and climax of the female orgasm. The woman—fiftyish, short-cropped silver hair, overalls, Birkenstocks – was murmuring low and gesturing intensely at the illustrations, then back to Hayley, who seemed peeved.

"Not at all," said Hayley in a deliberately raised tone. "I always come from vaginal penetration, okay? Maybe *you're* the one with the problem!"

Good Christ.

I slid the twenty feet between us like a penguin on ice skates. The poor woman's mouth hung open in stupefaction. I took Hayley by the arm.

"Time to go, darling," I said cheerily.

"Of course, my sweet," she smiled through gritted teeth, never taking her steely gaze off this dame. When the woman was still in earshot, Hayley tossed off, "Dyke," for good measure.

I said, "All that money for Dale Carnegie's course and look at you!"

"Who?" Then she did a slow burn. "Don't get smart-assed, Paxton. What time is it?"

"Nearly two o'clock."

"We gotta meet Malcolm at the tomb."

"I was about to say."

"Then let's move it."

We had only strolled down the stairs to the first floor when it became apparent we would not have to trudge off into the woods to Reich's monument.

"There he is—Malcolm!" she yelled, and actually rushed into his arms.

If I was startled by the exuberance of her greeting to this character—this was no Big Brother/Mentor/Friend embrace, oh no—then I was downright dumbstruck by the appearance of the motley cartoon himself.

She'd described him as twenty-five; he looked ten years older. He was tall—at least six-three—with a coxcomb of unruly brown hair, streaked with magenta, sticking out in all directions. Three days' growth scruffed an angular face, a beak nose supporting blue-tinted wire-framed glasses. His skin was the color of almonds, as if from too much sun but not enough soap. He wore dirty cut-offs, red basketball high tops, and a sweatshirt emblazoned with *Nanterrein Now*, all enveloped in a knee-length, multi-swatched coat of many colors that looked as if it might have been stitched together by the inmates of the asylum at Charenton. The man was dressed like a minstrel.

When tiny Hayley leapt into his long arms, she wrapped her legs around his midsection, then kissed him with an ardor that could only be considered brotherly by Caligula.

"Hello, darling. How are you?" she said breathlessly, coming up for air. Standing there still holding her little rump in his rough-hewn, pitch-stained hands, he intoned:

"I am ill—there's no doubt about it. And yet I felt so well last month. I have a fever, a terrible fever, or rather a feverish irritation of my nerves which afflicts my mind just as much as my body. I constantly have this dreadful sensation of being threatened by some danger, this feeling of imminent disaster or encroaching death, this state of apprehension which is no doubt caused by the onset of some hitherto unknown disease incubating in my blood and flesh."

"Oh, wow—that's awesome! When did you write it?"

"I didn't. That's Guy de Maupassant. But that's exactly how I feel," he said exuberantly.

"You're incredible," she said.

The incredible and exuberant Malcolm became aware that their Karma Sutra number seemed to be attracting attention from other, newly arrived Reich enthusiasts. He dropped her to the floor and kissed her forehead.

She took him by the hand and tugged him over as if bringing the new beau to meet her uncle. I thought I might puke.

"Paxton, I want you to meet Malcolm. Malcolm, this is my *friend*, Paxton Graham."

He pumped my hand with admiration.

"It's an honor. I think 'Michael Rockefeller' is one of the greatest pieces of its kind. I'm a poet, too, but nothing like your league."

The tinny, electronic trill of "Hava Nagela" in double-time suddenly erupted from Malcolm's quilt-pocket.

"Hang on, babe," he said, pulling a phone from the ridiculous coat. "Gotta check in." He kissed her, gave a nod-and-wink to me, and loped off in his big sneaks to a corner of the lobby to take the call. Her gaze trailed after him lovingly, mooned around the lobby with a sign of satisfaction, then finally came to rest on my steely glare.

"What?"

"Malcolm's a poet," I said acidly. "Who knew?"

"That bother you?"

"No. Yes. But what really bothers me is that this clown is clearly not—"

"Don't you dare call him—"

"Your brotherly mentor. What a load of bullshit you—"

"You're not fit to—"

"You lied to me, Hayley, why? Why—"

But Malcolm was back, sniffing trouble like a great, gangling gazelle, and noting the tears welling up in his little gnu's eyes, he took up a combative position.

"There a problem?" he asked. We were silent, Hayley shaking her head, crying now.

"No problem," I said pleasantly. But Malc was no fool.

"That's good," he said, "Because this whole thing is far too important for me to allow any kind of personal issues to compromise it. Now, I know that you've developed a lot of affection for Hayley in the last month, and I can understand that…" He tugged her close—her nose almost at his belt-level—in earnest of his humility. "But she's here now. With me. And we need to concentrate on what needs to get accomplished."

He had three inches on me and fifty pounds, with hands like two slabs, but at that point, I didn't care. I was still physically unsound from the drink, but with the perfect little twit sniffling symbolically between us (it was one thing I was ready to ditch her that very day, but now she was dumping me not for some goofy adolescent, but another poet a mere seven— supposedly—years my junior, thus making me thrown over for a relative, if ludicrous, compatriot, and this after discovering I had been cuckolded all along by this scarecrow travesty, with a wardrobe by Ringling Brothers, the keeper of her heart's flame, Christ, what a stinking world), the prospect of mixing it up with him right then and there gave not the slightest pause.

"Aw, save it *Guy de*," I snapped. "Where the hell'd you get that coat, Walt Disney?"

He took a menacing high-topped step forward, causing Hayley's head to bounce against his torso. Her eyes nearly crossed; I laughed.

"Listen, pal," he said all tough stuff, "Personally, I could care less about—"

"Couldn't."

"What?"

"You mean to say you couldn't care less, not could. You see if you say you *could* care less, that means that right now you do, in fact, *care*, and are capable of caring less than you already do. What you're wanting to say is, you *couldn't* care less, clearly stating that you *don't* care, you wouldn't care, you *couldn't* possible care less than you do now. Grasp the difference?"

Both just stared, mute.

"It's okay," I said brightly. "A lot of people make that error, dumb-ass mistake that it is."

He stuck a finger like a Brunei tuber in my face.

"Don't mess with me, Paxton. I admire your work but that won't keep me from kicking your alcoholic ass from here to Nova Scotia. We got a job to do, and unfortunately that includes you. That phone call just indicated that now's the time. So let's go finish the job and cut you loose. Until then, keep your mouth shut and don't let me catch you upsetting Hayley."

She sniffled once, little moppet, and he hugged her away.

I stood there, much stupid with disbelief. This unlikely concatenation of events had really begun with my destitution, my loss of job and home. And those losses were accrued through my boozing. I would still have gotten blown up with Chauncey, but I never would have accepted his Wicker Madness offer had I not been desperate, and I would not have been desperate had it not been for liquor, and had I not accepted Wicker Madness I would not have met Hayley (again) and would not now be way up in the middle of Where-the-Fuck, Maine, waiting to deliver Rasputin's penis only to watch Hayley be snatched away by the large, unwashed grasp of a kaleidoscopic ostrich. My pride was wounded, and I felt sick and tired. I was sick and tired of being sick and tired. I had to admit—*ya think?*—my life had become unmanageable, and I was powerless over alcohol. You bet I admitted it.

And then I followed them out like a squelched South African sad sack. What the hell else was I going to do?

4

Malcolm's shit-mobile was some sort of rusted Toyota. The fact that the Wrath-of-God interior hadn't been cleaned to allow even leg room, I found revolting. He gallantly shook out a mildewed, sand-filled beach towel to clear a space in front for M'Lady to plunk down her behind, but I was left to plough through the garbage of the back on my own. The paper detritus category— old newspapers, grocery bags, crumpled receipts, *The Celestine Prophecy*, copies of what looked to be counter-culture rags—was basically as objectionable as the overall sundry class—dirty sweatshirts, t- shirts, shorts, shoes, caps, baseball bat, insect repellent, soccer ball, badminton shuttlecocks, badminton rackets, Frisbee, sack of Vitapet Dog Chow. But it was really the beyond belief division—Taco Bell bags still filled with food, biggie-sized soft drink containers, a take-out box emblazoned, "Hong Kong Gardens," several banana peels, soiled girls underwear (Hayley's?), and a rusty, half-eaten apple—plus spills, stains and coagulated, caked substances the content and derivation of which one could only shudder to guess—that truly cemented my long-held conviction that one's car interior could prove as a keen measure of character. There was a scent reminiscent of a used diaper.

"You have children, Malcolm?" I asked from the back end of this hovel-on-wheels. He looked quizzically in the rearview mirror.

I said, "This car is a public health menace."

"Why don't you just zip it, all right?"

The thing started with a wheeze and a rattle—the poor Japanese bastard vehicle clearly being poisoned from the inside—and lurched out onto Dodge Pond Road. Hayley began fiddling with dashboard dials.

"Is the radio broken?" she asked.

"Yeah, it's a bummer, dude."

"The cassette player, too?"

"Ditto."

"Oh," she said, then added, "Major-league bummage, bro."

My face contorted in disgust.

"What are you lookin' at?" she snapped viciously.

She caught me off-guard, and I was going to let it go, but she kept staring, waiting.

"I was just surprised at the change in your syntax," I said coolly, but sounding really prissy. "But I guess that's influenced by who you hang around with, who and what you lower your level of speech to when you're—"

"I told you to zip it, Paxton!" he bellowed from the wheel.

She flounced around in her seat and began talking sunnily—ignoring my existence, never mind my feelings—about some (yo, dude) awesome new band she'd discovered.

I could feel my face hot and red with shame, anger, embarrassment. So this is how it was going to be. Bad Paxton in the back seat with Big Malc and Little Baby Mama in front calling the shots. I was enraged and despairing.

Well, fuck this. I would deliver this box, collect the money, and never, ever be in a situation even remotely, vaguely similar to this one again. You betcha. Right!

I stared out the window for what seemed a long time, simmering in my own resentments, when his surfer-by-way-of-Bread-and-Puppet narrative managed to slog through the ambergris of my self-pity.

"But really, babe, it all started with the Cramps."

"The Cramps?" Happy Hayley Mills tutored by stoner Dean Jones.

"Oh, yeah. I loved them from the first moment I heard them. They changed my life. Their anarchy, their style, their—anarchy, yeah—was very freeing. They were a bridge to other things. A door—they opened the door for me to Charles Bukowski and William S. Burroughs."

I closed my eyes to roll them. He continued.

"Cutting-edge stuff, you know? They made me realize the scope of my potential. So I went down to Mexico."

"What did you do in Mexico?"

"Drugs, mostly. But I read a lot. That's where I discovered Celine."

I couldn't keep my mouth shut. I attempted to convincingly modulate to chit-chat mode.

"Oh," I cleared my throat, "the French novelist?"

"Right," said Malcolm, pals again and perky to have found a peer. Hayley regarded me suspiciously. "Reading him changed my life."

"Again," I said. She shot me a barbed glance.

Malcolm said, "He's my all-time favorite writer. The man makes a lot of sense." I could feel the dawn of a gnostic smile.

"But, wait a minute," I said. "I'm sorry, I don't—Celine was anti-Semitic. A lot."

Malcolm glanced into the mirror, twice, waiting. I continued, "And your girlfriend here is Jewish. So you're in love with an anti-Semitic writer *and* a Jewish girl?"

Hayley looked momentarily panicked, glancing from one to the other of us. Malcolm didn't miss a beat.

"Oh, yeah, but he was really misunderstood."

"He wrote propaganda for the Nazis."

"A lot of it was taken out of context."

"Oh," I said. "I didn't know that." I gave up.

"Oh, yeah. The man was a scapegoat. You know, you shouldn't talk about racism, being South African and all. And besides," he said with a chuckle and a slap to her thigh, "Hayley doesn't read much."

She stuck her tongue out at me and turned back to her hero, unfazed by my provocations to him or his insult to her.

How could she let him say that about her? She doesn't read! I knew she had more literary smarts in her little finger than this waterhead did in his whole gangling body. This is what she loved? This smirking, pompous *artiste*? How could she be infatuated with this fatuous, unwashed *poseur*? And how in Christ's name could she prefer him to me?

"Anyway," he nattered on, "That's around the time I started with the Claymation. I was doing sculpture and shooting digital stuff, and I thought, hell, here's a medium. So I started working in the film industry. With all its fake, bullshit glamour," he added with a rueful chuckle.

"Hollywood?"

"No, Mexico City. Vampimation—vampire Claymation—was really big in Mexico. I did a lot of work for Emilio Hernandez, he's kinda the godfather of vampimation, and that was my apprenticeship. But there was never enough money and way too many drugs. That was my Beat period."

I asked, "Why did you leave?"

"The food was killing my stomach."

"Malcolm has a delicate stomach," added Hayley motheringly, as she not-so-motheringly caressed the back of his greasy neck.

"Yeah, but I've been off heroin for a long time, and I'm really driven by this next project."

"Oh, tell him about it, Malcolm!" she said with excited pride, then flipped me a look of warning. He seemed suddenly reluctant, all aw-shucks humility, then glanced in the mirror.

"Yeah, Malcolm, tell me," I encouraged.

"I wrote a verse-play adaptation of the Marquis De Sade's *120 Days of Sodom* and Hayley and I did it with hand puppets at Goddard College in Vermont, and it was a big hit. So that's going to be the Claymation film on digital! It's pornographic and kinda woke, but with an aesthetic sensibility."

"It's awesome," said Little Orphan Sycophant.

"Yeah," agreed the *auteur*, "I think people will love it. We just need the money to start shooting. That's where you come in, Paxton."

"Yes," I said, sounding as matter-of-fact as I could manage. "Speaking of which, how exactly is all of this supposed to go down?"

"Glad you asked," said Malcolm. "That phone call was from Dora Shannon. She's Chief Operations Officer for SLAV."

"Ah."

"We're all meeting at headquarters to plot out a strategy for when you make the exchange. So, I'm afraid it's that time."

He pulled the car onto the side of the road, yanked on the emergency brake, and spun around to face me.

"Afraid I'm going to have to ask your indulgence, Paxton."

He opened the glovebox of the rancid car and pulled out a black sleep mask and a pair of handcuffs.

"What the hell are those for?" I asked.

"So you can't tell anyone where headquarters is located."

"*Are* located. Forget it."

He said, "We figured you'd say that."

On cue, Hayley pulled a sleek black revolver up over the seat and pointed it straight at me. I almost laughed. But I didn't.

"You've been rehearsing," I said.

"The safety's off," she said. "But don't make me cock the hammer. That makes things dangerous."

"Nine millimeter Beretta with a hair-trigger, Paxton," he said, handing me the mask. I sighed and noted that the cold look in Hayley's eyes was far chillier and more metallic than the handgun she trained so dispassionately on the man she had made love to—if you could call it that—the night before. I put the mask on.

"Now put your wrists together," said Malcolm. I did, feeling the bite and hearing the click of the steel.

There was a long moment where neither of them said anything, but I could hear them both mouthing a conversation. Finally Malcolm said, "You can put that down now, Hayley," and she giggled. The animal rights movement's Bonnie and Clyde.

"Okay, not to worry, Paxton. Soon as we get there, you'll be free and out of the dark. Safe as milk."

I don't know what prompted me to say what I said next, but I said, "Why don't you just kill me and take the box for yourselves? That would really be eliminating the middle-man."

I could hear Malcolm chuckle uneasily.

"Come on, Paxton. Nobody's gonna kill anybody. Just relax." Then he added sternly, "Don't talk like that." Little Dillinger was quiet.

We continued driving for fifteen or twenty minutes, but it was disquieting to realize how difficult the passage of time is to note when you're deprived of sight. (Once on a trip to Los Angeles with Erika, we had visited a sensory-deprivation place in West Hollywood called Altered States. She'd found a float in the saline solution of an isolation tank terrifying and hadn't lasted five minutes. I savored the full hour as a singularly enlightening out-of-body experience. Now, however, the feeling was of helplessness.)

I heard an occasional car whisk by the open windows, but then came the stillness of backroads and late afternoon insects.

Finally, we pulled off the road and stopped, the car switched off.

"Are we there?" I asked. I was ignored.

"Wait here," he told her. "I gotta take a leak."

Then it was just the two of us sitting in silence.

"So," I began pleasantly. "You in love with him?

Nothing.

I said, "Are you trying to decide whether to answer me or whether you're in love with him?"

"Yes."

"Yes what?"

"What do you think?"

"I see." Then I laughed at that. So did she. I waited a forlorn moment before saying, "So you were just pretending with me the whole time."

She thought about this. "No," she said finally. "I like you, Paxton. I love Malcolm. I know I deceived you, but this is for a cause a lot bigger than you or me. You ever hear of personal sacrifice?"

"Close your eyes and think of England, huh? You said you hated me."

"Look, don't start in with any of your shit, okay? That was all real cute for a laugh, but I don't really go in for that crap. I'm a little more of the truth-and-beauty type, Paxton, rather than somebody who lives their whole life through books."

"So poetry's nothing to you."

"I didn't say that. I just think art without service is a load. You have to serve somebody, Paxton. Or something."

"I just can't believe you're such a lapdog to this grungy punk."

"Don't you dare talk about Malcolm like that, you loser!"

"He's as dumb as a box of rocks, Hayley. I just wish I was as sure about anything as he is about everything."

I could hear her struggling in her seat, then felt her slapping the side of my head, then Malcolm's voice.

"Hey—Hey! Hayley!" he yelled. She stopped, restrained. "What the hell are you doing? Every time I leave you two alone there's an incident."

"He provoked me," she said.

He seemed amused. "Well, don't converse with the prisoner, for Christ's sake. You read the Patty Hearst pamphlet. What'd ya say to provoke her, Paxton?"

"I said, 'The passion of the mediocre is to maintain stimulation at its own level.' Norman Mailer."

He thought about that. "Oh." And then, "Sit down, Hayley. And shut up, Paxton."

We drove off, and I was wondering if I might, in fact, end up dead. In only a few minutes, however, the notion was put aside as Malcolm announced, "We're here."

Chapter Nine

1

I was led from the backseat through tall grass, the setting sun warm on my blindfolded face, Malcolm carrying the knapsack, Hayley carrying the gun, each on either side of me clutching an arm and doing such a sterling job of guiding me that I tripped and fell flat twice before they seemed to get the hang of it. We didn't walk too far before we entered through a doorway into stifling heat—I had a sense memory of my grandfather's barn — musty timbers, rot.

Other voices arrived. There were mumbled greetings and monosyllabic exchanges. I felt pretty vulnerable as I was pushed backwards into a chair and Malcolm (I could tell by his smell) unlocked the handcuffs and pulled the blind from my eyes.

"*Voila.*"

I blinked and rubbed my eyes to get some bearings and saw intense, full light at the end of a large, dark space. I was seated in the front row of a theater. On stage, under full-strength theatrical instruments, were some set pieces—a pair of high-backed chairs designed to look like thrones, a long table around which were some folding canvas-backed seats, a dusty but once brightly-painted mummy case, and canvas flats with the striped pattern of a Victorian drawing-room. A bottle of Johnny Walker Black was set prominently on the table, possibly a prop. Above the proscenium arch hung a faded, tattered banner: *The Barnstormers Summer Players*.

Seated on a stool downstage was a swarthy, masculine woman with short black hair, wearing military boots, camouflage pants, and a loose man's shirt. She was dully tapping the end of a blackboard pointer.

Sitting cross-legged at her feet was a figure of indeterminate gender. It sported a stubble-haired skull, rimless glasses, and a sort of sackcloth blouse over dirty, oversized trousers. The ears and face were a metal minefield of multiple piercings. It seemed hostile, protective of the swarthy woman.

The last of the triumvirate was breathtaking in his uniqueness. He was a little person, about three-feet tall, posing near one of the thrones. He was clearly of black African descent, but possessed the gray skin, light hair, and opaque eyes of albinism. He wore silver shoes with six-inch platform heels, a Japanese kimono that dragged to the stage, a red fish-net shirt cut at the midriff, and immodestly brief red shorts. He stirred the thick air in front of his face with an Asian fan.

As difficult as it was, I tore my gaze from this bizarre tableau and glanced around the darkness. It was a barn all right, one of the many throughout New England that had been converted into theaters for the summer seasons. The floor was concrete, and the house looked about three hundred seats, but the place was badly in disrepair, leftover trash of productions past piled up with paint cans and coiled ropes. Several rows of seats were missing, and those remaining had torn or missing upholstery. My eye caught the movement of girls lining the walls on both sides—four of them, all female, shrouded in darkness, but there was no mistaking the glint of heavy firearms.

My hosts stayed silent, allowing me to take this all in. Then — again as if rehearsed — Malcolm and Hayley sat down a few seats on either side of me, and we all waited. At last the swarthy woman spoke.

"You have the box?"

Malcolm rose without answer and pulled it from the knapsack, clambered through the cluttered orchestra pit up a flight of steps to the stage, and wordlessly flourished it in front of her. We might have been in the court of Elizabeth I.

"Open it."

Malcolm snapped open the clasp and lifted the lid. Both the stubble-skulled androgyne and the black albino hurried over to peer. The little guy smirked; the stubbled creature looked revolted. The swarthy woman waved it away. Malcolm closed the box and took a few respectful steps backward.

The swarthy woman suddenly smiled and said warmly, "Introduce us, Malcolm."

"Oh, absolutely." He stepped forward to do the honors. "Paxton Graham—once promising but now drunken, washed-up poet—meet Dora Shannon, Chief Operations Officer of the Society for the Liberation of Animal Victims."

"You'll have to forgive me," said Shannon, "but I've never read you."

"No apology necessary," I said, chuckling nervously. "I been outta print for some time now. This is a great place you got here. Old barn theater, colorful atmosphere, sort of a Mickey Rooney-Judy Garland thing, huh? I love it. You're not going to kill me, are you?"

"What kind of accent is that?" asked the albino with a swish of his kimono and a practiced sashay on his platforms. He was outrageous.

Malcolm said, "This is Manfred—Manfred, " he hesitated. "Mumford."

"Can I call you Manny?" I asked, God knows why.

"You may certainly not!" he snapped, then smiled. "My friends call me Mumsy. I like it."

I nodded. "Mumsy."

Shannon said, "Why would we go to all the trouble of blindfolding you only to kill you?"

"Glad to hear that," I said. "My accent is—uh—" I said, addressing Mumsy, "Afrikaaner. South African."

"South Africa!" Mumsy said, horrified. "You mean apartheid?"

The genderless thing spread her filthy, sandaled feet apart in a defiant stance. "That's right," she said.

"Left there when I was ten," I said quickly. "Never been back. Nelson Mandela is a saint."

"And don't forget it," said Genderless. "Because we won't."

Malcolm said, "This is Komeda. She's artistic director of the Anarcho Theatrical Company."

"Oh, yeah?" I said brightly. It was a she.

"Yeah," she said. "And I don't appreciate the Mickey Rooney crack."

"How 'bout Athol Fugard?" My voice was strained. Hayley looked at me in curiosity, then shook her head.

"All right, people," said Shannon. "Let's knock off all the bullshit and get down to business. Obviously, you know why you're here, Paxton. To drop off that disgusting and perverse artifact to the freak Kureishi who's buying it from Fat Boy, correct?"

"Yes."

"Fine. As Hayley has informed you, we've received intelligence that one or the other is planning on cutting us out of our end. We put Kureishi in touch with Fat Boy, arranged the whole deal at considerable time, effort and expense, and now that morbidly obese rat or the Pakistani plans to double-cross us. We're going to see to it that doesn't happen."

"Visigoths," sniffed Mumsy.

"They're lower than whale shit!" piped Komeda.

The name intrigued me. "Komeda," I said. "That's an interesting name. Is that your surname, or your Christian name?"

"Nobody's Christian here," she said emphatically.

"Is it Polish?" I asked. "Reminds me of the late jazz and film-score composer Krystof Komeda. Did some Polanski films?"

"I don't know anything about that shit!" She was disturbed.

And then I noticed. I am far from the most observant fellow— my mother used to say a wildebeest could be in the room a week before I'd notice—but it was something about the rising superciliary arch when she spoke, the way she shook her whole head for emphasis when making a statement. This curiosity was tightly-wrapped, high-strung, fever-pitched. The shaved head, lack of make-up, pierced nose, lips and eyebrows, endless rows of rings, studs and hoops through each ear, the crap-cloth ensemble, and the glasses all worked to conceal or at least submerge the surface of the spoiled heiress, but the squirmy body language and ferret expression couldn't, ultimately, hide it: the lustrous auburn mane was gone along with the signature elaborate eye-shadow, the Ellen Tracy wardrobe—but it was her.

"Brieanna," I said with more astonishment than Henry Morton Stanley could have mustered. The room was still as a tomb.

"Don't call me that," she hissed.

Mumsy swatted his fan, Brieanna/Komeda glared, and Shannon smiled wryly.

Call me mercurial, but my attitude was undergoing a change as violent as the one experienced when I thought Malcolm was going to pull a Marquess of Queensberry. These desperate confederates had already distinguished themselves as kidnappers, terrorists, and thieves and were in possession of some obviously heavy firepower, but my fear had suddenly vanished. Looking at these three buffoons on stage (fitting, that) and the absurdity of this numb-skull situation I had been prim-rosed into via a waterfall of distilled spirits, an existential apathy was welling up to conversely tip my balance into action. They wouldn't kill me; they wanted the box and the money, and I would be hostaged again and sent off like a good lad. Until then, they were playing at silly buggers, and doing it well.

"Well . . . whatever, as you Americans are so fond of saying." (I was, of course, a naturalized citizen, but this lot clearly wanted the whole nine yards of Ian Fleming *schtick*, so I would play Bond to their SPECTRE or SMERSH.

"What precisely is the game plan, Ms. Shannon?"

She rose to her feet from the stool, bouncing the pointer from its tip off the stage and catching it, very Broadway. Not bad, clearly practiced.

"Same plan as all along," she said amiably. "You meet Saeed Kureishi or whatever stooge *he's* sent as courier—"

"Thank yum."

Shannon smiled, on firm firma. Hayley and Malcolm both looked a little uncertain at the studied manner and glib *repartee* now being passed between Shan and Pax like a saltshaker.

"No offense meant. You meet, whomever, at King Williams' Falls—that's about three miles from here—at seven o'clock sharp and hand over the box. We receive the money from said representative and take our cut—25 percent."

"Wow," I said. "Twenty-five thousand dollars? Chauncey's not gonna like that." Gangster point.

"I don't' give a damn whether he likes it or not." Counter-gangster point. "You looking out for his interests?"

Mumsy and Brieanna and Hayley and Malcolm and the troupe lining the walls all seemed to regard me with one go. I raised my hands, palms up.

"Not me, babe—"

"Don't call me babe."

"And don't call me Brieanna!" said Komeda.

Mumsy said, "You may call me Mumsy."

I said, "I'm looking out for myself. You said you had this deal, and you think you're going to be double-crossed, fine. You do whatever you have to do to get the money you think you're entitled to. Just give me a note or a videotape with you all in ski masks to that effect, so Chaunce doesn't think I ripped him off."

"Not to worry," said Shannon. "Consider it done."

"And we're not ripping him off!" said Brieanna. "He promised us that money and we need it!" She seemed about to cry, this once-privileged and en-titled mental case.

"What for?" I asked coolly. I was smooth now, all stammering, shaking, and sweating vanquished.

"You're not familiar with our work, Mr. Graham?" asked Shannon. She was Mr. Grahaming me now that I was coming off like Sean Connery.

"I know you're an extremist animal rights organization that was too much even for PETA."

She smiled.

"I also know you blew up the Schraeder Labs on Newbury Street and ex-ploded me straight into the hospital."

She turned grave. "An unforgivable mistake. We've offered formal, public apologies about that, but the media and the FBI seem uninterested in dissem-inating this information."

"A mistake?" I asked.

"Yes." She looked embarrassed. "The bomb was set to go off at twelve *midnight*, not twelve noon. At 12:00 A.M. on a weeknight the labs are closed and so is the restaurant and all the shops. We knew the damage to civilians would've been minimal. One of our operatives paid insufficient attention to the training session on setting the timer."

I almost laughed, but the heavy air of regret in the barn seemed to prohibit this. She looked at me intently.

"How are you?" she asked. She seemed genuinely concerned.

"Fine," I said. "Mending. My lung collapsed. Mild concussion."

"Well," she said. "I sincerely apologize about that. And, in case you haven't figured it out, we had no idea you were there."

"No, no," I said reassuringly. "How could you? We'd never met. Forget it."

"The agent responsible was terminated," said Shannon. I regarded her for a disquieted moment.

"You mean fired, I hope."

"No," said Mumsy, making a slashing motion across his neck with a pudgy forefinger and accompanying sound. "Terminated."

Shannon said, "He's joking. But that was a mistake, and SLAV is through with mistakes. We only kill the killers and torturers of the innocent. Accidental killing of innocents is done with – for good."

"The world is going to learn," said Brieanna, "that we hold the whip-hand for the murderers of the innocent. Have you read *Victims of Vanity*"?

"Paxton," said Shannon. "Do you know what little difference there is between animals and human beings?"

"Hardly any," I said, "Except we're not afraid of vacuum cleaners." She stared at me for a long moment.

"So you're not against us?"

"I'm completely neutral," I said, truthfully. "I'm getting paid for doing this, and like you, I need the money. Like I said, do whatever you have to, then cut me loose."

"Done," she said.

"I really just question why you had to orchestrate the whole sedeuction thing with Little Miss Community Panties over here," I said gesturing to Hayley.

"Hey!" said Malcolm, jumping off the stage.

"Shut up, Paxton!" said Hayley.

As Malcolm hit the orchestra pit, the figures around the perimeter of the barn moved from the dark into the spill of the stage lights. Black commando outfits, semi-automatic weapons — the median age mid-twenties — but some looked as young as Hayley. Young women, armed and dangerous. Malcolm caught their prepping for trouble and appeared to think better of clocking me for chivalry's sake.

"I really detest that word," said Shannon.

"Which one?" I asked. "Seduction?"

"Panties!" she almost spat.

"Oh?" I said, perplexed. "Gee, it's one of my favorites." Hayley rolled her eyes.

"It infantilizes women," said Shannon, a flash in her eyes.

"No, it doesn't," I said. "It gently feminizes them. And that's a good thing, right?"

"Sexist exploiter!" yelled Brieanna. The girl-guards menaced the area.

"How am I a sexist exploiter?"

"By defiling this innocent girl still in her adolescence!" And she pointed a fierce *j'accuse* finger at me. From her position downstage center, Brieanna struck what would have been one marvelous piece of blocking for a production of *The Crucible*.

"What does she mean *defiled*?" asked Malcolm. He turned to Hayley. "What does she mean?" Hayley stared at him, goggle-eyed.

"What do you think she means, Einstein?" giggled Mumsy. "Deflowered her—popped her cherry—took her maidenhead."

"Her virginity!" declared Brieanna.

Malcolm looked as if he'd swallowed his gum. He glared at me, then brought his burning gaze to bear on little Baby Bug-Eyes.

"You told me," he said evenly, "that you never actually had sex with him." There was a feel in the barn as if we were witness to a trial, a moment, hanging heavily, that was twice as intense as any so far accorded the Great Rasputin Double-Cross.

"He raped her!" shouted Malcolm. Hayley bit her lower lip.

"Did not," I said.

"All men rape under the right circumstances," said Brieanna.

I ran with that one. "Saying all men will rape under particular circumstances is like saying all people will eat human flesh under the right circumstances. Does that make us all born cannibals? Are date rapes comparable to rapes by soldiers in war? Isn't it likely some are sexually motivated and some purely hostile?" Sounded good.

"He's making a speech!" Brieanna thundered.

Shannon said, "You'd better shut up."

"Will do."

Hayley looked about to cry, then really pissed. She spun her head to everyone in the room—leaving a lingering look of hatred for Brieanna, spiller of the beans—and stalked off at a brisk clip backstage, Malcolm following quickly in the wake of her flouncing bum.

"You're disgusting," said Brieanna, disgusted. "I'll bet you read *Playboy*."

"I don't, actually," I said. "I hearken back to that by-gone era when the magazine at least had pretensions to sophistication, when the reader was actually to aspire to some kind of class through his dress, attitudes, and manner. Today the whole philosophy seems geared to slob frat boys who think wallowing in front of a kegger is the height of entertainment for men. And the women! You look at issues from the '60s or '70s, these women really looked like the so-called girl next door, sweet and wholesome. Today, they only look like that if the girl next door is a surgically-altered stripper. Cheap? Oh, *cheap*."

"Bravo!" cheered Mumsy.

"All right, enough with the speeches," said Shannon irritably, then wryly added, "Christ, you're verbose. Now I know where Erika gets it."

My stomach did a chill flip. Time, indeed, stood still.

"What did you say?"

There was a distant scream from outside. Hayley, it sounded like. Everyone tensed and looked to Shannon.

"Girls," she ordered, and on the word, all four commando guards raced out, two through the front and two the back. It crossed my mind to ask how calling armed women girls could be acceptable to this anti-sexist extremist, but I was startled by the sudden action and stunned from Shannon's last remark. Her pulling a pistol from her waistband and a clip of ammunition from her pocket was also fascinating.

"Hold it there, pussycat!" came an accented voice. "Hands up."

The four of us turned to see a tall, thin figure emerging like Max Schreck from the shadows. When she reached the light from the stage, though, I could see that she was one very sexy Max Schreck. About five-foot-nine and svelte, yet with the curvy contours that beautifully complement fine height. She had a short, black Louise Brooks helmet of hair with two sharply styled curls on each cheek. A pretty face, bright white blouse, and deep red lipstick matching the shade of her pants. She held what looked to be a .38 on us. We didn't move a muscle.

"This is loaded and real," she said, heavily Slavic. "Put your hands up, please!"

We immediately obliged, Shannon holding the pistol and clip in each raised hand. There came a startling burst of machine-gun fire from the distance.

"Shit…" said Brieanna.

"Throw aside that which you are holding please," the tall woman said to Shannon. Shannon frowned, sighed, and tossed both aside; they clattered out of reach.

"What the hell do you think you're doing?" asked Shannon.

"There's the box," said the woman with a smile.

"Not so fast," came a familiar voice from behind, and we all spun, hands raised, to see Hayley and Malcolm being marched in, raised hands, by a revolver and badge-wielding Janis Poplin.

"Special Agent Janis Poplin, FBI. You're all under arrest."

"I would prefer not to," said the Slavic woman.

"I don't' know who you are, lady," said Poplin, "but you're about to be in a hell of a lot of trouble. My back-up's going to be here any minute."

The Slavic slowly appraised Poplin, the entire room, and the whole situation. With great deliberateness she said,

"I don't think so."

Before the last word had passed from her lips, Malcolm swung one arm down and across Poplin's abdomen. At the force of the blow, her revolver fired with a pop and a smell of powder; Hayley and Mumsy screamed, and everybody hit the deck — all except the Slavic woman, who stood standing, swaying, and wincing, still training the gun in our direction, the stain of a dark red flower already spreading across the middle of her blouse.

"Why do you people always have to be such heroes?" she asked calmly.

2

Anyone entering the barn only twenty minutes later would have been met by quite a scene. The Slavic woman, who introduced herself as Petra, forced Shannon at gun-point to collect ropes from the pit and tie Hayley, Malcolm, Mumsy, Brieanna, and Poplin together, all seated in chairs in the center of the stage. Then she instructed me to tie Shannon.

When I was finished, Petra said, "Okay, buddy—uh, what's your name?"

"Paxton."

She paused. "Okay, buddy, you just sit down right there by the others on the stage, please."

"Why doesn't he get tied up?" whined Malcolm.

"How the hell am I supposed to tie up—shot and bleeding—with one hand holding gun?" she asked logically. I suddenly thought of Rocky and Bullwinkle. I sat down on the stage, nearest Hayley. Petra finally sat down with finality in the first row of seats. I thought it remarkable that a woman who had taken a bullet straight into the gut could remain standing all that time to supervise the trussing up of her captives before getting off her feet.

"My back-up's going to be here any minute," said Poplin again.

"You said that nearly half an hour ago," said Petra. "Are they on horseback?"

"They're late."

"Good thing this isn't an emergency," I said. Poplin glared. I turned to Petra. "You need a hospital."

"I know. My friends are coming to collect me. I can get help. It makes more sense for me to sit here and wait for them and keep you with me than to stumble out and bleed all over my nice rental car. My friends won't know where I am if I drive around bleeding. I'll be okay, I should think. I'm good with pain and bleeding."

"Women usually are," said Brieanna.

"My back-up is coming," said Poplin.

"Okay, okay, then I'll improvise. Stop badgering me," said Petra. There was silence for a moment, then Shannon asked, "So what happens now?"

Petra sighed. "You know, I love this country, I really do. But you people always need to know what's going on. I mean every goddamn minute. Can't you ever relax? The pace of life is far more pleasant—" she winced, "in Europe."

"Are you going to kill us?" asked Hayley, little girl-voiced.

Petra regarded her intently. "I don't want to kill you, but I will if I have to. Otherwise, if there are difficulties, I will simply shoot your knees. That's very shocking and painful," she sighed. "Trust me."

"I'm really sorry," said Malcolm. "I didn't know she'd shoot you."

"I didn't shoot her, you jerk," said Poplin. "The gun went off when you grabbed my arm."

Petra had opened the box and glancing quickly at its contents, closed it. Holding the pistol, she was attempting with her free hand, blood-stained from her stomach, to slide the box into a plastic Macy's shopping bag, but the wooden edges kept getting caught. She persisted diligently, and I was about to offer help when her determination paid off and the box finally slid into the bag.

"So, you're stealing that for Kureishi?" asked Shannon.

The question seemed to reach her through a long-distance delay. She finally looked up and squinted.

"Who?" she said. "Oh, that guy. Kureishi. Kureishi like a fox. Yes. No! He's not my friend. Do I look like a crazy Pakistani? I'm a crazy Polack."

"Oh, me too!" said Hayley.

"What's your name?"

"Hayley."

"Hayley?"

Hayley Glass. But Hayley Goroskowski, really, you see?"

Petra nodded dubiously. "Uh huh. Hayley... Hayley... that isn't Polish. What the hell is that?"

"It's for Haley Mills. The actress?"

"Oh, yes!" said Petra cheerily. "Walt Disney. Wonderful..." She turned back to Shannon. "Steal what? Who said steal? I'm simply repossessing."

"It's yours?" asked Mumsy.

"In a sense," Petra replied. "It belongs to the Russian people." Petra then spied the bottle of Johnny Walker on the table.

"Is that real?" she asked.

"Yes," said Shannon.

"Get that for me," to me.

"There are glasses in the green room—" said Mumsy.

"Just—!" She was impatient, and I scrambled to my feet and to the bottle, which I retrieved, scurried over to her, and presented it like a trophy.

"You drink some," she said.

"I'd rather not," I said. You see, I have something of a drinking problem, and I just managed to quit and—"

Her gun barrel touched the tip of my nose. I unscrewed the cap from the glass threads, smelled the contents, and took a conservative pull. A taste of copper pennies in syrup (or was it blood?) pooled in my mouth, then burned down my throat, and spread through my stomach. I thought this might have a deleterious effect on the Pole's innards. Mine rejoiced.

"Thank you," she said, palming the bottle. "I'm trying to practice caution."

She swigged from the bottle like it was ice water on a hot day, gasped in satisfaction, then gestured that I sit down. When I was settled, she heaved a large sigh.

"Well, this has really buggered things up. I abhor violence — I really do. I'm always afraid I'm going to get hurt. Now look."

"Can't you at least explain what's going on?" asked Shannon. Petra appraised her.

"Sure. We were prepared to pay you a very exciting amount of money for Rasputin's member, you know, since we found out it was in your possession. Now this government person has to be here. What kind of transaction can we now transact? Messy, of course. Look at us."

As in earnest, she looked dolefully to our group, the sadness of Mother Russia's (Poland's, Russia's) many centuries in her eyes.

"You didn't come here to steal it?" asked Malcolm.

"Certainly not," she answered indignantly.

Shannon said, "Are you telling me—"

"I'm telling you," said Petra. "They gotta lotta money, my friends."

"What d'ya want that thing for?" Brieanna asked testily.

Petra managed a laugh. "I'm shot, I'm bleeding, I'm behind schedule, clearly I am upset—and I'm holding a loaded gun on you. I could kill you; yet you still need to know the program. Well, that's what makes America great, yes?" She licked her dry mouth. "That penis has had a very interesting history."

"Oh, tell us about it!" Hayley asked brightly.

"Don't bother her," said Shannon.

"It's okay," said Petra jovially. "It's a good story. She took another slug from the bottle, grimaced, and whistled. I was impressed by how unconcerned she seemed, really, about the circumstances, how unafraid of the possibility of her own death, which, it seemed to me, loomed now like an actor in the wings about to make an entrance.

"One of the aristocrats—son-of-a-bitch bastards—was Prince Felix Yusupov. He was in love with Rasputin, but—the affection was not mutual. Always the way, huh? He led the aristos in the assassination. They poisoned Rasputin, beat him, shot him, but he was too strong for them. Fools. He was not your everyday monk, I tell you that. Before they drowned him, the maniac Yusupov cut off his magnificent organ." She sneered. "Jealous. One of the servants recovered it from the scene of his most despicable crime and gave it to a White Russian, nice old lady. She kept it in a place of reverence in her flat in Paris and gave it to Marie Rasputin, his daughter, 'round 1975. Maria lived in Los Angeles." She looked thoughtful. "Grigori would have loved Hollywood. He liked to have a good time. Anyway, she dies in '78 and that old fella's been in the hands of every freak in California, Thailand, Israel, California, and California ever since. We only tracked it down this year – your Pakistani acquaintance. I don't need to know what he wants it for."

"But why do *you* want it?" asked Brieanna.

"It's a means to an end." I noticed that Petra was beginning to sound weakened, that her breathing was becoming labored. Yet she pushed on with her narrative. "There's a political faction in my country—the one's that's correct. They're associated with the *Khlysty*, a religious sect, somewhat popular before the Revolution. The first one, I mean. They believed, believe, that Christ didn't ascend to Heaven when He died but inhabited another body on Earth to continue His work. They celebrate the body through ecstatic worship— dancing, drinking, and an enormous amount of sexual intercourse. Naturally, this appealed to Rasputin."

"I thought he was Orthodox," said Malcolm.

"He was also a man. These *Khlysty*, they feel the object in question would serve as a unifying symbol—a totem, icon, whatever it is—in the struggle against the oppression of the present corrupt regime."

"Oh," said Brieanna. "That's what you want it for."

"*Bozha moy*," said Petra. "I don't feel so good. Son-of-a-bitch bullet. What time is it?"

"Nearly 6:30," said Shannon.

"Bloody hell."

"So you're a goddamned subversive," said Poplin. "Your country finally shakes off the shackles of communism and has a fair crack at free enterprise, and you want to bring all that potential down around your ears."

"I don't think you understand—" said Petra.

"I think communism's terrific," said Malcolm. "The theory, anyway. I know things didn't work out in the Soviet Union, but it seems like there was a lot of mismanagement."

"Oh, baloney," snapped Poplin. "It never could have worked."

"It could too! I was reading this thing where—"

"Oh, blah blah blah," argued Poplin. "You haven't got a clue what you're talking—"

Petra suddenly exploded. "Okay, okay, okay! You try to transform a small-scale, fragmented, agrarian society into an industrialized state! What the hell you expect?"

There was a startled silence. Shannon and the Mumsy looked quietly amused. For a glint of a moment, all eyes went to Hayley when she popped her bubble-gum. Petra resumed, wearily.

"Lenin's dream of a classless utopia was more suited to the movies," then she added slowly, "I'm getting very tired..."

Even in the lengthening shadows of the fading sunset, her color was bad. She was dying. Surely she knew. She seemed no more resigned than the recipient of a particularly grim parking ticket. We then commenced to wait in silence, a death-watch.

I don't know how many minutes we sat with eyes riveted to her or averted, the only sound the passionate and mindlessly joyous humming, thrumming, and trilling of an endless host of insects, the heirs apparent to the planet.

Finally, Petra gently set the revolver down and lowered her head onto her folded arms across the seat next to her, like a weary theatre-goer at intermission. One small and dignified movement—even safely releasing the cocked hammer of the gun, then a phlegmy exhalation as a stomach full of black blood spilled from her mouth onto the floor—and she was finished. The rest was silence.

"Paxton," said Poplin's measured voice. "Could you untie us?"

I saw no reason not to, although I moved with the pace and purpose of a zombie. It took some minutes as I struggled with the knots, but all six waited without a hint of impatience. Hardly had the last rope dropped (as the others rubbed their limbs) when Poplin, ever-efficient activities director (could you imagine this bitch on a camping trip?) stepped forward with purpose, and picked up her gun from where it had landed during the struggle. She was into a purposeful stride towards Petra's body when, "Stop right there, Fed," said Shannon, an angry softball coach. She trained the Walther PPKS (my Uncle Nils was a collector), apparently pulled from thin air, on Poplin, who looked undeterred.

"Why the hell didn't you pull that out when she had the gun on us?"

Shannon smiled. "Like she said, who wants to get hurt? I had to wait for the right moment."

"And this is it?" asked Poplin incredulously.

"Talk about living in an alternate universe," said Malcolm.

"Hey, shut up, hippie." Poplin had a ready current of anger she could plug into at any moment.

"We just want the box," said Shannon, "and to get the hell out of here."

"Well, that's not going to happen," said Poplin with authority. "You're all under arrest— you bunny-hugger terrorists, the hippie and kid candy pants, the pedophile poet over there, and especially Ms. Crisco, who's being simultaneously rescued and busted at the same time."

I said, "That's redundant."

"Shut up, you goddamned South African child molester."

That really took the piss out of me: "Do you mean to say I'm a molester of South African children, or that I—"

And again burst the sickening *pop* of the real firearm, so much less dramatic than the sound effect in film and television. And again a hit body still stood, shocked, Poplin looking first at the smoking gun held in Brieanna's shaking grip, then down at the hole near her heart. Special Agent Poplin for once was at a loss for words, and with an adroit straightening of her arm, shot Shannon clean through the forehead, sending her body flying, the back of her head exploding. Brieanna shot Poplin again in the chest, and with this one she dropped like a sack of potatoes.

The only armed person still vertical was our celebrity hostage. She stared at the disintegrated flesh of her captor/mentor and the corpse of her rescuer/victim. She let the gun slip from her grasp and clatter to the floor. She ran with a guttural growl from the barn. Malcolm followed a vomiting Hayley out the opposite side. Mumsy walked around the corner of the stage, into the wings out of sight; in a moment I heard him weeping uncontrollably.

I confirmed that all three were dead, thus beyond help; then (we must be pragmatic, I assured myself, the illogical life being even more nasty, short, and brutal than alternatives) I emptied each wallet, culling $496 in bills. When I had done this, I collected all five revolvers and slipped them into the Macy's shopping bag along with the mahogany box. It took me a good fifteen minutes before deciding on a place of concealment for it in the barn.

Chapter Ten

1

About one hundred yards beyond the barn sat a broken-down farmhouse well beyond the point of being condemnable. This, evidently, in best hide-out fashion, had been serving as headquarters for the conspirators. A generator trailer was providing irregular power for lights, refrigerator, and stove, but portable toilets (nicked, I learned later, from a construction site with the generator) were the order of private comforts. If one wanted to be a proponent of bourgeois and capitalist repression and actually bathe, one had to stroll down to the clear, chill waters of Indian Pond. Good luck finding a bar of soap, as soap kills protective layers found naturally on the skin's surface (this from Brieanna).

Apparent attempts had been made towards habitation: broken furniture, sprung and torn; milk-crate shelving into which had been crammed, haphazardly, feminist tracts and communist tracts and Marxist-feminist tracts, much poor-quality literature on animal rights, good-quality editions on Reich, and plenty of books on explosives, self-defense, guerrilla tactics, armed aggression, and hand-to-hand combat, plus ancient issues of *Ms.*, *Off Our Backs*, *Gun Digest*, *Soldier of Fortune*, *Animal Lovers*, and a battered paperback of Machiavelli's *The Prince*. Dirty plates, empty pizza boxes, and the remnants of rancid fast food were everywhere, along with vast stacks of empty, unopened, and half-consumed cans of cat food. The place was swarming with cats—I counted at least three dozen—which any blind visitor could deduce, as the place was permeated by the stench of feline urine. A country hovel, squalid and miserable.

I was surprised how exhausting witnessing real-life carnage could be. I presumed that my generation and those that followed in our wake (having been weaned on simulated explosions, car chases/crashes, and automatic weapon fire in action thrillers, television, and video games; and torture, mutilations, beheadings and eviscerations in horror films, television and comic books; and an endless symphony of handguns shooting and shooting, bringing death and death and death, conducted through a tremendous, cascading, nearly voluptuous waterfall of blood) actually bearing witness to this kind of occurrence might be no big thing. Not so. The surviving quartet of Hayley, Malcolm, Brieanna, and Mumsy—all in their teens or twenties—were shocked and exhausted by the trio of violent deaths enacted before their eyes.

After Poplin took the last bullet, and it was established beyond doubt that all were dead, none of the young folks even suggested moving the bodies or brainstorming for a game plan.

Nothing.

What followed was routine, banal enough for Hannah Arendt: a spaghetti dinner (meatless sauce) with a large salad, quietly prepared, and even more quietly consumed. Then, dishes and pans left stained and unwashed on counter-tops and table, the sleepyheads trudged silently off to bed. After their mumbled goodnights and the closing of doors (Hayley and Malcolm in one room, Brieanna and Mumsy—oddly enough— in another) and the dousing of lights, I was left by myself at the kitchen table. I switched off the annoying threnody of the fluorescent tubes clamped to the ceiling and lit a single multi-colored drip candle stuck in the requisite empty Chianti bottle. I sat there for a long time in the flickering light, neither numb nor requiring sleep like the raw youths now slumbering around me. It occurred to me that it hadn't occurred to me to check the larder or refrigerator for alcohol. This, as if in a trance, I immediately did, devoid of practical intent or feeling, and discovered—with the lack of emotion of a chicken farmer with an ax—a half-bottle of Boone's Farm Strawberry wine. I left it as was.

2

The next morning, having only dozed a few hours (and discovering that the sofa was, naturally, a flea circus), I rose before dawn. I proceeded into the kitchen, discovered an almost-empty can of Maxwell House, poured one of the many gallons of distilled water stacked in a corner into a filthy Mr. Coffee, and settled back down at the table to await the filling of a thoroughly rinsed silex. The smell of the sticks of rancid butter congealing on a countertop—with aroma of the litter of a hundred meals I threw from the back porch—was soon replaced by fresh air from open windows and the strong aroma of the percolating coffee.

I heard a door open and the padding of little feet up the hallway. I held my breath in hope for Hayley, but the appearance through the doorway was kimono'd Mumsy, looking less exotic without makeup, jewelry, and oversized shades. He also seemed less threatening.

"My, my," he said, doing a subtle sashay into the room, one hand clutching the front of the robe, the other fanning a ferocious yawn. "We're up early, and I do mean we, honey." The yawn reminded me of Ignatz, and Mumsy's use of an endearment most favored by older waitresses helped dispel much of the lingering feeling of hostility from the night before. "My God, that smells delicious. How did you get it working?"

"The socket was shot. I just used another. I plugged Mr. Coffee into Mr. Socket."

He smirked and rolled his half-asleep eyes. "Mmmm…sounds too erotic for this hour. Might Miss Mumsy help herself to a Mr. Cup?"

"It's your kitchen."

"Bite your tongue." As he busied himself with the not inconsiderable task of finding a clean mug, I took the opportunity for some questions.

"I must admit, Mumsy, a person of your—uh—"

He stopped in his tracks. "My…?"

"Sense of style…"

"Oh, honey, say flamboyance."

"Ah! Very good—yes, your flamboyance—does seem a tad out of place in this decrepit farmhouse in rural Maine with a collection of…" I was cautious, as he had stopped again. "Militants," I said finally. He nodded approval.

"Not so unlikely," he said. "I'd die for the cause of animal liberation. My personal four-legged companions number two Persian cats, one Pomeranian, and an Afghan Hound."

"They're here?"

"Good Lord, no! I can't drag my preciousnesses 'round when I'm working, honey. They're with my mother, in Baton Rouge."

"Very chic. The pets, I mean."

"We don't use that word." He winked. "But an arbiter of style such as myself in the midst of the movement? Well, politics makes for strange bed-fellows. I mean, literally. Look at Komeda and me. Why else would we be sharing a bed?"

He poured himself coffee and sat down across from me at the table, cross-ing his squat legs demurely. I nodded and smiled as he sipped his, when this last remark packed its punch.

"Sharing a bed?" I actually stammered. He peered at me bleary-eyed over the tipped edge of the mug as he drank. I asked, "You don't mean…?"

"'Deed I do, honeychile. They do get it on, Komeda and Miss Mumsy."

"But I thought she was—I mean, I just assumed—and that you were…"

"A little man-hatin' dyke and a ravishing drag queen? Yes, baby, strange bedfellows as I said, and nothin' I'd be wantin' to make a habit of, but it's been fun goin' for the ride. Alleviates my boredom. I think Punky's just a kid explorin' all the avenues. She sure been explorin' mine." He winked one tired eye.

It is mean-spirited to say that the mental image of this unique being cou-pling with the scrawny, angry girl of the shaved and knobby skull was, at that hour, unsettling, but there you are.

"'Punky?"

"That's what we call her when she's not in the room. I tried tellin' that child that some people got no business shavin' their heads when they got awful-shaped skulls. And looks has always been somethin' of an obsession, bein' an albino dwarf nigger queen. I belong to a support group with only one member—me." He let loose a high-pitched cackle. "But, no accountin' for taste, as I'm sure *you* might agree."

"What do you mean?"

"What do I mean? Oh, please! I mean you and Shirley Temple, honey. Ole' Bug Eyes herself. Like 'em short, do you?" he asked, batting his eyelashes.

"She's quite pretty."

"Oh, sure. A sorta half-pint Peter Lorre in drag."

"That's rather unkind."

"Well, I wouldn't say it to her little moon face, baby. I avoid deliberate cruelty at all costs. It's a code I live by, first instilled in me by my Aunt Mathilde in the French Quarter. And don't be givin' me that look," he said, changing moods abruptly. "I didn't know anybody was gonna get hurt in Boston. Wasn't s'posed to happen that way, and I'm regretful. I'm regretful *you* got hurt, Paxton. We meant no offense."

This last ridiculous comment was made with such sincerity that all I could say was, "None taken." He smiled graciously, then switched gears again.

"Oh, but child, you were very funny! I never seen anybody stand up to Shannon like that! Weren't you scared?" He giggled energetically, but this dwindled to a sad sigh: "Poor Shannon..." and he looked then as if he might cry.

I asked, "What did she mean when she said, 'I know where Erika gets it'?"

He looked at me dully. "Well, just that. L'il Reeka talks a lot, jes' like y'all do. She's been with us from the beginning."

He took a sip of coffee, then caught the look in my eyes, then his own expression went from one of pique to disbelief to confusion to something akin to fear. He realized. He knew. He said, "My God—you tellin' me you really didn't know she was alive? That all this time you been thinkin' your pretty little wife's been dead? Oh, you poor baby—" and he stretched out his squat hand and clasped mine across the table. We sat in silence for some moments. He kept shaking his head, but never took his hand nor his eyes from mine.

Finally, I said, "Would you tell me why she faked her own death?"

"What you talkin' about?"

"For the last six years I've been living with the conclusion that she drowned in Bar Harbor. In a car accident. I was driving."

Now he looked frightened. "Paxton, I swear on the sainted grave of the Lady Chablis, that I don't know nothin' about any o' that. I thought you two were just bust up. Oh, Lordy, this must be quite a shock."

I groped for a good response. Failing this, I groped for any response. Then I just said: "Yes." He nodded slowly.

I asked, "Where is she?"

He put one hand across his heart and held the other up in oath. "Now, you gotta believe me when I say in all honesty that *I do not know*. SLAV's got an adjunct headquarters somewhere."

"And you don't know where that is?"

"No, honey, I do not. Shannon wouldn't tell none of us 'cause she felt if we operated in separate cells, none of us know too much. But I'm sure Reeka'll be along, once we're in contact."

"And when do we make contact?"

He looked blank, then said, "Shannon's the only one knew how to do that." We stared at each other. "I see."

He seemed to view this predicament from several angles, then asked with a right deficiency of attention, "You like animals, Paxton?"

"Of course. I love them."

"So y'all an animal *lover*." He caught the bestial lilt to his statement, and quickly amended, "I meant that nicely."

"I know. Yes, I had dogs, cats, mice, goldfish, like most middle-class kids. My parents were very serious, strict even, about my brother and I being responsible for animals. I'd resent changing a little box or walking the pooch when I wanted to go ride my bicycle. But the repetition of chores, I'm convinced, instilled in me a sense that these creatures were defenseless; that they depended on me."

"Amen to that, honey. Sounds 'though you had some decent folks."

"They did the best they could."

I must have weighted that with enough subtext that he cocked his head winsomely, which encouraged me to go back even *foyther*, as his accent would have had it.

I said, "I tried to rescue moths. Even as a tow-head in South Africa."

"Oh, that's right! He's *African*," giving this last a ghetto spin that made him chuckle.

"*Afrikaaner*, technically."

"Love the way you talk, baby, and a native of the Dark Continent can go a long way with me, *Mistah*." And he let peal that infectious laugh, so I was laughing as well when he chimed, "Rescue moths from what?"

"When it rained, they'd cling to the screen doors, their dusty wings all sodden and useless. I tried to help them without hurting them. I'd set them outside again in a dry place, but they'd fly back again and again, attracted of course by—"

"The light."

"Yeah. These foolish things."

He quoted, "'But ah my foes, and O my friends—'"

"'...It gives a lovely light'."

"What a sweet thing you are. 'A friend of the furred ones free of blemish.' Some sweet stud in Bangor laid that one on me."

"Not free. A grisly exception."

"How's zat?"

"When I was sixteen, I went on a camping trip in the Adirondacks. I was with a friend, and he'd brought along his BB gun."

He was alert, hard principles at stake.

"I'd never fired any gun. Funny, my youth gone in a place of hunters, poachers, killing as part of the culture. I come to the U.S. where guns are cheap, plentiful, easily had. I took this innocuous BB gun into the deep jungle of upstate New York, the Great White Hunter fresh from the Veld."

I proceeded slowly. "I spied a chipmunk sitting on a branch, busy with an acorn. I drew a bead on him, and honestly, without the merest second's reflection upon what I was about to do, all the while carefully aiming, pulled the trigger."

He sat silent, careful, motionless.

"I shot it. It fell from its perch. I ran pell-mell to my kill." I paused, yes, for effect. Not for Mumsy, for me. "This innocent thing lay twitching, convulsing blood spilling from its mouth and nose. I watched it, frozen, for the ten or twenty seconds it took to die. And immediately felt *my* convulsion of horror and shame. I wasn't some nine-year-old wannabe cowboy. I was a high school student, a young adult. I knew what I was doing."

Now I continued with difficulty.

"I killed a harmless creature out of bloodlust. I cried in real remorse, then buried the poor thing. And I have yet to forgive myself."

He stared at me with considerable cool, and chill, then said, "You haven't forgiven yourself for two deaths."

I trumped him. "Three, actually. My wife, the chipmunk, and a pet hamster who just died as a result of my inactions. His name was Ignatz."

Mumsy solemnly closed his eyes, sighed, and gently patted my hand.

"You're no worse," he started, faltered, then ended, "than anybody. Fact. I think, y'all ain't too bad a boy, at the end o' the day."

"Thank you," I said.

"But listen honey," he said. "What the hell we gonna do? We got three dead bodies in the red barn and I got a feelin' somebody from somewhere's gonna come lookin' for the cop or that Russian or us right quick. Got any ideas?"

3

"I do, as a matter of fact. I've been thinking about it all night."

"Lay it on me, baby. I'm all ears, with a few remarkable exceptions."

So I told Mumsy my plan: Despite the double ambush of Petra and Poplin, we could still deliver Rasputin's remarkable portion to Kureishi's courier as planned and collect the money. Mumsy's monkey-wrench confederates would get their cut; we would part ways, leaving the bodies in the barn with typed ID tags (I'd glimpsed an ancient Royal with dusty black-and-red ribbon unused on a desk amongst the squalor) and a brief account of what had, if not accidentally, then at least *misadventurously*, gone down. Then destroy the typewriter, wipe clean all, and make the drop. We would separate, neither faction knowing where the other was thithering.

"Thithering?" Mumsy asked.

"Where we each be goin'," I said in imitation.

"Oh."

I would then appraise Chauncey of the details of the disaster and tip off the local cops out of respect for the corpses before they became too ripe.

It was a preposterous plan, riddled with a thousand flaws, but it was the best I could come up with given the circumstances. And I knew now that I had to find Erika. She was alive. That was all I owned of purpose.

Mumsy saw neither flaws nor idiocy in my schematic—he loved it, said he would rouse the others, and lay it on *them*, baby. I voiced concern about their complicity.

"Now don't you worry 'bout that. Those chilluns listen to Mumsy when she talk."

I'm not sure which bothered me more: the warm, effeminate manner in which Mumsy coddled me, like, well, somebody's Mumsy, or the argot that I felt awkward having employed on a square, straight (anyone would be square compared to him) white like me. (Clearly the legacy of apartheid had left me dented, and for all time, but good.) Despite both, I liked him.

Enthused, he fairly skipped from the room, banged loudly on both doors down the hall, doing a dead-on Amanda Wingfield: "Rise and shine! Rise and shine, you children!"

I smiled to myself for the first time in some time and poured myself a cup of coffee, the most and least I had earned. I was struck by how good it felt to be free of a hangover. Perhaps there was a glimmer of hope amidst all the despair.

4

My starting point was that I knew where the guns—and much more important to the cause, Rasputin's property—were hidden. Once this was established, the rest was easy.

Mumsy was right. The l'il chilluns was a docile and eye-rubbingly pliant bunch this morning, as they'd been after their post-mayhem repast the previous evening. Mumsy sketched out my plan—now our plan, as he co-opted it—on the filthy table alongside breakfasts of Mountain Dew, tortilla chips and Ring-Dings, and the three listened as if a parent were explaining the preliminaries and precautions for a weekend camping trip. Not a single nod or murmur of assent; all spirit was gone, fled with the spirits gone from the barn. I prayed those spirits fled; if they were lingering in anger or confusion, this was no place to dawdle.

I did look carefully for even a flicker of dissent in the wide, crazy eyes of "Punky" Brieanna "Komeda" Crisco. She looked, as she crunched handfuls of dry Cocoa Puffs like a reticent dragoon, that she might be thinking that the halls and dorms of Palo Alto perhaps weren't so repressive after all. At least there was milk, if she drank it.

I next turned a gaze of intent to my little muffin. Her big, lovely eyes reflected only melancholy and devotion to Master Malcolm. She looked like a forlorn cocker spaniel. Her hair mussed and skin dry, nonetheless, she was achingly beautiful. My fickleness was revolting to me. For this I'd cashed out the stirring and morbid account of feeling for my dead girl, now truly not dead.

But as she rose from the table to fetchingly fetch more tepid soda, in the pink thermal-underwear outfit she'd sensibly packed (it was summer, but cold up north, practical chick), the curves of her perfect behind brought back a publicity snap of Marilyn Monroe from some '50s film (*Niagara*? Who cares?), and a sad pang of desire to recapture what I swore was love, to devotionally kiss that lovely ass (my honor to the Devil), rose up in me, and it was all I could do, on the instant, to keep from letting loose a howl like a gut-shot dog.

Once more, I'd received exactly what I'd asked for. This time, I had cast myself in a black fairy tale by James Ellroy on speed. What a jackass.

She plunked that bottom (once my property, as if stamped? Ha! Not no more, buddy-boy!) back onto the peeling kitchen chair, and all the magic swirled away; good. As she gulped deep the green, sugary swill from a plastic travel mug, I followed her canine gaze to the object of her devotion.

This asinine would-be ex-Beat was consuming half a soggy cantaloupe without the aid of a napkin; not a care in the world. To be sure, the corpses of three young women were stiffening close by; he was caught in the tide of a sordid, if not arguably sick, criminal situation; but given the price of melon, all was well in Malcolmland. The sloppiest of beasts has too much dignity to allow for any valid comparison to this asshole. How I hated him.

Of course, I was jealous. I envied him his muse in the pink thermal pants.

The dimwit did make the case that his shit-box and Hayley's wheels might be far more traceable should anyone, as we spoke, be already looking for us; so it was determined that the gang's VW van would serve as transport, as it was—amazingly—registered, inspected, in good shape, and not hot.

I told Mumsy to give them thirty minutes to pack. He laughed. Pack what?

I dusted off the Royal and addressed "To Whom It Might Concern" on a found sheet of old onionskin. It took all of three seconds for me to see the futility of attempting an explanation of the horrors awaiting discovery in the barn. Forget it. I tore the sheet from the roll, folded it carefully into my pocket, then took some lined three-by-five cards I found in a drawer.

I typed, "Petra, Polish/Russian Political Activist" and "Shannon Dora/American SLAV Terrorist," and "Janis Poplin/American FBI Agent" on the cards.

I wiped down the keys of the Royal, hefted it from the desk, trudged it through a wild waist-high field, and hurled it like an anvil into the pond. They'd find it, of course.

In the barn, clenching imaginary pipe between set teeth, I wasn't sure how to affix the cards to the bodies. I thought of slipping them between dead fingers, but this reminded me of *Apocalypse Now* and seemed to implicate me in this triple-homicide. I tried leaning Petra's name-tag against her folded arms, but this took on the air of a greeting card; we were back in Boston Strangler country, and a shiver went through me. I finally settled on slipping each into a pocket as quiet identification. Petra's suede jacket was easy.

Poplin lay face down, and slipping the card into her pants back pocket, my involuntary (now truly necrophiliac) appraisal of her backside brought an instant pang of revulsion. I felt horrible that a young woman was dead. I had disliked her intensely when she was alive; I did not care to appreciate the contours of a woman I disliked who was also dead. Out, out . . .

Shannon lay on her back, and as I unbuttoned a breast-pocket on her black epauleted, epicene shirt, I felt a sudden terror that her hand would reach up and grab my wrist with the strength of the undead.

I also did not care to linger on the sight nor memory of the flies buzzing busily over the coagulated grue. Out, out, out...

But first I retrieved the shopping bag. I grabbed Malcolm's filthy knapsack and transferred the firmly-latched box and the guns—checking that all safety-catches that I could actually identify were on—zipped it up and secured it to my back as if ready for a hike through edelweiss.

The Gang of Four was gathered in the drive, packed and waiting to be picked up for two weeks at summer camp. When I emerged and Malcolm saw me, he gave a curt nod—one member of the team to another—and trudged off to the last crumbling structure of this forgotten Yankee spread, a garage harboring the gassed-up, pea-green Big Bug. As we stood on the back porch watching him reverse the van, my self-disgust decided to provoke Punky.

I said, "Do you cultists get some discount from Volkswagen for pea-green vans? Seems like every lunatic-fringe bunch from the Manson Family to Proactive Vegans has owned one."

Maybe she was too tired to take me on, but in truth, I don't know why she said nothing, but quietly offered me one of the Watermelon cigarettes she was puffing on. Perhaps to shut me up. After a startled and embarrassed pause, I accepted it, and then a light from her zebra-striped Zippo. A small gesture of kindness from her: unexpected, inexplicable. I will never understand anyone.

Malcolm backed the van up to our doleful group.

"Hop in!" he yelled cheerfully, off for a picnic.

Mumsy told him to climb out.

"I'm driving," said Malcolm.

"The hell you are," said Mumsy with command.

"Why not?"

"'Cause you ain't got no valid drivin' license, Komeda's a recognizable hostage, Hayley'd fall apart like a wet papersack if a cop stops us, and I can't reach the pedals! We too close to a shitload o' money and the end o' this muthafuckin' nightmare to blow it now. Paxton drives. Out!"

Mumsy may have suspected I also lacked an official driving privilege, but if so, he may also have sensed I would never be so stupid—as so many fugitives on the run—to commit a traffic violation. How many wanted killers *hadn't* taken simple precautions and driven lawfully, only to be captured running a red light?

Malcolm clunked into the back, and I slid behind the wheel, awash in memory, the smell of Volkswagen upholstery, insignia, the clumsy stick-shift. My parents loomed up suddenly, faded. Sentiment for the vanished past amidst a body count.

I placed the knapsack on the floor beneath my legs.

Mumsy rode shotgun, chain-smoking Benson & Hedges menthol 100s. The three kids (yes, that's how I would now think of them) lolled in two rows behind. The radio played a French Canadian station. As I rolled the vehicle bumpily off, an old Serge Gainsbourg was replaced by golden age classics "Moonlight Serenade," "Begin the Beguine," and my father's favorite, "Canadian Sunset." Mumsy sang and hummed along wistfully with the lousy speakers, blissfully transported. When Brieanna meekly suggested that maybe a station more appropriate to the living might be nice, she was barked down by the little Pekingese with the long cigarette. All was quiet after that.

Close on two hours of travel—Mumsy soberly navigating the network of routes 16 to 27 to 16 again to 201 using my instructions from Chauncey—Malcolm seemed to stir. He suggested coffee as a Cumberland Farms approached, and we stopped to all tank up on an array of exciting blends. When we were back in motion, Malc began talking a blue streak.

"It's true," he said. "Beings from other planets have been visiting the Earth for centuries. Those huge spaceman carvings done by the Incas—or the Aztecs—one of them; maybe the Mayans, I don't know—the point is the scale and perspective. I mean, how could they do that with such precision without a full-scale view from like a mile up or something?"

"You seen them?" Brieanna asked moodily.

"I don't have to. It's all in books by Erich von Daniken, who's the world's leading authority on this stuff. I have a pipe that belonged to him. The South American-Mexican thing's the most obvious, but there's Easter Island, Stonehenge, King Charlemagne—who knew all about extraterrestrials. You got polarity here that's astounding—Christianity and paganism, science, and the fucking unknown universe."

"Polarity?" Brieanna, irritated. "Like polar bears?"

"No, stupid," said Malcolm. "Polar like opposites. Us and them, heaven and hell, God and the devil. You know the Gnostics thought the devil was actually God's, like, evil twin? Consider the stuff in the Bible that's so utterly fantastic but now has valid extraterrestrial explanation."

"Fantastic? You mean really great?" Brie was out for him.

"Fantastic like fantasy. Don't you read?"

"What stuff in the Bible?"

"Like the Nephilim, mentioned in Numbers 13:33."

I was impressed. The *manqué* knew Scripture.

"Who were *they*?" Hayley asked quietly. Her voice was rapt, but silence did the rest. As we sped down the winding, tree-dappled road with only the hum of the engine as accompaniment, the feel in the van took on that of a ghost-story around a campfire.

"The Nephilim?" Malcolm asked with flair, a grungy Rod Serling. He paused. "The Nephilim were giants who roamed the Earth in ancient times. Literal giants, ten stories tall, that the Earth's gravitational equation could not possibly have supported. Yet they were here."

I glanced in the mirror. Hayley had placed one forefinger inside her moistened, lower lip, riveted by Malcolm's horseshit. What sweetness in the imagery; I wanted to smack her.

"Even Adam and Eve—" he started.

"Oh, come off it! If that's not a bunch of crap, nothing is," raved Brieanna. "The whole goddamn race springing from incest? It's anti-feminist and it's fucked!"

Malcolm was indignant. "Man, you don't even know about the Magyars coupling with aliens! That's Adam and Eve for ya! It's a metaphor, okay? Grays are the result of Magyars and humans, the start of this race! It isn't that whole Cro-Magnon and Neanderthal Darwin/Leakey cover—that's just a smokescreen."

"And Apollo 11 never landed on the moon!" Hayley chimed in, trying to be helpful, but Malcolm looked distracted.

"Grays?" asked Brieanna.

"That's what they're called 'cause of their skin color," said the poet.

With Laurel & Hardy timing, Mumsy and I exchanged a glance across the cockpit of the van. He lowered his shades with two fingers. "Don't be gettin' no ideas."

"They're not green?" asked the wiseacre Brieanna.

I tossed in my thrup'nny's worth:

"So Malcolm…if these beings from another world were so helpful in getting us Earthlings propagating and all, why are they so utterly vanished now? I mean, except for the occasional Roswell crash or backroads abduction?"

"How the heck should I know?" he answered reasonably.

"Tell them about the Philadelphia Experiment!" Hayley just gushed encouragement, but Malcolm only seemed irritated by her well-meaning endorsement of his life philosophy, poor slob.

"What's a shitty movie got to do with anything?" asked Punky. I suddenly remembered a flash of her watching Hayley's lovely butt in those pink thermals, too; which figured, of course, she being attracted to women, with the exception of her bizarre coupling with Mumsy, who could be taken as yonic as well as phallic; and I also realized that she, Malcolm, and myself were all attracted to the same dope; or Brieanna at least appreciated a nice piece, who could blame her.

Malcolm was frothing. "Not the shitty video, you culturally illiterate dip! Polar bears, Jesus! I'm talking about when the United States government was experimenting with electromagnetics during World War II, hoping to render battleships invisible. Well, they screwed up big time. They created a forcefield of invisibility all right, but they accidentally sent a U.S. Navy ship into another dimension at the same time. Albert Einstein—"

"Oh, Christ." Brieanna's amused disgust was infectious. Malcolm grew more strident.

"—warned them! They tore a hole in the fabric of time and space, and the guys on the ship encountered some very startled grays. All the sailors involved went mad or disappeared. It was all covered up. But people knew. Even the Soviets knew."

Surprisingly, Brieanna shut up. Malcolm, sensing victory, continued in a low monotone, fraught with conviction.

"Their planets aren't in our galaxy, or even near it. But they don't travel these huge distances like we thought, these impossible light years. They're interdimensional, from a contiguous world—a parallel universe—completely non-tangent. They simply travel through another space-energy continuum to get here. And I think, Paxton, they've probably actually stepped up their visits since Roswell and Betty and Barney Hill in '61."

Another stretch of silence.

"It's spooky," said Hayley.

Brieanna then performed a marvelous imitation of a Theremin, the woozy electronic instrument of '50s horror film scores. We all laughed, save for Malcolm.

"It's not funny," he said.

"It's a scream," said Brieanna.

I was glad for the small change in atmosphere, as a shitty case of *contemptus mundi* was starting to settle in.

My hopeless hope was calcifying. A dark cave beckoned, and I felt brutally stupid. I asked myself sincerely, then rhetorically, by turns, *What the hell am I doing here?* Oh, yeah—my life had become unmanageable. Chaos, insanity, penury, dead wife not dead, dead hamster; I was in love with and had been fucking a teenager. While all the former might merely mystify decent folk, the latter would most definitely be viewed beneath contempt. True love would not conquer all, except me, and my fantasy child bride was throwing me over for a not-much younger, dumber and smellier poet, who I hoped was a bad poet, but if Robert Frost could write so lyrically of birches, draught-horses, and woods on snowy evenings, while all the while being a dyed-in-the-wool-son-of-a-bitch, anything was possible.

We were all well beyond anything that had even a semblance of what used to appear as reality. I was all too happy to see the sign announcing the approach of the Greater Desert of Maine.

Chapter Eleven

1

The sands of a barren stretch called the Great Desert of Maine blow near Freeport, not far from the steady sales of L.L. Bean, but the *Greater* (and only quantitatively) Desert spreads its dusty wastes at a barren region called Khartoum. The convenience store brochure informed me that failure to rotate crops properly combined with massive land-clearing and overgrazing resulted in severe soil erosion that subsequently produced exposure of a hidden ten-thousand-acre wasteland of sand. "Visit Maine's Two Famous Natural Phenomena for an Unforgettable Journey!"

And *Khartoum*, no less. What clever wag chose the scene of "Chinese" Gordon's suicidal siege in Egypt in 1885 as the name-place for this grainy freak of nature? I remembered what I'd written about Gordon, cribbed from a book, in the narration of a high school skit deemed so precocious that it toured area schools for a year. In the *Crimea* and in the savage hand-to-hand fighting against the Taiping rebels in China, he invited death at almost every step, exposing himself to totally unnecessary risks, unarmed except for a rattan cane.

General George had obsessed, yes, along with Michael Rockefeller and myself, but I had never even been near Cairo, or Tuscany—certainly not Khartoum; but here we both were in Maine. I shook off thoughts of my recent nightmare.

I pulled the iconic van into the still environs of the obviously long-abandoned Khartoum drive-in theater, its torn, disintegrating screen, overgrown lot, and empty speaker poles still waiting for the next show, never to come.

It looked to have been closed for at least thirty years. Swing sets rusted in front of the huge screen. Landscaping and a scheme of shrubbery could be discerned amongst the wild, consuming overgrowth. This place was even sadder than the derelict theater in the barn. I thought of all the theaters—cinemas, drive-ins, pantomime halls—of my childhood. But I couldn't tarry there long.

Mumsy seemed so confident, so happy, so determined. As I threw the clutch into neutral, he turned to me with the ebullience of a tour guide.

"Now you jes' wait, honey. These are my people! Everythin' gonna be jes' fine."

He snapped open the passenger door, hopped with a grunt from the van, and skipped with aplomb toward the one-story, dilapidated building that had housed a snack-bar and projection booth, a distance of roughly one hundred feet.

He was halfway there when a shot cracked, and he spun convulsively, then fell flat like a child pushed from a slide.

"Jesus!" It was Malcolm's voice, the two women screamed.

The instinct came to throw myself on the floor of the cab, clear of the next bullet, but I didn't. Malcolm, Brieanna, and Hayley were already down for the count. Hayley's voice bellowed up from the floor.

"Get down, Paxton, for Christ's sake! You wanna get your head blown off?!"

No, I didn't. But I turned to look at the tangle of limbs behind the front seat. She was splayed over him, her skirt up around her waist, bottom up, sexy as hell. The impulse to bury my face in the slick between her legs, then sink myself inside her was tangible, disturbing and acute, and about as close as I ever hope to come to the concomitance of sex-wish and death-wish. This was unbearably stupid: my skull right in the cross-hairs of a sniper, Death's hot breath on my neck, and I looked to her small body. I deserved my head blown off.

I stared at her delicious behind but for a moment more. She actually glanced over her shoulder to follow the trajectory of my gaze; she looked as put-out as a babysitter saddled with a recalcitrant brat. She actually flipped herself from the floor of the van in a sort of gymnastic hand-stand and grabbed me forcefully by the hair, a whole handful painfully prompting my scalp to chide the loins, and dragged me roughly to the floor with the rest of them, me having at least the presence of mind to grab the knapsack.

A shot exploded the glass of a side window, and I felt a searing in my face, a flash of terror that I'd been blinded, a warmth spreading quickly in the flesh, then blood down my cheek. I was down, but not out. Brieanna screamed for a brief and hysterical moment, then lapsed into wracking, hyperventilative sobs. I felt as resigned and pinned-down as Vic Morrow in old episodes of *Combat*—we were all gonna die—when Malcolm did a most amazing thing.

He looked from me to Hayley, then raised his head to confirm Mumsy's plopped corpse out in the dust', paused to give due consideration, all of six seconds; quoted Warren Oates ("Fuck this") and leapt—no, *sprang*—into the cab, clearly in the sights of whomever'd fired the shots, landed in the seat, turned the key in the ignition, threw the gears into first, and hit the gas without having his head exploded. Those few seconds took ten years off my life, I'm certain, but it was worth the rise of pure joy that came up in me as I found myself actually *whooping* as Malc drove that bug, hunch-shouldered and fit for the screen, the hell out of harm's way.

The back wheels fish-tailed and the sides of the careening vehicle were whipped by startled branches as he steered the VW up a sandy path barely wide enough to accommodate it.

What I glimpsed through the windows as we bounced from side to side (finding irregular purchase on the taught, slippery, upholstery) looked to be an old logging road.

"Where are you going?" I yelled over the angry engine and the grinding of the gears as he downshifted and worked the clutch and gas pedals as one whose life depended on it.

"Away!" he yelled back, and he could have been a knight on a charger in the sword-and-sorcery fantasy novels he surely consumed, along with his science fiction and Fritos. "Away!"

And we were going away. Away from the sound of gunfire and the gunshot wounds and the already putrescent corpses, and poor, decent Mumsy back there, spun like a top and dropped in the dirt as the small batch of peculiarities of which he was immensely proud. I could have been in the midst of a Central American revolution for the time I could expend mourning Mumsy, though it struck me like a eulogy that the world would not see the likes of him again.

But a revolution, no matter how wrong-headed or barbaric, is still anchored by the integrity of political change. Even an abomination like Pol Pot must have warmed himself with the flaming notion that the killing fields of Cambodia were ultimately for the best, strange monster. But us? We were fleeing through the brush of Vacationland, not Vietnam; life and death had become the stakes over money and nearly abstract pointlessness. We were all now dumb animals with blood on our hands, home at last.

As Malcolm slowed the speed of the van to a careful crawl, I braced my back hard against a seat and reached a tentative, trembling hand up to my cheekbone. The tips of my fingers brushed the splinter of glass embedded there, sending a volley of high-speed, furious needles through the temporal network. I gasped.

Brieanna came up, and like Hayley, took a handful of my hair, but gently, and eased my head against the wall of the cab to steady the bouncing from our bumpy movement.

"Close your eyes." Calm but firm, like a nurse.

I did as told, felt the shard move sharply, followed by a fresh trickle down my stained cheek. I opened my eyes.

"Look at that," she said, awed, holding an inch-long, quarter-inch thick sliver of the window, glistening with blood. I felt sick.

She pulled a Handi Wipe from the floor's trash, ripped the foil wrapper with her teeth, and swabbed the disinfectant-soaked sheet across the wound, which stung with relief.

I couldn't thank her before we noticed Malcolm nudging the VW into a tight copse of thin poplars. It had barely settled to rest when he clambered across Hayley in the passenger seat, unlatching the door, and spilled out of the van and off into the woods.

"Come on!" he stage-whispered. Hayley trotted.

He watched me grab the knapsack, then lumbered off. I was right behind them, spidery Brieanna skittering after me.

"Where are you going?" I hissed to him.

He stopped dead, sending Hayley bumping into him, sheer slapstick.

"To the castle," he hissed back, then stood waiting for any further inquiry.

"Castle?"

"That's what they call it. It's an old battery, probably a quarter-mile from here, up a hill. If we can make it there— " None of us would finish his sentence with *alive*. "I'll bet somebody will be there to make the exchange." The cool of the man!

"Oh, okay." Our rasped whispers in this sunny forest really sealed the terror-in-broad-daylight creeps working their way through my bowels.

"Erika will probably be there too, I'll bet," he said. I grabbed him by the arm, and he didn't resist.

"What do you know about Erika?"

He broke the whispering, and said in a faint but deeper tone, "We don't possibly have enough time for that now. We need you and that box. You need us to get out of here safely. We need each other. Now let's finish this. Help me."

Hayley stood shortly between us, looking up from the tall one to the taller. I half-expected Malc to add something like, "As poets and gentlemen who have both loved her, there is honor in this," but we both just glanced down at her, and her bangs swished on her forehead as she swiveled her gaze back and forth between us.

I too spoke softly but firmly, but my intended Errol Flynn "Agreed," came out as a Don Knotts, "O-kay!" How lamentable. I could have kicked the dirt in front of me.

Okey-doke, artichoke, let's go give 'em what for!

Self-disgust: the extreme had just provided a once-in-a-lifetime moment; a scene I had played poorly. Punky smirked.

Malcolm said, "Let's move."

And he ducked beneath some branches and wound the way through bracken and brambles, occasionally reaching back to tug Hayley's little hand through a particularly difficult clot of growth. I took up her rear, and each appreciative savor of that baby-fat bum seemed to be answered by the whistling slap of a birchy stem or slender limb right in the forelock or kisser, until my face was equal parts stung or numb. After about ten minutes of this I complained, muttered something about tree-branch etiquette, which was met by her asking irritably whether I thought she was a goddamned Campfire Girl. Malcolm *soto voce'd* for both of us to shut the hell up: people were dead and other people were trying to kill us, so *shut up shut up shut up! Sssshhh!* Sharp and sibilant like a rhythmic lawn-sprinkler, or a snake in the grass. Brieanna frowned, noticed my face with mild shock, and thanked me for being such a good scout with my handling of the hind-directed branches, as she was the genuine caboose of this nature walk.

Malcolm moved steadily and stealthily through the thick woods; he had been here before, and knew where he was going. He plunged on with Hayley not flagging now, in as much of a loping stride as she could manage to earn that merit badge from her mentor, the two of them the Mutt 'n' Jeff of the Maine jungle.

It was hot, and I was sweating heavily, plus being grimy, dusty, itching and bleeding. I daubed at my check with the handiwipe 'till it fell to shreds. Tiny insects swarmed in shafts of sunlight and stuck to the slick of sweat on my arms and face.

We came to an incline in this pseudo-path we were following, a step-up over an exposed, moss-lined root. Malcolm sailed over it in his high-tops and Hayley followed suit, little frog. I too—soft Back Bay poet, true, but with the copper stomach of ancestors who crossed the African Continent—stepped up and cleared the knot. Then I heard Punky crash and cry out. Young Love took no notice, continuing onward.

I paced back and found her splayed on the ground.

"I fell on that stupid rock."

I helped her turn herself. She had torn the knee of her overalls and a good deal of skinned, bloody pulp was already visible through the tear. As vicious mosquitoes settled on us and I got her to her feet, she discovered she had twisted—probably sprained—an ankle. Unkindly and unthinkingly, I said, "Jesus Christ, I don't believe this. Are we in a horror movie? We're running for our lives and you twist an ankle? You're really dimming my enthusiasm for living, here."

She looked equal parts ankle-hurt and feelings-hurt. I felt instantly mean, ungrateful, ashamed.

"Here," I said. "Put your arm around my shoulder."

Whether touched by my contrition, her fear, or the blubbery arms of a privileged upbringing that, despite her militant pretentions, had left her woefully unprepared for roughing it beyond a sleeping bag (she had once confessed in a notorious Tweet that she had never once made her own bed), she began to cry softly.

I helped her limp along a few yards, trying to support her and clear the branches as we lurched haltingly along, and I found myself saying, "It's okay, don't worry, we're going to get out of this….Everything's going to be all right…really…" What a bill of goods I was trying to sell to this poor little rich girl! She surely had my number from the moment we had met, but there are times when we all need the blanket of hollow reassurance, and clearly Brieanna Crisco just wanted the party to be over so she could go home. Whether home was the sprawling mansion in Marin County or the squalid digs of the Revolution, I knew not.

As we rounded a steep turn in the path, she nestled her head—for a fleeting moment—in the hollow of my shoulder, leaving my shirt wet with her tears.

My mind should have been nailed to survival through animal instinct; but as we passed a thick patch of lady's slipper, I saw a fat bumblebee lazily investigating the curled pink petals, and I remembered cutting a lawn when I was a boy (my very first occupation; perhaps one day I would take it up again) and witnessing a large, furry *bombus* accidentally sucked up into the blades and spit out the side of the mower in a torrent of cut grass, wings askew and utterly dazed, but perfectly intact. I stopped and watched it as it sought rest and repose on a clump of clover and soothed itself. This unbidden memory was followed by the sodden moths on the screen door in the rain, as told to Mumsy. And lastly, the garden slugs that would slither out to get drunk and bloated on the dish of milk set by my mother on the porch for a feral cat.

Brieanna, too, seemed to be daydreaming, evident from her next remark: "There was a gay bar in New York called the Crisco Disco…" She trailed off.

"Yeah?"

"No one would ever tell me why they called it that. I mean," she said limping, "Was it making fun of my family?"

"Um…no," I said. "They were just rhyming with *disco*."

"But why?"

I hesitated. Should I? Why not? "In honor of the popular sexual lubricant."

I had no idea how she'd take that, presumed hater of all things phallic and penetrative, but she actually laughed.

"Oh. I didn't know that."

"It's true."

We were combat buddies. If I'd had a cigarette, I would have lit it and placed it between her lips. I asked, "It's not broken, right? I mean, how do you feel?"

She said, "Pointless. How do you feel?"

I thought for a moment, then answered pointedly, "Like some eunuch with a pin-wheel hat, sitting around in his basement with an electric train set, trying to get a sugar buzz off a root beer."

I could feel her stare. She shook her head and gave an exhausted sigh. "I never know what the hell you're saying, Paxton." I turned to smile at her when she said this, so witnessed the startled shift in her expression: "Oh my God, I don't believe it."

I saw what shocked her: Not fifteen feet ahead of us the path parted to a clearing which became a shelf—which I saw as we slowly drew nearer—gave way onto a deep, deep ravine—a drop of possibly seven or eight stories. One did not want to approach too closely to see just how far the drop plunged. Shafts of sunlight exultantly lit angles in both directions. Here was a true crack in the earth, as though separating one world from another, and the heart-stop-ping view afforded confirmation that one would have to travel a good long distance in either direction to find the spot where the crevasse ended or might be forded.

"Not to worry!" came Malcolm's voice, at once near and far.

I looked across the immense fissure. He stood dead-straight across, a dis-tance of some sixteen feet, and I immediately had the notion that he was, in point of fact, of supernatural powers and had flown there, or walked across, Emperor of the Air.

"How...?" said Brieanna.

"Up here!" came Hayley's voice. Malcolm stood on a mirror-image of the cliff on which Brieanna and I uneasily shifted. Hayley was perched on a higher rock above Malcolm's head. I was reminded of a parrot on a pirate's shoulder. She clutched a thick rope with a wooden disk set above a large knot. I followed the line of the slack up and up to see its connection disappear into the leafy folds of a very high tree-top above her.

"Oh my God."

"Fear not," said Malcolm. "A rope-swing is firmly and permanently an-chored up there— not too old, it's in good shape and safe as milk. After you swing over to this side—" He stepped back to indicate what looked to be an adequate, grassy landing-area for such a feat, my heart now racing—"You take the thin rope with the weight attached to the main rope, and you hurl it back to the other side to await the next swinger."

Malcolm, so young, was surely ignorant of the outdated '60s meaning of the term, but I had an image of Hugh Hefner in silk jammies nodding sagely behind him, puffing his pipe.

"That's how we got over!" piped my little elevated goddess.

"I can't do this," Brieanna said, loud enough for just me to hear. "And I don't mean my ankle."

"Yes, you can," I said quietly, then to Hayley, boy to girl at lake. "Well, send it on over!" What cheer I displayed!

"Not so fast," said Malcolm, less friendly.

"Yeah," said Hayley, not friendly at all.

"What?"

He said, "Toss over the knapsack with the box and the guns."

"Why?"

"Because I don't trust you Paxton, and that stinks, but it's the truth. Now, obviously I need you to make this exchange. Mr. Kureishi or whoever he sends is only gonna deal with you. But I'm feeling a mite dispensable in all this right now, and I gotta look out for me and Hayley." He paused. "Now, I know where Erika Wikki is. And I know a lot more about her and what's been going on and what hasn't happened yet than you could ever imagine. I want you to trust me enough to give me the box and the guns. Then we can make the deal, get our cut, I'll set you straight about Erica, and everybody'll live happily ever after."

Brieanna seemed to have stopped breathing; I just stood there.

"You *do* have a choice, here," he said. "You can go back; but somebody's obviously got bad plans for us, and I'd say that somebody's coming up close behind you. You can't stay there, obviously. And the money and your ex-wife—sorry, not ex-wife, I didn't mean ex-wife!—are straight ahead. I suggest you don't take too long to think about it."

Hayley pleaded. "Oh, Paxton, please, we really just have to just get—"

"Yes." I let Brieanna disengage from me and steady herself on a birch tree, then she quickly pulled the knapsack from my shoulders.

"Good man!" said Malcolm with fine *bonhomie*. "Now, *please* – throw it far enough! If you don't make it, our dreams fall into this pit to die."

I had been a champion bowler at cricket in South Africa and later, on an eccentric team here in the States—my pitch had once been powerful. I took one measured step back, then swung the case in practice—once, twice, three times—and on the fourth, a cold and sweet feel of icicles in my stomach, I released the bag, and it sailed in a perfect arc over the deadly drop beneath and landed with a soft clunk in the grass at Malcom's feet.

He said softly, "Nice throw!"

Hayley casually dropped the rope behind her on the tall rock and scampered down the side to join her poet. As he slung the knapsack over his arms and they beamed at each other and kissed, I knew in the instant what was happening. Brieanna didn't quite yet.

"Send the rope over!" she demanded like an angry child.

"Don't waste your breath," I said to her.

"Sorry, guys," said Malcolm, "but I absolutely have got to cut our losses, here. This is getting too fucked up and too dangerous, and if Hayley and I are even going to get down to Cozumel, this has to be done, and right quick. You'd do the same thing." (Cozumel?)

"But there're going to kill us? They killed Mumsy!" Brie was coming unglued.

"At least throw us one of the guns," I said.

"No. You might shoot us right across this ravine. In revenge."

"Then toss over an empty gun and throw over some bullets. You can be out of range before the thing's even loaded." I couldn't believe what I was saying. Where the hell was this shit coming from?

Malcolm considered this. "No. Too risky."

"What about Erika?"

He seemed to just remember. "Oh, yeah. Well, I lied. You have the damndest luck with women, Paxton."

I gripped the urge to cry by the vocal-chords. "Where is she now? And what was this future stuff you mentioned?"

"What?" he asked impatiently.

"You said you'd tell me about what hasn't happened yet."

"Oh! Right. That was bullshit, too. I know nothing. Last I knew, say two weeks ago, she was in San Francisco."

"San Francisco?" I said incredulously. "You're lying."

Apparently lying in the service of an end was a trait Malcolm could stand by with Machiavellian practicality, but he clearly now took offense at being accused of fibbing when he had, in fact, elected to tell the truth.

"Am not!" he said. "She's in fucking San Francisco, okay? There's some Brazilian consulate guy, looks like Humphrey Bogart out there who she's got funding some new save-the-bunnies caper. Word is he writes checks and boffs her."

I don't know how I looked—hurt? Stupid? Both? He seemed to momentarily pity me and said, "That's the truth, Paxton. Cross my heart." He looked sheepish, then added, "And that's all she wrote. Literally."

He looked right into my eyes across the divide.

I said, "They could kill us, you know. Her, too," pointing to Brieanna.

"You'd do the same thing, Paxton. You know you would," he said again with a considerable measure of conviction.

"No, I wouldn't."

Something must have resonated in him, some faint echo of doubt in the grand hall of his smug self-righteousness, for the surety drained from his face, and his eyes clouded over with a mist of hesitance, turned quickly to shame, then annoyance.

"Come on, Hayley," he said, and trudged off into the deep and waiting forest. She started after him, and a pang of anger stabbed me when I realized she would not look back. Yet my heart leapt as if hit with a pistol-shot when she did stop, then turn, and smile at me as if to say that all was well because she knew—*she knew*—we were parting as friends.

"Good luck, Paxton," she said, blew a kiss, gave a wave, and was gone. I stood, silent and unfortunate for only a moment before a small sob caught in my throat. Brieanna gingerly lowered herself to the ground and sat down, occasionally and feebly swatting at insects. She reminded me of a photo I'd once seen of an African plantation worker who'd been chained and exposed to the heat as punishment. Surely he'd died of despair before exposure.

I turned from her. "Snap out of it," I said angrily.

"Who're you talking to?"

"The both of us."

"You're such a sap, Paxton. If we were smart we'd just kill ourselves now."

I can't say I was too enthused by that idea. I was disgusted enough to ask, "Didn't I read about you trying to kill yourself once? What happened?"

"Botched it."

"How?"

"You try to fill up a four-car garage with carbon monoxide using an MG."

Neither of us heard them approach, so they were on us strategically—the four commando girls from the barn, and three others—so help me—in all variance of pretty or cute, in direct-to-video guerrilla gear, toting heavy guns.

One stepped towards me, an amazing woman of Robert Crumb proportions, voluptuous legs and hips and boobs squeezed into the camouflage fatigues, an Amazon for sure, but you could melt into all that curvy pulchritude, and if there was room at the inn, the vacancy flash was her sweet face: dimpled cheeks, tiny overbite, almond-shaped eyes that twinkled. She would be the most popular item on the menu of a Bangkok brothel.

Two of them wordlessly helped Brieanna to her feet, which heartened me for all of one second until the lead lethal plush-toy held an outstretched pistol straight to my forehead and cocked the hammer. I believed she would pull the trigger and I would fly backwards all dead and silly and flop into the ravine a bloody heap, maybe stay there for weeks for maggots and animals, so ignominious an end, but somehow so much a part of not learning from my mistakes, and I hated my panic and fear, and the feeling I might cry, and Malcolm's pity, and hated above all the pity I wanted from this girl.

"This just ain't your day," she said coyly. Without taking her eyes from me, she asked, "You okay, Komeda?"

Punky looked at them for what would turn out to be the last time, then said, "Twisted my ankle and gashed my knee. I'll live," a world-weary warrior.

"May I ask your name?" I asked politely.

"Put your hands on your head."

I could have quipped, *Italian, is it?* but who cared? I was very tired; I was through. I put my hands on my head.

"You may call me Chloe," she said. The others giggled girlishly or gave a masculine guffaw. I didn't get it, so she added, "Even if it's not my name." More giggles and guffaws.

"Shannon's dead," said Brieanna.

"I know," said Chloe. "We found them all, in the barn. What happened?"

"They all kinda shot each other," said Brieanna. "It was horrible."

"Yeah. And Mumsy, back there—revolting. Well. Guess we all knew this day was going to come."

Brieanna looked a bit perplexed by that, but recovered quickly to nod small and slow, her thin lips set. Then she asked, "Who killed him?"

Chloe looked puzzled and actually turned a glance to Bri. "You mean this clown didn't?"

"No," said Brieanna, sounding a bit put out. Misinformation, it seemed, ruled the day.

"I thought maybe you girls—guys—women—did," I said, not trying to sound cute.

Chloe pressed the gun barrel to my head. "Hey! Don't get cute. Why would we kill Mumsy? Just keep your trap shut."

I wasn't sure how to do this and also answer her question. She didn't wait, instead saying, "It must be that goddamned Paki's goons—animals. Animals—no, I should never say that! Animals aren't pigs like people! I don't know, I don't know." Her cool seemed to be heating up in the fatigue of battle. "Okay, come on," she said, making a leader's decision. "Let's get up there."

They led us out and back down the strangulated path to two waiting Jeeps. If I had been inclined to mock these suburban anarchists, their hardware was beginning to inhibit my mirth. We shoe-horned into the Jeeps, which lurched out to follow the same logging road but took a fork that gave way onto a more serviceable gravel drive that spiraled steadily up, around and up, until after only a few minutes of travel the stone structure on the high hill came into view. I squinted up at it.

"The Castle of Khartoum," said the chocolate-skinned Special Ops chick next to me, and grinned.

Both Jeeps pulled up in front of two large, rusted doors that were designed to accommodate big things on wheels. The outside grey-and-white mottled façade rose ominously up three stories to open turrets and windows and a balcony extending around all sides of the structure. The roof was flat. The ground beneath us had been paved at one time, but that was long ago; dirt and weeds had cracked and crumbled the beige-colored pavement. Like the two theaters before it, the place was forgotten and neglected, but standing silently, as if counting on the day when its former inhabitants would return to put it again to use. Dust rose as the first Jeep emptied and the girls leapt professionally to the ground and swiftly moved to apparently preplanned positions—again with the impressive!

"What is this place?" I asked Chocolate Tone.

"Used to be an army battery during World War I."

"Why the hell would they build this in the middle of Nowhere, Maine, for World War I?"

She shifted her Marlin pump twelve-gauge (just like Unc's) from palm-to-palm swiftly, pulled a piece of gum from the corner of her mouth to chew with focus, then said, "Do I *look* like a fuckin' history teacher?"

Best to stay friendly. "Sorry." But, oh no (when-will-you-ever-learn?), an apology only inspired contempt, of course, and judging from her expression, we were now in even worse shape together. I glanced at Brieanna, wedged on the other side of my new pal, but she refused to meet my gaze. I looked away. Non-history-teaching Chocolate resumed her lesson.

"Then for a while it was a national guard armory, but then they closed it down, sold it to the town of Rockwood—Khartoum ain't actually incorporated as no town—and it's mostly been a hangout for teenagers drinkin' beer—note the Satanic graffiti—'till we laid claim a year ago."

From this hilltop the isolation of the place was clear in all directions, but isolation also meant vulnerability.

"Don't the local authorities know what you're up to?"

She snorted. The two women in front chuckled indulgently at that one, too.

"We rent the place," Chocolate said finally. "They think we're a paint-ball club."

They all roared at this, and Punky joined in, back as one of the cool kids.

One of the women in front, a pretty Asian with swept-up silky black hair, turned her full attention on me suddenly, and declared, "I always have one question I ask a man when I meet him," she said, assessing me, giving the impression that she was weighing whether to ask the Question. She seemed to be waiting for a reply. I cleared my throat.

"And what is that question, I wonder?"

"What did you think of the movie *Titanic?*"

I stared at her, scrutinizing her dark eyes for a clue to this most mystical of queries. Where was the hook? What was the angle here? I wanted to do Edward G. Robinson: *Say, sister, what gives?*

I said, "I thought it was good."

She shook her head tolerantly: "No. What did you *think* of it?"

"You mean, like a critique?" She stared levelly. I said, "Well, I mean, the effects were top-notch. You felt like you were really there. I guess the whole jealous-boyfriend subplot was a bit contrived."

She shook her head again, while one of the others indulged in poor mimicry of my accented "a bit contrived." She patted my hand, which made me notice her long, perfectly manicured nails. How the hell do you operate a Savage 440 rifle with long nails?

"No, no—listen…"

"*Listen* to her," said Chocolate tersely.

"From the heart and soul, now. Hear me and respond. What did you think of the movie *Titanic?*"

I wasn't sure which tumble of the dice would get me struck, killed or worse. When in doubt, go with the truth.

I said, "Well, actually, I tend to like the cinema of ideas. Films made outside of the U.S. are best for that. I mean, how much intelligence does it take to watch a goddamned boat sink?"

She wailed like a maniac. To say I didn't know what hit me would be untrue, as the pummeling hands and scratching nails and yelps of bloody murder were all emanating from this China Doll turned to Dragon Lady, and man, was she crazed and pissed off. The other two women laughed uproariously at her hysterics, and Chocolate leaned away from me into Punky to avoid being flailed by blocking her and shoving her back into the front seat. She too, had descended into satisfied laughter, leading me to believe that the whole thing had been a set-up, an inside joke. No matter what I'd said, the answer would have produced this same insane reaction. These girls sure knew how to have fun. My nose was bleeding.

I said, "Since we're on the subject, my favorite film is actually *Rat Pfink a Boo-Boo*." My fear was crashing and ebbing like I was bipolar.

A sharp whistle sounded from above. We looked up to see Chloe signal us in with a wave worthy of Mussolini.

We flung ourselves from the vehicle like the gang from *Hatari!* and entered the "castle" through a rusted doorway.

Inside, one lethal Powderpuff was already posted at the center of the big, damp, crypt-cool, piss-smelling, airplane-hangar-sized battery. Another stood sentry at the foot of a wide stone staircase, rather regal for a utilitarian structure: You could announce the guests for a royal ball from that staircase. Count Dracula would feel right to home welcoming Renfield up there. Chloe offered a welcome of relief as she skipped kittenishly down the steps towards us, her lovely breasts bouncing all the way.

"All clear," she said. I was tempted to salute. "If they show up now for the swap, we're ready. If they attack, we're ready."

"Attack?" said Brieanna with alarm. Clearly one afternoon to Hell and back was all the poor little rich girl could handle.

"Why the hell do you think they killed Mumsy?"

"But who's *they*?" I demanded.

"I don't *know*!" she yelled. Then she turned to the commandos: "Take up Plan R positions. Komeda, you come with me. Hayden and Phoebe, as planned. Anita, take the prisoner to the South Wing."

Anita seemed to get quite a kick out of sticking the barrel of her semi-automatic in my back, smiling and giggling like a kid at play, up the stairs, down a filthy hall until we came to a large, thick, oaken door set on massive hinges.

"Open it," she said. Gun in the back, then a giggle.

"You know, you don't have to keep prodding me with that. I'm not resisting, moving sluggishly, or disobeying your orders. And since we're not in the Japanese camp on Blood Island, you shouldn't be doing that just for shits and grins. It's sadistic."

Given her *Titanic* question of only a few minutes earlier, this clearly was not the most prudent line of reasoning to pursue, but Christ, I was fed up. I, too, was feeling something akin to despair that had been so evident in Brieanna when she'd collapsed to the ground before our (my) capture, the life was being sucked, along with the spirit, right out of me. What would she do, slap and scratch me again? I was a mess already. My face felt swollen to the size of a football. I was feverish, and dozens of insect bites on my arms and ankles itched and stung intolerably. I needed a cold shower, a hot bath, and serious rest. And this female Sessue Hayakawa was deliberately cruel.

"You're saying I'm like a Jap soldier?" She didn't seem upset—cool and collected, in fact.

"You're acting like one."

"Do I look Japanese?"

No, she didn't. Living in Quincy, I had become (so I thought) rather adept at identifying the subtleties of facial discrimination in Chinese, Vietnamese, Koreans, even Burmese.

"No. Chinese. But I didn't make that crack because you're Asian."

"Oh, give me a break. Then when didn't you say I was acting like a Nazi?"

Good point. I hated to concede it. I didn't. She said, "Anyway, I *am* Chinese. Good for you."

"Anita, huh? Anita what?"

"Chu."

"Ah. Wait a minute. You're 'A. Chu'? Ah-choo? Like *Gesundheit*?"

She cracked up laughing and blushed slightly and regarded me as if for the first time. I said, "Don't tell me you never heard that before."

She began to laugh again even harder, and I was suddenly and sadly reminded of my Erika.

"No," she said. "I mean, yes. I never noticed and nobody's ever said anything." Again she started laughing.

"They were probably too terrified of you."

"Politically correct," she said, "and you'd know about that, wouldn't you, apartheid boy."

"How'd you know that?"

"Your little wife told me."

"When did you—"

"Open the door."

The door stuck, but I gave it the best two-handed, upper-body shove I could muster in my wiped-out and dispassionate state, and it swung slowly open with a creak.

The room that came into view screaming at a thousand miles an hour straight into my being was enough to cause a loss of consciousness. There was no moment of fuzzy recollection, no reaching for a memory just inches from the outstretched fingertips of recall. No, I knew dead-on that instant: this was the room from my dream, my nightmare, the open-air villa in Tuscany.

The bed, canopied, was before the same wall, but its curtains and a torn tapestry were blown by a large rotating floor fan plugged into a small generator. Carpets were spread over the rough floor, open fenestrations cut into one wall. I went to them. The view was certainly not Tuscany's fabled landscape, but a lovely succession of small meadows, hillocks, and trees. If one had no scruples, the place would be perfect for condos. Differences, sure, but small details. This was the room. I suddenly knew a great sense of foreboding at the sound of the heavy door slamming closed behind me.

"Take your clothes off."

I paused, back to her, then turned in as close an approximation of calm as I could manage.

"I'm sorry?" Annoyance to imply noncompliance.

"You heard me."

"I don't think I did."

"Strip. Now. Everything."

"What the hell for?"

"A lesson."

I thought about that. I had always hated the swoony masochism evinced in the heroines of Sade, and males and females both in Roquelaire's spicy volumes. Yes, it was there, in everyone, and herein me, surely, in spades, to be revealed like the genitalia of the crucified, should I care to dive down into the murk and muck of my own sexual cesspool. But I always found the punishment-and-dominance, bondage-and-discipline, tie-me-up-and-humiliate-me trip a bit much.

"A lesson? I already know how to take my clothes off."

She stepped forward carefully, still smiling as warmly as she had been when I'd made the sneeze jape on her name, but she struck me hard with the back of her hand, quick and practiced, drawing blood from my lower lip. Now even my teeth felt bruised. She said nothing else.

I slowly unbuttoned my shirt, trying to control an obvious tremor, and folded it as if it had been freshly dry-cleaned and pressed. I deliberated over pants, socks, shoes, folding and placing all carefully in a small changing-room pile, then, finally got down to the shorts. These I removed with stoic resignation. What I could not retain of my clothing I would of my dignity. I casually placed both hands in front of me, but tried to affect a Gurkha at ease rather than a nervous fifth grader in a line-up for a physical.

"You're not in very good shape," said A. Chu. "I mean, you haven't developed the muscles of your limbs or chest, yet you've let your stomach sag. You look like one of those starving kids in Africa."

Even naked, one may mount a high-horse. I said, "Is that why I'm standing here bloody well bollocks naked, so you can critique the inadequacies—in your opinion—of my physique? Well, fair play, darling. Why don't you strip off that ridiculous Soldieress of Fortune get-up and let's see what you've got, eh?"

I was really steamed now, even removing my hands from in front of me, though not quite sure next where, pocketless, to place them; standing hands-on-hips starkers conjured images of Third World street urchins or girls in pornographic videos—it wouldn't do.

I continued, "And for your information, a rather exquisite young woman has recently found me attractive enough, thank you very much."

She grinned. "Yes, we know. That's why you and I are up here. To teach you not to prey on young girls to satisfy your disgusting urges."

"Prey? What the hell are—?" I actually started at the notion of some fresh trump-up; then light dawned, and I scowled in disgust. "Don't tell me you're talking about—"

"Hayley. Little Hayley—that virgin you spoiled."

"Oh, for God's sake, you're all completely mental—"

"Lay down on the bed."

"This is ridiculous."

She took a scary step forward. It wasn't so much out of fear at being struck again—my body seemed to be in the last stages of complete benumbedness, along with my spirit. A self-destructive drive to get this—all of it, whatever it was—over with was now foremost in ruling my actions, edging out any survival instinct for a photofinish. Would this end in death or castration, as prophesied in my nightmare? Both? Or simply more pain and humiliation to be followed by arrest as an accomplice to murder, then prison, and more pain and humiliation? Perhaps I should attack her, or run for it, prompting the automatic weapon's fire that would shred my viscera to ribbons and allow my life to stream out messily in seconds? Now there was an idea. Like crazy Sade said—the first inhibitor is always the fear of death. Overcome that, and anything is possible. Sure.

I went over to the bed. The thin coverlet over the sheets of the mattress was chill. I stretched out on my back, even saucily placing my hand behind my head as if awaiting snack and remote control. She smiled and shook her head, in charge.

"No, no. Your hands. Wrists together."

And for the second time in two days, I was back in handcuffs.

"Now face the wall—on your knees."

This I did and realized on the instant the fate that had been bubbling in her as a twist of debasing retribution for what was perceived as my debauched ravishment of Little Red Riding Hood.

Behind me I heard the zipper of her tight trousers, then a rummage under the bed, the clunk and unzip of an article of luggage. The sound of tightening straps brought the sensation of not wanting to look down that gorge that Brieanna and I never crossed. But I turned.

She had not bothered to pull her pants off over her heavy boots, so waddled in tiny duck-steps to the side of the bed. She had put down the Savage 440. She held a long chain—a leash—— and strapped to her crotch was a rather sinister rubbery pink phallus, at least eight inches long and two inches thick, glistening as if oiled, firmly rooted in a leather base that enveloped her loins like an inverse chastity belt. Straps on both hips secured her artificial manhood to her pelvis.

Predictable, really, and biblical in the Old Testament sense of vengeance. She would show me what it was like, and the evil of humiliating me and thrusting convulsively into my pain would fuel her pleasure. She, of the theoretically formerly oppressed, now emancipated, behaving as some libertine in eighteenth century France. It was perhaps the twinge and twinkle of that very swoony masochism rising now in the back and base of my loins that dashed off that split-second notice to the brain that if this was the order of the moment, then so be it, but it would be a rape, bloody and damaging, and not the passive acquiescence of the trussed-up lamb. Time to be or not to be.

She shuffled forward, dragging her pants across the floor, the huge comic prick wagging with each movement like the tail of a Saint Bernard. She held the chain out towards my handcuffed wrists and spoke like a nanny about to administer an enema, the perversity underscored by a Mary Poppins tone:

"Now we just loop this chain through here—"

And I was on her in a flash. I jerked my balled, chained fists hard across her face, sending her flying backwards onto the floor. I rolled on my arms off the bed and onto my feet, then onto her, knocking the air out of her. I clamped my knees astride her waist, the thick fake cock merrily erect against my very real and detumescent one. Blood was spilling from her nose, which looked broken, the result of my blow, which sickened me. My weak sympathy sickened me even further; I grabbed her throat hard with both hands and roared, "Where's the key to the handcuffs?"

She seemed dazed by the blow, choked, and shook her head from side to side. I took this to be uncooperative. I repeated the question, tightening my grip on her trachea, and she began asphyxiating in earnest, complete with popping eyes. My fatigue vanished and was replaced by a rage that fired on all cylinders. I was yelling—incoherently over her gasping, gurgling, strangulating sounds—and when I began rhythmically banging her head on the floor in time to my indecipherable demands, the noise had reached such a volume that I wasn't aware of the heavy door being blasted open nor the swarm of Furies that descended screeching upon me.

I was dragged furiously from behind and slammed aside, my handcuffed nakedness making for a painful tumble. I don't know how many there were, but at least three sets of fists were felling blows, and knees in the groin and stomach and once even the forehead, and any attempts to flail out with cuffed wrists, shins, et cetera, were feeble and useless. I was awash in a sea of nails and boobs and tummies under a thick cloud of shampoo smells and delicious scents—it was like being stomped at the perfume counter at Macy's—militants with a dose of *Faster, Pussycat! Kill! Kill!*

With blood running from cuts, eyebrows, and nose, and both ears ringing from hard-fisted pelts, the spirit ebbed for what surely was the last time.

I was blacking out. So this was it.

I heard a faint professorial voice say, as if addressing a lecture hall: "*The marriage vows and his wife's fate, so inextricably linked with his own, led to this sorry and sordid end. Had the body ever been found—it wasn't—in its unmarked and degraded grave, the details would have provided a most tawdry coda to the episode: naked and hand-cuffed, ruptured testicles, penis ripped from the body, rectum savagely buggered, probably after death; nipples lacerated beyond recognition, along with the face, of course. Remaining teeth were eventually matched to dental records. Oddly, despite being nearly torn to pieces, the actual terminal event was a cutting off of the air supply through nose and mouth due to the forced application of an—um—vulva. Death by 'queening'. We all heaved a sigh of relief that both parents were dead. One surviving sibling, a brother, expressed little remorse and no surprise, as the deceased had an addictive personality.*"

Now the voice took on the emphatic tone of a eulogy: "*Yes, dearly beloved, he loved perhaps too well, but was still a third-rate poet no matter how you slice it. He let his emotions get the better of him, tossing into the shitter all reason, intellect, or rationality.*

'When, by the rout that made the hideous road,
His gory visage down the stream was sent,
Down the swift Hebrus to the Lesbian shore' . . .

"Amen. The would-be Chief Mourneress could not be here today, as she is busy getting laid in Cozumel by a second-rate poet who smells. The departed's ex-wife—sorry, wife!—is dead but feeling terrific and living in San Francisco."

So this was it, then, and why not? I was played out, finished. I had clearly failed to cope and had brought upon myself and others much misery. Which was fine.

As I lost consciousness and the chorus of female screams receded from my numb and swollen ears, I welcomed the black infinity that I knew awaited me, a state that would so resemble my time long ago floating in an isolation tank in West Hollywood, when finally my body had melted to nothingness, evaporated, and I was left as pure ethereal spirit, all thought non-linear and acausal, and I approached a bursting of starlight in the epicenter of an endless void . . .

Chapter Twelve

1

Imagine my surprise when I came to, again in a hospital bed, to hear a familiar voice ask, "Hey, hey! Alive after all, eh?" And again a pause, and then, "Aren't you?"

It was Chauncey, although not, this time, in the next bed. He had squeezed his great girth into a tight plastic visitor's chair; on his opposite stood a nurse in hospital greens that were blue. I knew she wasn't Julie, but I was reminded of my English Crumpet from Boston. Her stethoscope was measuring somatic thumps in my chest and neck. The name tag over her breast read *Rachel*.

"A biblical name," I said groggily. My vocal chords sounded as if they hadn't been worked in days.

"Whadja say?" she asked with a broad Yankee accent and utterly charming smile, snapping a wad of gum. She was as British as a California beach bunny. She looked about twenty.

"Don't listen to him," said Chauncey. "He's delirious even when he ain't drugged up." This said with great affection by my Uncle Digger. "Now you just take it easy, Paxton. Gotta get fit and get you outta here."

"Another job?" I managed to lift my head, but it fell, a thousand pounds, back onto the pillow.

Chauncey chuckled. "Think not. You best just concentrate on convalescin' for a bit."

I was all hooked up again with clips and drips and blips. Rachel reached out one cool hand and brushed the hair from my bandaged forehead. Such a pretty girl. Really sweet. This was how one got in trouble. At least this one.

2

Three months later, I was steering a new Nissan Sentra onto busy Castro Street in San Francisco.

I'd been in the Maine Medical Center in Portland, in the hospital for a week (again) with the same lung collapsed and a concussion (again and again) plus many stitches and a nasty hernia and several broken toes, cracked ribs, and chipped teeth. I was a mess. My young but motherly doctor sternly warned me that if I didn't learn to manage the stress in my life, my damned lung would collapse for good, and they'd then need to stitch the thing to my rib-cage. She suggested I investigate the benefits of yoga and meditation. I told her I would.

Chauncey allowed me to recuperate at his magnificent seaside home in Bar Harbor. Spending the remainder of the summer there proved invigorating. I gained twenty pounds, promptly enrolled in a yoga class, pedaled bicycle paths, and abstained from the grape and grain, white-knuckled. For ninety days I lived in a suspended state of eight hours sleep a night, healthy meals, meditation, and large portions of Dante and Mishima. I was preparing.

It turned out Chauncey had received word after our departure from Rangeley that Mr. Kureishi was scotching the deal. When Special Agent Avery came looking for Poplin at the shop, Chauncey'd had a bad feeling and headed up there himself. Avery had followed Chauncey. After discovering the massacre at the Barnstormers, both the Fat Man and the F.B.I. agent traveled together to the Greater Desert of Maine, evidently right on our heels. Avery had called in state troopers, and when they'd found Mumsy's body, they rang up what passed as the local S.W.A.T. The boys and girls in flak-jackets had saved my unmanaged life. I was actually flown to Portland by helicopter, an experience I'm sorry to have missed.

Hayley and Malcolm were apprehended within a mile of the castle—they had become hopelessly lost. Malcolm had the good sense to toss all the firearms into a deep bog upon the first sound of a voice through a bullhorn, but he did manage, he told Chauncey later, to conceal the mahogany box and its unique piece of history in a very cunning hiding place in the wilds of Khartoum. Now if only he could remember exactly where.

At the baffled inquest, Chauncey, Malcolm, Hayley, and I gave consistent but apparently infuriating testimony to angry and disapproving inquisitors but were each cleared of complicity in the deaths of Janis Poplin, Dora Shannon, and Petra Wajda. Petra had been wanted for questioning by both Russian agents and Interpol, Shannon by the F.B.I. for the Crisco kidnapping. Agent Avery told me during a break that Poplin was considered at the Bureau to be what twisted J. Edgar Hoover used to call "a loose cannon." Brieanna was returned to her crestfallen handlers in California. I read in *USA Today* that she was an intern working in fashion design for Vivienne Westwood and was out on bail, awaiting trial for SLAV shenanigans.

Hayley's mother packed her off to college in Sydney, Australia. I find the idea of her studying amongst the wallabies, 'roos, and koalas very fitting.

Ek is life vir jou and *Totsiens* to my little friend—farewell, my darling.

One day, facing the blue Atlantic from the balcony of Chauncey's retreat, I took up pen and paper and wrote:

Once, walked on black crow's feet,
Your mean touch caught me, came
To break fast fingers, to lay claim
And there we were. All done, complete.

A spooky story, proctored
Without eyes or ears, the classroom
Your old doll set, a dusty tomb
My finger-prints have lettered.

We could wait to hear a clear
Sound. No Mozart, strings or soft bell
To clasp in panic. Oh, well.
Face the music, pay the fiddler, dear.

It was a start.

In late August, I again visited the bridge where Erika Wikki had drowned. I never mentioned to Chauncey or the tired folks at the inquest what Malcolm had said about her. It was especially tingly, then, when Chauncey announced one morning that I seemed healthy and recovered, and, "That yogi stuff's a buncha nonsense, but seems like it's nonsense you can't do without," and he had another job for me.

His daughter Amanda had flown in a hurry on business to the West Coast and was, for the time being, relocated. Chauncey had closed up and sold her house and shipped her belongings, but her new car, the Nissan, needed to be delivered. How about if I took a leisurely, no-pressure drive across these great United States, spent some scenic time—all expenses paid—out West, and flew or Amtrak'd back? The choice was mine. Delightful. And where was Amanda?

"Out ta 'Frisco."

Kismet.

My trip took a calm and sane week, a leisurely crossing of the continent in lovely weather. If Chauncey imposed pecuniary limits on accommodations ("It's Motel 6 all the way fer you, fella"), he was most generous with time: I was able to meander and dawdle, at times stopping for hours to appreciate mildly disturbing wide-open spaces in Kansas and Nebraska (childhood recollection mixed with adult agoraphobia). Montana was indescribably beautiful, so I shall make no attempt to describe it, but I spent several days there feeling as if I was renewing some long-lost connection with the Earth itself.

The journey came to an end with my arrival in San Francisco. I met Amanda in front of the Transamerica building at 600 Montgomery Street. A woman in her forties, she was as pretty and pleasant as Chaunce was round and eccentric. Despite knowing I had been well taken care of by her father, she tipped me five hundred dollars in cash.

I decided to stay in the North Beach neighborhood and checked into the San Remo Hotel.

The first day I went sightseeing, drank much *l'eau fines*, ate countless crabs at Fisherman's Wharf, and saw a new print of *The Vampire Lovers* at the Castro Street Theater.

On the second morning, I docked myself from 8:45 to 10:00, then 12:00 to 1:00 in front of the Consulate General of Brazil at 300 Montgomery Street.

On the third day, a man in his thirties who bore more than a passing resemblance to Humphrey Bogart exited the building at the beginning of the lunch hour. I followed him six blocks to a restaurant called And That's All She Wrote, where he joined a short, pretty woman in her twenties with jet-black hair, full breasts, and darkly tinted glasses, dressed in green cashmere sweater and beige skirt, a woven bag slung loosely over her shoulder. A beige beret topped her off with a Gallic touch. They met as eager lovers with an embrace, much kissing, and he a furtive, stolen caress.

I left my hovering-point on the edge of the restaurant in a nervous flurry. I had not prepared for stakeout work despite this stakeout, nor such quick results. I hurried to a nearby chemist's and purchased black sunglasses and a fishing cap I would originally not be caught dead wearing, but this was an extraordinary situation. I returned to see them—via a quick duck in and out of the doorway—romantically consuming, from the looks of the bistro, an expensive luncheon. I loitered outside.

An hour later they left together, walking the sunny blocks to the consulate. Then, a lingering kiss goodbye and she was off strolling solo. I followed, carefully.

We walked for many blocks from Montgomery Street up Columbus to Lombard, until we reached 1201 Mason Street, and she entered the San Francisco Cable Car Museum. She hadn't noticed me, so I barely needed to hang back before entering the free exhibit.

I didn't know who she was. Erika? No. But she could lead me to her, and this was probably dangerous. I patted the side pocket of my jacket as if for luck and felt Shannon's Walther PPKS, the only weapon of the clutch at the barn I had purloined. It had survived capture by the Girls, collection during near-rape by A. Chu, and managed a safe return in the pocket of my denim jacket, courtesy of the Maine State Troopers, to the snug of the hospital room in Portland. There my shock manifested itself by a short shriek of a laugh when I searched the filthy coat and discovered it. How the hell? I could hear the tin-star tones as it might have been handed back:

"Think this'n's yers, pardner."

"Might powerful obliged, Sher'f."

A marvelous country.

She was not browsing as a first-time visitor, but moving, not quickly but steadily, with intent. I followed as she made her way down to the level of the cable-winding machinery. An observer might have wondered at the small woman in dark glasses and hat being somberly tailed by the not-small man in dark glasses and hat.

We traveled down and down farther, the clack of her heels soon smothered by the industrial chug of the huge sheaves, the wheeled pulleys that endlessly drag the immense length of massive cable that streams just beneath the surface of the streets of the city to carry its passenger cars up and down its perilous hills in safety.

She went as far as possible on the walkway beneath the sheaves, then surprised me by calmly twisting the latch on a metal gate marked, *Danger: No Admittance Past This Point*, smartly swinging it open and closed behind her and marching on as if she'd entered her grandmother's garden. I let her tromp ahead, checking in all directions to see if we were being watched (she certainly hadn't), then I followed.

We were now on a gangway or catwalk that ran the circumference of the machinery room. She was well ahead of me, apparently unconcerned by the possibility that a museum employee might notice her unauthorized presence. She rounded a corner and disappeared beyond a high brick wall. The pulleys hummed in infinite revolve.

I stealthed gingerly up the remaining length of catwalk, confident that I hadn't lost her, though I could no longer hear her step. A glance back to ascertain there was no witness, and I rounded the corner.

"A little closer."

She held a pistol. She had been waiting for me and now stood a trained ten feet of killing range from the corner where I stood.

She was pert-nosed (unlike Erika's pug) with a small white scar through a corner of her upper lip. The glasses concealed her eyes. We were in an alcove, the catwalk rounding the corner and coming to an abrupt halt above a deep pool into which a waterfall of heavy drainage tumbled: an intimidating spot.

She repeated, "Step a little closer, please, so you can't be seen."

She had an accent: Scandinavian? Russian?

I stepped forward as instructed. She stared at me. She had the gun, and I awaited her questions, orders, comments—but she said nothing. I allowed a few more moments to elapse and suddenly felt that she was afraid to speak; was, in fact waiting for me to say something.

I said, "I don't mean you any harm. I followed you because I thought you might be able to help me find someone."

She just stared (or I presume she stared; her eyes might have been closed for all I could tell behind the black lenses).

I continued, "My wife, Erika Wikki. I'm looking for her. I came all the way from the East Coast. I was told she might have some connection to the gentleman you were having lunch with. I just want to find out where she is."

Something seemed to shift in her, causing a change to her stance, which I at first took to be readying to shoot me clean through, but happened to be a more relaxed grip on her revolver. She shook her head before she opened her mouth, gearing up for speech.

"She is dead. I'm sorry. I don't know anything else."

It was an odd voice, deliberate and inflected by something artificial. I was reminded again of Natasha Fatale in *Rocky & Bullwinkle*.

I asked, "Do you at least know when and how she died? You see, I've been under the impression she died years ago way out in Maine, but..." I paused. "Several people I've spoken to refuse to share that opinion."

She waited again, and again shook her head. And she shook it falsely, un-convincingly, poorly—like a little girl caught in a lie, and I knew at once—I *knew*. My darling Erika was always such a lousy liar! How many screaming matches had we shared during which I reminded her that one as sociopathic and prone to dishonesty as she should take acting lessons, of such poor quality were her performances. If you can't lie convincingly, don't lie. A one woman Gang That Couldn't Shoot Straight, and here she was holding a gun on her husband.

"It's you," I said, finally.

She stood frozen, but now I could feel that behind the shades, her nerve was slipping. She tried to rally, to control the modulation of her cartoon voice.

"You don't know me," she said.

I tempered my voice to Boris Badenov's: "Fearless Leader mebbe pissed." I grinned. "Lousy Garbo imitation, Erika."

And she laughed, spluttered actually, her torso weaving for a moment back and forth in a sweet undulation to accommodate her giggle.

She was so much alive! New nose, new hair, new boobs, and a charming scar on her wide, sensual mouth—but it was Erika. It was Erika.

"It *is* you."

She still held the gun on me, but carelessly, an after-thought. With her free hand she removed her sunglasses and her beret and shook out a long, thick mane of black hair. Then she bore her gaze straight into mine. Two lavender-hued eyes (contacts) I had last seen clearly as we plunged off a bridge into the sea six years before. I took off my glasses and hat.

"Hello, jerk," came Erika's smooth, clear tone, a voice from the dead.

"I've been looking for you," I said. "Where's the girl I used to know?"

She chuckled, but mirthlessly. "Yeah," she began, slightly embarrassed. "I had to change my appearance...you know— "

"I don't, actually," I said like a customer dissatisfied with a dry-cleaner. "I was hoping you might explain."

Now she was laughing heartily. "Oh, my. It's what you would call, 'rather a long story'..."

I stood smiling. "I have plenty of time."

She turned steely. "Well, I don't. That's why all this happened in the first place."

"I don't understand."

"You never will. That's always been your problem. And your problem was mine while I was with you. That and your drinking 'problem,' nice polite term you always used. I had to get away. Not just from you, but all of it."

"Couldn't you have just divorced me?"

She smirked. "It's complicated. I was in love. Still am, actually. Evidently you've seen him."

"The guy who looks like Bogart."

"Yes, he does. He's Brazilian," she said with pride.

"Just tell me why."

She sighed. "Before the trip to Bar Harbor, I knew it was all over. A shaman explained the numerology to me—I was twenty-two. You'll scoff, cynic that you are, but I had a vision—a clear vision—that my first life was over. What had I been? A college drop-out with no direction, saddled with a pathetic drunk for a husband. Wicca was just a path, but it showed me if I could save anything of our planet, our first Mother, starting with the most primal elements of fire and water, or true *nature*, then I might be able to save myself. This is all lost on you, isn't it?"

She looked away, thoughtful, and said to herself, "I just might." She paused, listening to the heavy cascade of the waterfall.

She said, "I met Hermes at the Earth Day conference I attended—remember? Oh, wait— you thought I was visiting my friend Tinny. Anyway, we were kindred, soulmates, me and Hermes. He outlined his plans to save the rainforests of Latin America. And I was hooked, heart and mind."

"And soul."

"Yes," she said, cocking her chin, "that's right. I went to work for him—with his movement, his wonderful people, the formation of SLAV—but also on paper, for the consulate. My life insurance was what you'd call, uh, considerable."

She smirked again and beat me to it: "I was worth more dead. On paper."

"How in hell did you manage the car crash?"

She slid its safety in place and dropped the gun in her woven bag like a compact, then took one slight step forward, her expression the old prelude to the placement of her hand on my face to make a point, cruel or kind. But unlike the past, she went no further.

"I didn't, darling. You did! Isn't that too perfect?"

She paused to savor my expression.

"I was as shocked as you, you asshole—you could have killed me!" She laughed. "Hermes was working on all sorts of schemes for my disappearance. It was supposed to take place in the Andes, if you can believe it. *Mucho dinero!* And then you drunkenly swerved us right into the ocean and—*splash!* I mean, if that wasn't a sign, then I don't know what would be. Don't you think?"

I felt slightly sick, but managed, "Uncanny."

She laughed. "Well, yeah! When I realized I was alive, I swam and swam—without being able to swim!—in that freezing water and made it to Hermes' hotel. No one saw me. No one ever sees you, you know?" She was quite matter-of-fact.

"He was up there with us?"

"Sure. And from there it was just details—the coroner, the undertaker—just details that were addressed less by *how* as by simply how *much*."

She looked pretty pleased, then said, "You've gained weight. You look good. You still drinking?"

I ignored this and stumbled ahead:

"Didn't you care what I was feeling? I love you. I thought you were dead. I thought I'd killed you."

"And you might have!" she snapped, her anger flashing. "Serves you right. I didn't owe you anything. I put up with you for a long time, and gave you at least *some* happiness, which is more than you ever gave me. It was all hell for me, every horrible minute. I figure we're even."

She took a moment to test the resiliency of this while I stood there.

"Now what?" I asked.

"None of your business," she said decisively. "And if you know what's good for you, you'll just let the whole thing pass. Otherwise, you'll probably be killed. I have a new life. New face and body, too, if you noticed, and—knowing your all-consuming sex-drive, dear—you must have noticed."

"Oh, yes."

"Nice, huh? I always thought big boobs were somewhat silly. Perhaps they are, but I've grown very fond of these."

"How'd you get the scar?"

She brightened. "It was deliberate. Done with a dental instrument. For authenticity." She smiled slightly. "What the hell are you doing here?"

"Just delivering a car. You know...I was at Newbury Street," I said slowly.

"Jesus, was that a shock! What the hell! I couldn't believe that one."

"But you blew me up anyway."

She cleared her throat with impatience. "Couldn't be helped," she said tersely. "Not my fault you were boozing before noon at the wrong spot—stupid. I thought it was fair turnaround— you'd almost killed me. And you survived, right? You weren't injured for life or anything? We're even."

"Are we?"

"Yes, we are," she said, her anger rounding again. "And we were finished long before Bar Harbor. Silly Erika's gone, and so are you, you drunk. Hermes and I are leaving the country soon. I have work to do. I'm in love." She softened for a moment. "Can't you be happy for me?"

I stood there.

"Sorry about the little girl," she said without conviction. "I heard."

"There isn't a single moment—since I thought you'd...not a day that I haven't thought about you."

She caught the weak catch in my throat. She knew I was on the edge of crying.

"Oh, Paxton," she said, shaking her head, and laughing, with full indulgence. "You're such a loser. Everyone takes advantage of you. You let them. You're a jerk, and you always will be. Don't you know that? I mean—can't you say that's *true*?"

Kenneth Butler

I had eased back the hammer of the Walther in my pocket, pulled it out now and pointed.

"That's true," I said, and pulled the trigger.

She had no time for any reaction. The shot caught her shockingly in the chest; she stumbled, leaned for leverage at the railing, collapsed, and tumbled over it into the pool, the gun's report echoing around the machinery.

I glanced down to watch her body float for a moment, then sink in a fluid cloud of crimson, then disappear into the dark depths. There was no struggle, and no swimming this time. She was dead.

I slipped the gun into my pocket and put on the hat and glasses and retraced my ex-wife's path back through the museum. In the lobby, no one seemed to have seen or heard anything. She was right.

I entered the North Beach autumn afternoon and walked and walked to Fisherman's Wharf. There I surreptitiously stole to an empty slip, wiped the gun clean with my shirttails, and let it fall gently from my hand into San Francisco Bay, the many around me oblivious. Seals barked merrily.

I found a payphone and called the Carmel detox where I had earlier arranged to check in for their thirty-day program. I confirmed I would be arriving sometime in the late evening, drunk, by cab. Chauncey would be paying the expenses, though he didn't know it yet. I had no worry that he would be unhappy.

I walked to City Lights Books, where I purchased Robert Lowell's *Selected Poems*, then went next door to Vesuvio's, famed watering hole of the Beats, appropriate for one last bender.

I settled in with my book at the bar and ordered a whiskey sour, as dated a drink as a highball or Tom Collins or gimlet. It had been my first cocktail, seventeen years earlier, and I was feeling nostalgic. I followed this with several Jack Daniel's on the rocks and remembered an afternoon in New Hampshire months before and thousands of miles away:

Hayley and I had picnicked at a spot called Wagon Hill Farm she'd been eager to show me. She'd said it reminded her of her one trip to the Forest of Dean in the British Isles.

After lunch and a drowse in the shade, she had plucked us both up, and

210

dragging me by the hand, then releasing me, flung herself pell-mell down the long, steep incline of this fabulous hill, her light summer dress swirling around her delectable legs and hips and bottom.

At first hesitant and lastly awkward, I finally did follow, rolling, and collapsed with her at the foot of the hill, her skin damp, sweet-and-sour smelling, grass-speckled. She laughed uncontrollably, clasped and kissed me fiercely, and I knew there would never be a moment finer than this one, the happiest time: now, always.

And I took the time to cherish that moment—one hand behind my head, the other on her soft breast—and gazed at the clouds in the brilliant, bright blue sky.

And I knew then that she would always be there: my girl wrapped in my embrace; the sunlight warm, the day endless, and the hill rolling on forever.